A Hunt for the
GREAT NORTHERN

HERB NEILS

Hunt For The Great Northern

By Herb Neils

Copyright 2000 by Herb Neils

ISBN 0-912299-95-9

Library of Congress Control Number: 00-131502

Published in the United States of America

Cover and Design: Carol Colbath

Dedication: To Pat. We have learned much together.

Acknowledgments: Special appreciation must be made to three individuals. They are Bud Journey, who encouraged me to write from early on; Elaine Cummings, retired editor of Safari Magazine, whose enthusiasm and editorial help were a great contribution; and Blaise Szekely, a fine critic, a lifetime friend, and full of good ideas.

This book is a work of fiction. Any resemblance of the characters to actual persons is entirely coincidental.

STONEYDALE PRESS PUBLISHING COMPANY
523 Main Street • Stevensville, Montana 59870
Phone: 406-777-2729

Foreword

The events take place in the late 1940s, just after World War II. Some of the story was lived by Herb, and some is written just as things were in that backwoods country as modern civilization was making its way into the Northern Rockies.

The desire of a man to roam free in the wild country is portrayed by the many scenes of hunting, horse wrangling and fishing in the unknown Kootenai country. There are crimes needing attention, but handled in a different manner than one would expect nowadays. There is love, which basically never changes, and there are hate, heroism and all the rest of the human emotions.

The four distinct seasons that are part of nature in the north country play a role in the lives and deaths of the people involved. There is a time for everything in that wild section of mountains; from love to hate, from respect for life to the taking of it, from making hay in summer, to survival in a snow-covered wilderness, but time mostly for the building of a person's character.

One man's lifetime ambition is fulfilled, but another's is denied. A central theme in the story is a life revolving around a special river, a place apart, where a man still is free to do what he chooses in the rapids, or on the ridges forming the scenic valley. His horse is his best companion until a woman shows him a different way and helps him to recover from the ravages of war.

The story is written from the heart, from experiences that few men in the United States will ever witness again in their own lives. Times change, the weather changes, the country changes, but some things of value, like honor, are rare but eternal. A man must quickly learn respect and self-reliance under the harsh teachings of a northern wilderness. He can learn to endure, or he can succumb to the temptations of the "easy" life of crime, gambling and dissipation.

It is all in this book, with a moral for those who wish to read about how it was, when the old was catching up with the new, but when a man still had more pride in honor than in possessions.

Introduction

The crew of our B-24 Liberator bomber was jubilant. Our worn-out aircraft touched down for the last time, with everyone alive, which was not always the case. The European war was over, and we would be sent to Florida for a long period of training in a new aircraft called the B-29. We were told that it was a long-range, high-altitude aircraft with pressurized and heated cabin, unlike our B-24. It was, for its day, a high-tech machine, capabilities still classified.

Physical problems and stress were evident in nearly all the air crews. We were given a period of time to recover before starting the training in secret, for what we deduced would be a massive raid on Japan. By the time we were completely familiar with our new aircraft and had been given our overseas orders, the first and then the second atomic bombs were dropped. Our particular crew was scheduled to drop number four, which would eliminate Tokyo from the face of the globe, as we learned after peace was declared.

I took my discharge after being lectured for weeks on the good reasons to reenlist. How I missed the mountains where I grew up! The horses, camping, elk hunting alone without noise or people present, and the rhythm of the seasons along the Kootenai River were integral to my soul. The river was in my veins like my own blood.

Chapter 1

At approximately two a.m. on a cold, black, February night, the scheduled freight express was barreling along in a blinding snowstorm. Johanson, the engineer, was late getting out of Whitefish, and had been crowding his speed limits a bit coming down the Kootenai canyon. He was proud of running his section on time, and knew these tracks like he did his own horse pasture, but, sadly, it was not to be Johanson's night. Nature was soon to play a cruel hand in the lives of those she met on the night express.

There were a lot of narrow stretches along this hundred miles of Great Northern right-of-way, but the worst part ran just west of the junction of the Fisher River and the Kootenai. Tony Mountain guarded the narrow river mouth with rock bluffs and nearly vertical slopes rising two thousand feet above the water. The tracks had been placed here on a narrow bed, hacked out of solid rock, and just wide enough for swaying boxcars to clear the uphill side. There was barely enough room for a man to safely walk on the downhill side before it dropped a hundred feet into deep, swirling water.

Johanson could hardly see the front of his locomotive from the blowing snow, but he knew that there were about a couple hundred feet left to go before clearing this dangerous run, and he started easing forward on the throttle. Right where the last bluff opened into a flood plain, marking the end of Tony Mountain, is where Johanson's tandem locomotives ploughed into an avalanche, forty feet deep, laced with logs and giant boulders.

Two steam Malleys, followed by 110 loaded freight cars at fifty miles per hour carry with them an incredible amount of momentum. The train burst through the avalanche, slowed somewhat by packed snow and ice, but derailed by thick logs and granite boulders. For nearly two minutes this dynamic force hurled itself onto the flood plain amid a great shower of splintered wood and broken steel, spilling wheat and diesel oil, furniture and machinery. Countless other items disappeared into the vast burial ground of snow.

Boxcars continued piling one on top of the other in seemingly endless procession. Couplings were breaking with rifle-shot booms, and steel rails, jerked from their moorings on frozen crossties, screamed in the winter wind like incoming artillery as they twisted into inconceivable shapes. Eventually the silence became as total as the darkness, any possible sound muted by the still falling powder snow. The midnight run had become a total disaster.

Johanson's locomotive was on its side, but he was alive, although scalded some by live steam. Somehow he and his fireman managed to crawl out of the wreckage before they would be burned to death, and they collapsed when they reached the railbed. The caboose, nearly a half mile behind, was still on the track by some miracle. The conductor was on the floor, waking up after being thrown the length of the car and being knocked out by a blow on his head. He was feeling for broken bones, but could not find any. He put on his parka, lit a surviving kerosene lantern, and started up the tracks looking for the engineer and fireman who he thought must be dead.

Oscar was pulling night duty in the Libby depot. He kept dragging his Waltham railroad watch out of his vest pocket, checking the time, and nervously trying to wind the watch several times against a tight spring. He was worried. His watch had always been accurate within a few seconds per week, and now the night freight showed late, very late. He sat staring at his telegraph key and thinking for a moment what would happen to him if he sent a false alarm. Then he wired the Whitefish night man for the second time. He told him that the freight was an hour late, "And for God's sake, stop all westbound traffic in Whitefish. There must be an accident, and I will keep all the eastbound stuff in Troy. We sure don't need any collisions. Be quick now, and wire Ed Scharpe in Minneapolis, get him out of bed and tell him we got troubles."

Charlie's phone was ringing, but nobody answered. Oscar tried another number with the operator, let it ring a dozen times and finally heard a female voice. "We got bad problems down at the railroad, and I need help," Oscar pleaded, "and right now! I sent a speeder up the line and they found a wreck and brought back the crew who are now at the hospital."

Charlie climbed out of Alice's bed and started dressing. He threw a big chunk of wood into the stove before pulling on his mackinaw and boots, muttering about how he was going to clobber that dumb telegrapher when he got a chance. Little did he know that Ed "Chaps" Scharpe, his boss, would be transmitting on the line by the time he waded through the blizzard and reached his office.

"Charlie, get hold of Walt immediately. Tell him we have a wreck by the Fisher River, as the semaphore on your side of it was not activated.

All our salvage equipment is in Seattle and we cannot get it up there for at least two days. We can use all the help he can give us to clear the main line and get our trains moving. I want to know every hour what is happening up there. Ed Scharpe."

Walt, who ran a lumber outfit, was wide awake when he reached for the phone, and he started right out by giving Charlie his orders for the day. "Get your local train crew together and hook up a dozen flat cars for machinery and a boxcar for shelter for our men. Keep those cars in front of the engine, as we will need some rail and ties pushed up there later. I am going to get my logging crews down there with six bulldozers and at least one crane. Pull your train up to our loading dock and we will get that equipment aboard within an hour. Call Bill and get his cafe cooks busy making breakfast and lunch boxes for thirty men, along with coffee, hot soup, and anything else they can come up with. Get one of your portable cookstoves loaded into the boxcar for heat. We will need all the lanterns you have and I'll send our camp generator for light. Move on it!"

A tougher group of men was never assembled for a job like this one. They were told what the problem was and were promised double pay to take care of it with no wasted time. There were Swedes, Norskies, Danes, and a couple Germans thrown together on that night, with heavy snow, and zero degrees F. to contend with. Nobody complained, but put their best efforts into loading the cats and a crane onto the flat cars in record time. These men had spent their lives working in the woods under extreme conditions, and they were hardened beyond most people's imagination.

Within the predicted hour, the salvage operation was in motion. The men were huddled around a big cookstove in the boxcar trying to keep from freezing. A cold draft from a slightly open door, which allowed air in and a smokestack to protrude horizontally, was biting at feet and fingers, but a coffeepot set on the hot steel partially made up for it. By the time the short train made it to Tony Mountain, the men, under the leadership of their hard-bitten Irish woods boss, McRell, had their plans all made. Everyone knew exactly what to do, and it would be a race against time and money. Chaps had mentioned once that it cost the railroad a million dollars a day to have the main line closed down.

The crane was the first machine put into operation. It was used to drag uprooted crossties into place alongside the flat cars, making a ramp for unloading the bulldozers and skidding cats. The snow had quit falling, and the brightening star-filled sky gave a little light. That, combined with the arc lamps from the generator, made possible a construction job like few had ever witnessed before. The log-skidding cats were outfitted with power winches and heavy duty drawbars for moving timber off mountainsides, and now the same technique was used to drag broken cars out of the way. The bulldozers soon had about twenty acres of level ground cleared of snow and the remains of the wreckage. This would be a staging area for new track, ties, dry gravel for ballast, and a workshop of sorts with a tent for equipment and tools.

Acetylene cutting torches flashed in the darkness, burning away useless rail while the crane lifted it and then dropped it out of the way. A clear day was slowly arriving, bringing with it a drop in temperature to minus ten degrees. Trees started to snap as they do in very cold weather, but nobody noticed that or the brilliant sunrise that illuminated the high peaks with gold. Heavy timber on the lower slopes, still black with shadow, created a contrast that enhanced the great beauty of the mountains. It was difficult to look at the massive destruction in the foreground when all one had to do was lift his eyes to see God's perfection in the distance.

Pride and urgency were pushing the workforce now, and the results were showing. By noontime, McRell had the right-of-way cleared the half mile back to the caboose, which was now being used as an office of sorts. He had all the broken cars and much of their contents stacked in one area to make it easier for salvage operations in the springtime. The work train had returned from Libby with all the rail and ties needed for repairs, along with a gondola car full of gravel, and the men were soon laying new track.

Walt and I were on this train, along with one of the cooks from Bill's cafe, who soon had a very hot and very large lunch going. It was apparent to us that this line would be open around nightfall for some slow traffic. The work train would then have to retreat a couple miles to a short passing track while the back-to-back traffic came through. We intended to make a full progress report to Chaps the minute we returned to Libby. The line would be upgraded during the next forty-eight hours by the Great Northern's own section gang, with Charlie in attendance. McRell and the crane operator offered to remain until the job was completed and then supervise the return of all the mill's equipment.

Ed Scharpe was ecstatic when he heard the news, and he declared then and there that he and the Great Northern would never forget this day. He was able to keep his word the following summer with lumber orders and hunting expeditions. Ed Scharpe was an expert at buttering his bread on both sides.

Chapter 2

The scene was wild in a rugged land. From here it would take a good horse a day of hard travel to carry his rider to any kind of settlement, and even then a man would be lucky to find much more than a sparse meal and a warm homebrew beer. It was early summer, and I was riding through the last patches of bluebells, which thrived in the shade of countless tall yellow sunflowers. There was a constant hum of bees as they worked the elderberry and serviceberry blossoms that my mount gingerly brushed aside.

High timbered peaks rose endlessly into the mist from both sides of the narrow valley. Their dark green and distant blue slopes contrasted with the pale green of the clear glacial waters running in the Kootenai River. The numerous drainages that entered the valley from both east and west were trackless except for game trails leading to old burns, well defined by the ancient forest surrounding them.

These burns, in various stages of regeneration, were the lifeblood of the area, creating food and open space for the vast numbers of deer, elk, moose, and bears that roamed the country of northwestern Montana, undisturbed by hunters. A high population of grizzlies ruled the huge mountain huckleberry patches, unaware that their cousins from the prairie had been shot off along with the buffalo. Game was everywhere, and each time I took up another notch with my belt buckle, I was reminded how good a handful of late summer mule deer chops would be, broiled over coals. The bolt action Winchester under my left knee could make it possible.

My horse, Buck, was standing askew on three legs, resting from the long, difficult trip south that had started where the Tobacco River hit the Kootenai. Buck's normally sleek buckskin-tinted hide was now stained with dust and sweat, but he was still alert, with his head and ears pointed toward the river. We were both listening to the same splashing noise, with Buck wondering about it, while I was figuring how to catch the large cutthroat trout that was disturbing the peace by feeding on emerging caddis flies.

By standing in the stirrups, I could just make out the trout through the bushes, as his huge head appeared under an insect, jaws open to suck it in. His two-foot-long body would then roll over while his palm-sized tail made a splash like a young beaver as it propelled him back to the depths. The longer I watched, the more I could feel my pinched stomach, and the nearby fish dinner looked easier by far to this tired rider than a deer hunt. My mission here was to scout out some good hunting country, but that could wait another day while I rustled up some vittles and made a camp. There was enough grass around for Buck to get his fill after I hobbled him, and he would find welcome shade under some spreading cottonwoods along the riverbank. Maybe I could generate the energy to roll away sufficient boulders to lay my two blankets flat. As an afterthought a couple days ago, I had dropped some line, leader, and a few hooks into my saddlebags.

Buck seemed to appreciate being unsaddled and then rubbed down with a burlap sack that I had rolled into a cylinder. After watering below the riffle where now a dozen trout were working, he started in on the best grass first, making sure he wouldn't have to leave any of it behind if we departed in a hurry! With every step, he jumped up several grasshoppers, which gave me a good idea. I caught a dozen and dropped them into the riffle above where the immense cutthroat had been feeding. It wasn't long before the fish spotted those diamond-backed hoppers and savagely tore them off the surface of the river. "What a display of greed," I said to myself. "And that, old boy, is going to put you into the skillet."

After selecting the longest willow I could find, I cut it off with my axe and trimmed the branches until I had a smooth fish pole, maybe too limber, but worth the try. I tied on all the line, attached the leader and a number ten hook with grasshopper installed. I dropped the bait into the current and let it drift into the riffle, hoping for a strike, but not prepared for what happened next.

The river erupted under my grasshopper, which disappeared in a flash. My line gave a heavy jerk, throwing me off balance, and I found myself face down in ice-cold water with a six-pound trout towing me downstream. I was a good enough swimmer, thanks to my father, so I wasn't in trouble, but I had no intention of losing that huge fish either. After drifting into slow water, I finally got to shore and played out the trout, eventually beaching him. "Nobody would believe this," I muttered later, while squatting before the cook fire naked, with my clothes adorning the surrounding bushes. Buck, luckily for him, declined any comment.

A small steel grill with folding legs worked like a charm when placed over a bed of coals. Fish fillets browning on one side of it and a pot of water boiling on the other was all the kitchen I needed. The water that my potatoes boiled in became soup stock, while the remaining fish, a slice of bacon, and a leaf of wild mint from the riverbank would make it a meal. This would have to sustain me all day tomorrow while I was chopping out a route to mountaintop hunting country.

The obscure trail we were riding was made during the course of many centuries by nomadic Kootenai Indians while heading from the interior lake country to the vast buffalo-hunting prairies to the northeast. The month-long trail followed the valley across the Canadian border to the mouth of the Elk River, and thence east along the Elk to Crows Nest Pass. From there it was downhill through extensive badlands, finally reaching the endless great plains.

Hornet Peak dominated the area that I was now traversing. It was a towering mountain, formed by numerous cliffs, benches, and avalanche chutes. Its base rose directly out of the river, making travel through here impossible during the high water of spring and early summer. Even after the river receded, one had to saw through the countless deadfalls, and slowly pick his way across rockslides with his packstring, which often became a dangerous undertaking. The back side of this mountain had three very long ridges leading for miles to its summit, making for better travel, with easy hunting. It was worth the trip to these subalpine ridges to view the breathtaking scenes, reaching all the way to the backbone of the snowcapped Cabinet range, days to the south. Numerous springs were used by bighorn sheep and mule deer in the high areas, and the creeks in the lower, more dense cover were frequented by elk and whitetail deer.

No wonder that the big cats here were fat from venison and grouse. I hoped also to harvest some of the surplus from this wild land, to put away my bit against hard times. My immediate problem was to locate a horse trail from the river to the high country behind Hornet Peak. The best chance was along the one nearby stream that didn't come down from the peak in a long series of waterfalls. My future hunting companion was not going to be a mountain man, or a horseman, which facts bothered me a considerable amount. He would have to ride all the way to the top, on a very large horse, and my trail needed to be wide and gentle or we would not get the job done.

Numerous benches facing the south or west were open enough for good horse travel, as the dry sides of these mountains produced great old ponderosa pines that kept the underbrush away. Sweet bunchgrass, like candy for elk, mule deer, or horses, covered the ground to knee height, giving the area a fine parklike appearance. The big trick was to find a way up from one bench to the next without having to navigate a twenty foot cliff or a steep rockslide.

Several times I was able to move large logs out of the way by putting a loop of rope around an end, taking a dally around the saddle horn and letting Buck pull them across the hillside. This saved hours of work, and Buck didn't seem to mind, as we had done similar things before while making firewood. Blazes put on appropriate trees, and stone cairns, which I erected in the open areas, would help to find the trail in the dark or during snowstorms in the late fall hunting seasons. There are times when one can hardly see two horse lengths ahead, and to get off the trail then could very well bring a disaster.

Two days of intense effort brought us to the top for a well-deserved rest and a great chicken dinner. I had managed to shoot the heads off of two blue grouse with my .270 Winchester and soon had the birds roasting on a spit over the coals of dry lodgepole. This wood gave no pine flavor to the wild birds, and with the addition of a little salt and pepper, I ate them both down to the bare bones, leaving the remains for a sharp-eyed raven. A heavily used game trail led us to the north slope of the ridge, where we quickly found a nice, cold spring and a fine patch of ripe huckleberries. It didn't take long to turn my fingers and face into a purple mess as I satisfied my craving for a good dessert.

Here was a perfect place for an ambush, a hunter's dream spot, and by great good luck I had walked right into it. There were innumerable deer and elk trails converging on the spring. There was cover, shelter from the wind, browse and grass close at hand, and no evidence of anyone ever hunting the area. Big Ed Scharpe, "Chaps," would shoot his game from this location, using a blind that I would build for him and his fabled lady friend, Teresa. He could make his own mythology here, he could make venison, or he could make love in the seclusion of this glade of two-hundred-year-old firs. Nobody except Johnny Bates and I would ever know of it.

Chaps was no ordinary man, and I contemplated his extraordinary demands with their commensurate rewards or punishments. This was as good a place as any to ponder these things while sitting on a soft hummock of bunch grass with my back against a three-foot-thick Douglas fir. Buck's main concern was using his long tail with unerring accuracy to dispatch some pesky deer flies. I fell asleep and hardly moved until a late afternoon breeze cooled the air. It was time to go, but Johnny Bates and I would be back and nothing could stop us!

Chapter 3

Chaps was the superintendent of the Western Division of the Great Northern Railroad. He was a king in his domain, and he used his influence to further the interests of his employer and also of himself. Chaps was an imposing figure with an untrained body of six feet and six inches and two hundred seventy-five pounds. In contrast there was nothing untrained about his mind, which had the quickness of a bobcat trap. He was endowed with a lifetime memory, much to the sorrow of his enemies or to the benefit of his friends. His position as the division manager gave him power over towns, businesses, farmers, ranchers, lumbermen, and the U.S. mail.

Nothing moved into the area or out of it without his knowledge or approval, as his railway was the main link to civilization between Seattle and Minneapolis. Grain, lumber, coal, food, ore, oil, gas, and automobiles, all were transported over the Great Northern, and woe betide anyone who needed a boxcar or other equipment if he was on the bottom side of the "ledger." Some, on the other hand, had been rewarded in a princely fashion for favors done above the ordinary, and my mind was working on that possibility. I was also wondering about using Johnny Bates on this difficult assignment. Bates and Scharpe were like day and night to each other, like winter and summer, or like thoroughbreds and mules, but both were very good at what they did.

Johnny Bates was my horse wrangler, a rough-cut independent spirit who answered to no one but himself until he was on the verge of starvation. Whenever that stared him in the face he quit his endless rounds of horse training, parties, and women, more or less in that order. Somehow, he took a liking to me, and would take orders for the duration of a couple paydays, which was usually long enough to get my hunts or wilderness expeditions completed.

Johnny's expertise with horses and pack mules was second to none, and he served me well while in the back country. After that, he would disappear like a shot-at bull elk, fading into the mist to resurface when one of his basic needs became too compelling. It seemed like he never stood close enough to his razor, and his copious red hair constantly moved as though caught up in a whirlwind. An obvious bowlegged stance, along with a pair of worn-down Acme boots and an aversion to walking, gave him away as a born horseman. Johnny could be a likable sort, mostly, if you were able to stay upwind of him. More than once I threatened to throw him, boots and all, into the Kootenai River before our big hunt began, but he smiled through it all.

Big Ed Scharpe was a southern gentleman from New Orleans who carried his southern drawl into Montana, where it was heard with great suspicion. He had also learned the four-letter language of the section hands, which he used with astonishing results when smooth-talk was going nowhere. Chaps could identify practically every French wine worthy of an expert; he knew all the works of the classical composers from Chopin to Tchaikovsky, and he could charm a lady out of her petticoats, which seemed to me to be often enough. Chaps, with his bright, exquisite companion, Teresa, were welcome in every important boardroom. They knew the best restaurants and boutiques, and attended most major sporting events.

What had eluded Chaps up to now were the skills and the abilities of a hunter. This was bad for his ego, as he wanted a macho mystique that would make him a real man's man. He was now ready to devote a great deal of money and energy into changing his image. We figured that Teresa had something to do with this new adventure, but I had the feeling that Chaps was too much of an aristocrat to really get his feet wet, or to harden that huge body with extensive physical effort. Johnny and I were true cowards though, when it came time to mention something like that to the giant we had signed on with.

Besides, there was the Creole cooking in his private railway car to look forward to, and the chance to taste fresh crabs, Gulf shrimp, and lobsters, all washed down with rare wines that neither of us had ever heard of. We had little proper education, but we weren't backward enough to endanger our chances for money, great food, and glory.

Chaps' wardrobe was hand tailored by the best clothiers in San Francisco and New York. The impeccable needlework done on rare, imported fabrics made Chaps stand out in any gathering. His hunting clothes were also elegant, but inefficient. His tailors had likely never seen a dense north slope in the Rockies, much less hunted or ridden a horse in the bush. My own woolens were by comparison well mended but durable, loose and easy to move in, layered to fit any weather conditions, and completely without style. What jeans and cotton shirts I had showed plenty of hard wear. As Chaps jokingly pointed out, there was "no way" my outfit could "make the grade at any royal shoot on the European continent." Still, through a lot of trial and error, our local, drab equipment was the best yet devised for the Rocky Mountains. Johnny and I would show this visiting "royalty" a thing or two before we finished with him.

A great stir went through the community of Libby when a sixty-foot-long private railway car with a white mountain goat artistically painted on each side was spotted on the sidetrack behind the depot. It had been dropped off by the transcontinental Empire Builder, the crack passenger train that never stopped in places like Libby, but this time it did for sure. There couldn't be many reasons why an executive with a palatial traveling office like this would want to stop here. The car was freshly painted a pale green, with gold trim liberally applied in filigree style by a very talented artisan. No one would doubt that money and power flowed from this car like high water in the Kootenai River. There was a thin plume of white smoke coming out of the stack, indicating that Richard, the black cook, was preparing breakfast for two.

Teresa by now had treated her companion to the sort of wake-up call that he could never describe, and would be laying out the clothes for the day while Chaps attempted recovery in the hot shower. Her morning attire was fifty years ahead of time, sparing and filmy. It revealed her tall slender body and full breasts in a way that would make any man forget about breakfast. She had long and shiny brown hair falling to her shoulders, outlining an intelligent, strong face with piercing blue eyes. The unblemished skin of her entire body was perfectly tanned. A woman such as this was a very rare item indeed in this backwater region, and she would be talked about for years. Richard sighed, and forced himself to look out the window as Teresa entered the dining room. He set the sterling silver coffee service in place and slowly disappeared into the kitchen, trying, but failing, to forget what he had seen.

Charlie MacDougal, the Scottish depot agent, roughly grabbed the maddening phone as he rolled out of bed a bit late that morning. He had spent too much time the previous evening evaluating the new shipment of Scotland Mist that had reached the Mint Bar very recently. His head was throbbing, and his short temper wasn't helping soothe his feelings any. Charlie looked and felt a lot like the numerous snarling grizzlies that decorated the barroom walls, and he did not take kindly to being called before having coffee in the morning.

"Yeah," he growled into the receiver, which he held an inch from his mouth, likely sending fumes across the line, "What the hell do you want?"

"This is Ferd, down at the Mint. I been cleanin' up your mess this mornin' and when I looked out the window I see this private car parked by the depot. I never seen nothing like it before, and I figgered it must be your big boss. I wanted to let you know about it so you could sober up in a hurry and get your rear end down there before I lost one of my ornery customers."

"Go jump into the river, I'll get there soon enough," was the nasty snarl that would have done Ferd's grizzlies justice. There was a wide grin on Ferd's face as Charlie rammed the earphone into its holder and then hammered the whole machine down on the pine tabletop. He just added another deep half moon scar to accompany the rest of them on his table. "Ed Scharpe is not who I need hanging around here today with me bein' a week behind," he thought, while cussing his luck. Charlie would soon show a dramatic change in attitude when he got a good look at Mr. Scharpe's traveling companion, a woman who could melt stone.

"MacDougal, I want to talk to you in your office, now," Chaps commanded as he entered the depot. "And shut the door. I do not want your telegraph operator clicking this conversation up and down the line."

"First of all, my, ah, friend and I took a walk all along your sidetrack right after breakfast and do you know what we did not see? We did not see one single fifty-foot double door boxcar waiting to be switched into the lumber mill. I have it on the best authority that your local mill is supplying all the lumber for a new shopping area in downtown Chicago. That is fifteen hundred miles from here, all on our railroad! Do you have any idea of the money involved in this? I promised this outfit some boxcars, and by all that is holy, they are going to get them, and fast. Get your operator on it." Chaps was shouting by this time. "You got my orders for this last week!"

"All them ranchers east of here is shipping grain to Minneapolis and they got most of the rolling stock along the HiLine between Great Falls and Fargo," Charlie replied, his face turning pale. His gut was in bad shape from last night, and now it was feeling even worse.

"Then get some of it transferred here on today's number twenty-seven," Chaps roared, while pointing his finger directly at Charlie's nose, " Or I'll have you swinging a spike hammer on the section along with all those Swedes this winter. Maybe you are sitting too close to your warm stove!"

Charlie stood up and staggered to the door, shouting through it, "Oscar, you heard the man. Get on the line to Fargo and get us a dozen fifty footers per day for the next two weeks, or someone is likely to get hung." Charlie had visions of leaving home before daylight, using a hammer and crowbar all day, freezing his hands and feet, and getting home again long after dark. He couldn't survive the Arctic weather again as he had during his youth, and his now overworked liver rebelled along with his pounding head. It never entered Charlie's mind that Chaps might have a share in the Chicago shopping center.

"Now that chore is done," Chaps said in a new tone of voice. "Get the manager of the mill on the phone, and then get that Herb somebody, who is the best hunter around here. I want them for lunch in my private car, and you too. I have some business to transact with them that you will know about sooner or later anyway. By the way, here is my written order to build a spur off the main line at any point that Herb tells you to. Do you get that? I am going to have a major hunting trip around here this fall and you will be the first critter to get skinned if you foul anything up. This man has been in my pay for half the summer, and I want to know exactly what he has found. Get yourself shaved and put on a clean shirt. We will have a lady for company."

Charlie sank down into his beat-up old swivel chair and wiped the sweat off his scowling face as Chaps stalked out of the depot. He had not been asked to show the books on ore and lumber shipments for the past month, books on which he was behind, and on which his commission depended. In a close scrutiny, he was going to have trouble defending his past six months' paychecks, and now he was sure that before sunset, the axe was going to fall on his well-exposed neck.

After a bit of thought, the answer to his immediate problem came to him. Create a diversion, find the one weak spot in his boss's armor and attack! Charlie raised the phone and spoke to the operator, "Get me Alice, over at the greenhouse, and when I am done with that, get me the manager down at the sawmill."

"Alice," Charlie said in his sweetest manner, "you got to find me the best and biggest bunch of mixed flowers, roses, and iris, and such that you can, and get them over to the private car on my siding before noon." There was an ominous silence. "No, Alice, I'm not trying to spark a new fancy lady. You still are the prettiest blossom in Montana."

"Quit the blarney, Charlie, I know you would take up with a young tart if one gave you the eye, and besides, you forgot my birthday last week."

Charlie was sweating again, and he was trying hard to stay calm, "Alice, my job probably depends on this, and I'll pay you for it."

"Hunh," Alice replied. "I heard from Ferd that you spent your money at his place on a wild night, and you're probably broke by now, but I'll see."

"Now, that's my old sweetheart," Charlie crowed, "and there is a free pass to Spokane for you just waiting in my desk drawer."

"Maybe I am making progress," Charlie mused, "I hear rumors that Chaps cannot take his eyes off that woman, and maybe if these flowers make her happy, he will forget about me." Charlie rubbed his stomach. It still hurt like the devil.

The phone rang in the sawmill manager's office and the secretary answered. "Walt is out right now, and I don't know where Herb is. I have hardly seen him around all summer and nobody knows what he has been doing. It is all so very secret."

"This is Charlie, down at the depot. Please tell Walt and Herb, too, if you can find him, that their presence is requested for lunch today at Ed Scharpe's private car on our siding, and they better be there."

"Yes, I know your voice, Charlie, and you sound bad, like you been eating sand or something."

"If it was just some sand I been swallowing today, I'd be soundin' lots better," Charlie replied in a very agitated Scottish brogue. "You better get them two down here, and tell 'em both to put on a clean shirt. This is supposed to be a high-class private meeting, and don't you go blabbing to nobody about it."

"Why, Charlie, this sounds like there is going to be a woman there, and you know I just love private meetings, too. Mind if I come along?" Walt's secretary wasn't too busy these days, and she was just itching for something new to occupy her mind. This news was just like giving raw meat to a cougar, and her phone would be busy the rest of the morning.

Chapter 4

Teresa entered the waiting room of the Libby depot on the bright summer morning to find it empty. Number 27 wasn't due for a couple hours, so the mailman had not arrived yet, and none of the regulars who just liked watching trains were sitting in their accustomed spots by the bay window. Teresa had on a beautifully crafted flowered dress, with a tight waist and long flowing skirts, perfectly accenting her tall, trim figure. Her plunging neckline, which was partially obscured by dainty, handmade lace, finished the portrait of elegance. Oscar heard her footsteps and looked up to see the most astonishing woman of his life leaning over the counter, smiling at him.

"Hello, Oscar," she purred, "I was feeling bored this morning, and I thought it would be fun to learn how to operate a telegraph machine. I heard that you were about the best in the company, and hoped you could teach me a few things." Teresa's blue eyes were sparkling, and Oscar was melting.

Oscar wiped his flushed face with a red bandanna kerchief, and tried to say, "No," without any success. He had never had much to do with women, but this one put him under her control before he ever thought about it.

"It isn't usually allowed, Mrs., uh, Ma'am," Oscar choked out, "but seeing as you're Mr. Scharpe's, uh, very good friend, it might just be possible." A faint touch of Teresa's delicate perfume, the best from New York, found him now, and he had to back into his chair to keep from falling on his face. "Please come in," he whispered. "Charlie went home to get himself cleaned up for your luncheon."

"What if I want to send a message to my sister in Portland?" Teresa asked sweetly.

Oscar explained, "Well, it can be sent to our agent there if it is an emergency. He can get your sister on the phone, and then send her answer back. It wouldn't take more than a couple minutes, but it is against regulations to send a personal wire without Charlie's okay. I could be in bad trouble if I started something like that."

Teresa had sidled up to Oscar's chair, and now let her long hair brush up against his face. "I really wouldn't want to cause you any problems, with you being so kind and all, so why don't we just send one of your regular messages? I used to practice the Morse code, you know."

Oscar was losing ground fast. He was blocked from standing up, and did not dare turn his head toward Teresa. That would press his face into her breast with her being so close, and he could already feel some swelling between his legs. In desperation, he finally came up with an idea. "I have an extra key that has never been hooked up to our private line. I could get it out of the storeroom and we could practice on that if you like."

"Oh, that would be loads of fun, and maybe I can remember just how I used to talk with my sister in school by tapping a pencil on my desk. Why don't you just hurry up and find your new key, while I wait right here."

Oscar felt like a drowning man who had just been thrown a rope, as Teresa backed up a bit and sat on the edge of the desk, crossing her legs. Oscar couldn't move his eyes away from this new set of curves as he headed for the storage closet with visions swimming around in his head. A surge of cold fear in his heart was all that kept him in check. By the time he returned, Teresa had removed a small, partially filled flask from her handbag and deposited it in the bottom desk drawer.

"It's coming back to me, already," Teresa said, looking Oscar straight in the eyes with a smile while she patted him on the cheek, "and maybe after everybody goes to lunch, you could just send this little note to Abigail, in Portland. No need for an answer. She is getting married, poor dear, and I just can't seem to find her a good seamstress!"

The depot door opened and Chaps saved Oscar from himself. "Oh, here you are, Teresa," Chaps said, "I thought maybe you had walked to town to dig around in some of the shops, so I was going to do a bit of bookwork in here, and earn my wages." Oscar stood up and moved away from his temptress, trying to regain some composure. "Where do you keep your pen and paper?" Chaps asked, as he walked to the desk and started rummaging through the drawers.

Suddenly Chaps' manner changed. He was feigning intense anger and a black scowl crossed his face. He pulled a half-filled bottle of Scotch from the lower drawer, waved it around in the air, and strode over to Oscar, who was watching in disbelief. "What in the hell is this?" Chaps demanded. "You know the regulations on keeping alcohol in the office. I want all my operators sober and alert at all times, do you understand? I could send you to Siberia for this," he shouted.

Oscar was staring dismissal and starvation in the eye. A couple minutes ago he was experiencing great passion, and now within the blink of an eye he was on the verge of disgrace and unemployment. "I don't know, I can't remember putting it in there." Oscar was pleading for his life. He had given up drinking over a year ago when he saw what troubles it got Charlie into. The thought suddenly hit him: it had to be Charlie who took it out of his own desk and put it into mine when he saw the big boss arriving. Wait till I get my chance, and I'll kill him!.

Teresa put her arms around Scharpe, pulled him up tight and tilted her head back. "Don't be too hard on the dear man," she whispered, "he was being so nice to me."

"Yeah, it sure looked like it, all right," Chaps growled. "Okay, I'll let it go for now as I am crowded for time and can't be bothered with finding another operator. I want to go over the books on ore shipments and lumber. Where does Charlie keep them, Oscar?"

"He says that they are his private business and he always locks them in the file cabinet and takes the keys with him. I might be able to find the spares, though." Oscar was afraid of Charlie, but not nearly as afraid as he was of big Ed Scharpe. Now was a great chance to get even with Charlie for hiding that booze in his desk. No one would ever know of it, either. The spare key was on a high hook behind the door to the john.

Chaps had a degree in accounting along with his business education, and it was a matter of minutes before he figured out the deceptions that an untrained depot agent had made in the records. There were a few hundred dollars here, and a few hundred there, nothing large enough to create any real problems for the company, but enough to allow Charlie to entertain Alice in Spokane from time to time. It also could make Charlie look like a big shot among his drinking and poker partners at the Mint, where he usually lost most of his money.

Chaps made some notations on a pad, which he now confined to his briefcase, and then replaced Charlie's books and locked the cabinet. Teresa, in the meanwhile, had gone to help Richard decorate the dining room before all the guests arrived. "We shall remain quiet about this entire affair," Chaps instructed Oscar, "and for your own sake, get rid of that bottle right now. Don't let this happen again, you hear?"

"Yes sir," was all Oscar could manage, as he rubbed his face again with the bandanna. Chaps tried to hide a satisfied grin as he headed for lunch.

"That woman is a winner," he thought to himself, while still remembering her passionate efforts and his own exhaustion early that morning. "Too bad I'm not in shape, but she could get used to living in luxury and would likely do anything I ask her to get it. There are a lot of people waiting to be relieved of a lot of money, and they won't feel so badly, losing it to a beautiful woman," he mused.

Chapter 5

Richard had planned this meal for several days, ordering the fresh salmon on ice from Seattle, and the world's best prime corn-fed beef cut to his specifications out of Chicago. His master's touch in the kitchen started years earlier in New Orleans restaurants where he had learned the hard way from several domineering chefs. He kept his mouth closed and his ears open, and tried to maintain a good humor through it all. His big break came one night while he substituted for an absent chef, producing a great meal for Chaps and guests who happened to choose the right restaurant on the right evening.

Chaps was impressed with the food and special service, and asked to meet the chef, who also impressed him with his confidence and quick wit. It was shortly thereafter that Richard was offered a job with the Great Northern Special Services, Ed Scharpe, department head. Richard's pay was doubled as soon as he graduated from the Great Northern's cooking school. After a short apprentice time on the Empire Builder's dining cars, he was reassigned to Chaps' private car, where his great imagination was the outer limit on his productivity.

The fame of Richard's creative cooking spread, and soon he was being tempted by other executives of the company to change bosses, but there was a loyalty in Richard and an appreciation by his benefactor that formed a very firm bond between the two. Richard was happy where he was. It also gave Chaps a great deal of joy to be one up on his contemporaries, and he never missed a chance to rub it in. Richard had rapidly become a master at No-Holds-Barred cooking, with little restraints on costs.

Alice made a real effort to put together a fine bouquet of fresh cut flowers and ferns, and delivered it in person before noon. Teresa accepted the gift graciously, and put Alice at ease with her genuine and friendly manner.

"My God," Alice thought to herself, "When Charlie gets a good look at this beautiful woman he will never take another look at me; but then again, that old Scotchman surely couldn't handle anything like her without having a heart attack in the first five minutes. Maybe it's time I tried a new hairdo, myself."

Walt's secretary had done her job tracking us down. I took a fast shower, put on my best checkered plaid western shirt and found a clean pair of jeans in respectable condition. I pulled on my new boots, which were long overdue. My old ones were worn out from the constant use in the mountains, so I junked them on the way out. All in all, I didn't look too shabby in the mirror, the way it seemed to me. My body was lean and tough as buffalo hide, darkened by the sun, and well muscled up from the long days working in the timber. I was wondering if I would make a reasonable impression on the unseen lady at lunch as I clapped my old 4 X Stetson on my sun-bleached, still damp hair. I knew that my new boots would be dusty when I arrived at the depot, but I would take them off at the door. The old, thin socks and worn-out underwear arched through the air toward the same can holding my tattered boots. A perfect basket brought a smile to my face, and I thought it might be the sign of a lucky day.

We all arrived on time and could smell some wonderful aromas emanating from Richard's kitchen. When inspired, Richard could do things with a cookstove that most people could not even imagine, and today was no different. The meal started out with broiled grapefruit halves, the world's best from southern Texas. The pink meat was sweet without sugar to hide its subtle flavor. No knife was ever needed to extract the large juicy sections, which seemed to go down one's throat in endless succession. Next came a cold seafood soup, light, with a taste that demanded second helpings, but none were served. Richard figured that a man was actually satisfied when he still wanted more, and he teased us with this philosophy.

The salmon and steak were served side by side, each with its savory sauce made with ingredients I never identified. Up till now, we had been treated with what normally would be a terrific lunch, but we all were reaching for large helpings of these additional courses like starving savages. A heaping salad was served in wooden bowls that had been rubbed with garlic before being filled with the finest lettuce and herbs. The aromatic dressing was a new experience for me also, as was this entire affair.

There were two kinds of French wine, one being proper for fish and the other for corn-fed beef. I had no way of knowing which was which, having never tasted anything but homebrew before, which I disliked fervently. I had to watch Chaps and more or less copy what he was doing to keep from making a major gaffe.

Charlie was having a lot of trouble with the three sets of knives, forks, and spoons which were set at each place. He used his salad fork for the fish while I elbowed him in the ribs, but I had to kick him in the shins when he buttered his fresh baked rolls with a steak knife. Even I had that one figured out by then. The manners expected here were a far cry from clamping your teeth on to a tough, dripping piece of moose flank and cutting off the extra with a Remington sheath knife. Carefully sparing your nose from a six-inch blade while your eyes were watering from a smoky fire became a highly developed skill, but not exactly in place at this elegant affair.

The dining table was set with English bone china decorated with the Great Northern mountain goat, very artistically done in the center, and offset by a gold band on the rim. Using gold on dinnerware was something that had never occurred to me, but I had heard of sterling silver implements even though my rough hands had not held any of those before. I could just see the wheels going around in Charlie's poker-playing head, with all this precious metal sitting here within easy reach. The spotless tablecloth of pure Irish linen was hand monogrammed E. S., with napkins to match. Charlie's floral gift was on display in a delicate cut-glass vase on a side table, where Teresa had skillfully made an oriental arrangement of it.

Behind the vase on a hardwood wall was an original oil by Charlie Russell, depicting a herd of buffalo being run over a cliff by a dozen Indians on horseback. I was duly impressed by the beauty and realism of this famous work, and could hardly guess at its great value. Charlie was obviously taken with this painting, also, but the artistic qualities were submerged in his mind. The grain sack full of dollars it represented was the thing that had him thinking new thoughts. He had been to Great Falls a couple times and had seen the works of Charlie Russell in the museum there. One picture could get a man a ranch, and a fancy new woman to show off with it. Under a long thin display light on the opposite wall hung an early original Picasso.

Teresa broke the spell by serving the dessert. She moved in front of Charlie and leaned over a bit as she set the plate before him. Charlie's eyes widened and his mouth opened as he stared down that lovely valley that was exposed to him with nothing hidden, and he momentarily forgot all else. All talking stopped. There was complete silence, any sounds being muffled by the thick oriental rug. Time was standing still, but finally Charlie broke, as everyone's eyes moved to his face, which was now dotted with sweat, brought to the surface with pure lust. He clutched a napkin to his mouth as I raised a glass of water, clinking the ice cubes. Charlie would never recover.

Dessert was a fresh apple pie topped with ice cream, scarce enough in that country, but at least we all could relate to it. Richard probably had that in mind when he made the pie. Walt had been around a lot, and seemed perfectly at ease with the whole situation, while I was as nervous as a boy on his first date, worrying about making a mistake. Thinking ahead, I could see that nobody would want to get out into the woods and go hunting while the best food in Montana sat in camp. I was wondering, too, just how good Richard was as a security guard, since he was alone in the car so often.

How anyone could live like this on a daily basis was beyond me. Then, after the mild effects of the wine I drank started to wear off, the whole affair came into focus. Here was Chaps' way of showing off his world-class lady friend, his private car with its priceless oil paintings and appointments, his appreciation of fine food and wines, and lastly, his hospitable way of telling us that he demanded the best of everything and would get it. My mind was catching up with his, and I knew what had to be done to satisfy a large ego. Give him a great hunt and make him look good.

"Gentlemen," Chaps said, bringing us back to reality, "I trust that you all appreciate Richard's contribution to our enjoyment, and now we have a bit of time to discuss the immediate future. Walt, I wish to use this opportunity to tell you just how much I value your efforts in my behalf during the train wreck last winter. I hope that the lumber orders for the Chicago project will compensate you in some small way." He looked out a window before continuing. "I did use a little timely persuasion in getting those orders, just in case you want to know."

What Chaps forgot to tell us was that the contractor had a rapidly approaching deadline, and there were no boxcars available for lumber shipments out of Montana due to the heavy grain crop being moved. Walt was hurting too, and when Chaps offered him a huge order at prices somewhat below the market, it was accepted. The shopping center owners reluctantly agreed to give Chaps a five percent ownership in the project if he could get the lumber for them, and on time. Their bankers were about to recall the loan. The contractor paid Chaps the market price for the lumber.

"Well, Charlie, that brings us down to you," Chaps continued, "and I can see a way for you to do the Great Northern a big service. Herb, here, will fill you in on all the details, as he has spent a lot of time this summer researching an expedition for us. It involves building a spur into a roadless area so we can spot my private car there and hunt in complete privacy and comfort. You will be in charge of the construction."

"But sir," Charlie was already complaining, "that spur will cost a whole lot of money, and besides, the job as agent is taking all my time." The longer Charlie worked in the office, the more he hated the physical labor out on the tracks, and he would do about anything to avoid it. His nightlife wasn't exactly compatible with hard work, and he was revolted by the idea of getting out of some lady's warm bed at five-thirty on those freezing mornings.

Chaps flashed a warning look at Charlie and put some heat into his reply. "You are getting out of shape, and that job will harden you up and increase your appetite. It will likely add ten years to your life if you stay away from the Mint at night and do a man's work during the daytime. I have no doubt that you will be thanking me for this before very long."

Charlie still did not tumble to the fact that maybe Chaps had something on him, and he stepped into yet deeper water. "I'm not feeling all that well, lately, and I know that Ingvar, our section foreman, could get it done just as well."

"MacDougal," Chaps commanded in a very stern voice, "you will do this on your own time on weekends, without pay, and the section gang will be there with you. As it so happens, I have been auditing your books, and they do not add up. It appears to me that you owe the company about six months pay for overcharging your commissions. I also discovered that Ingvar knew about this somehow, because you have been paying him and his crew overtime pay for work not accomplished yet!" Chaps was angrily waving his notepad as Charlie's face turned chalk white. "This spur will be built immediately. Is that clear?" Charlie was not feeling thankful as yet.

I noticed that Teresa was hiding her face behind a fan, and not doing a very good job of concealing her laughter. Somehow I knew that the beautiful creature in front of me had something to do with Charlie's exposure, and I quickly learned that beauty and danger could be close playmates. Like everyone else, though, I could hardly take my eyes off her.

No one had to tell me that it was time for me to break into the conversation. "Mr. Scharpe, Walt has already agreed to send two of his best men and a couple D-8 cats to the area that I selected and surveyed for the hunting spur. The rates for the crew and the cats will be slightly above market, but you will have the best job possible done quickly and done right the first time." I gave Walt a little sideways smile. "We can have the roadbed roughed in during one weekend, as I have found a route with very little earth-moving to do. It will put us within a couple miles of the access trail that I cleared for our horses, and there is good grass and fresh water nearby.

"Johnny Bates and I were out there the past couple weeks improving the trail, and scouting out more of the hunting area. We also built a corral and made us a good campsite with cover for hay and horse tack. There is game up there that you would not believe, and most of it will likely die of old age. It's a long ways in, though, so I am thinking of putting in another small camp on the ridgetop for overnighters. You should start doing some riding now, or the first few days of hunting could be very painful, to say the least. Running wouldn't hurt you any, either." Chaps didn't look to be too quick on his feet, and I sure as sin didn't want to pack him out of the hills draped sideways across old Sally, my best pack mule.

"I knew right off that I could depend on you, Herb," Chaps said, ignoring my advice. "I am sure that Charlie will be glad to start working on the spur, as soon as your cats get there on Saturday. By the way, you will be getting your first check tomorrow with a nice raise in pay." Ed turned his face toward Charlie, now, and gave him a stare that could stun old Sally. Charlie knew he was trapped, and he sat there glassy-eyed and mum, wondering where he had gone wrong. About then, hate started replacing the lust inside his head.

"Gee, thanks a lot Ed," I said in pleasant surprise, still smiling at Walt. We now figured to get most of Walt's missing money back from the lumber deal. "I took the liberty to order a really fine rifle for you and it's here, waiting at the hardware store. It might be a good idea to pick it up and get in an hour of target practice this afternoon. We can zero it in and shoot at the old gravel pit across the river where I built a good solid bench."

Iver Iverson ran the local hardware store, and also carried a few lever-action Winchester deer rifles, some Remington shotguns and .22 rifles, and always a variety of Colt handguns of various calibers. He had never sold a bolt-action Super Grade Winchester Model 70, but he had seen pictures of them in his catalog. I had him order one in .30-06 caliber, complete with Lyman sights, sling, and a case of 180-grain Silvertip ammunition. This rifle would have a highly figured French walnut stock, a deer engraved on the floorplate, surrounded by classical scroll work, and Chaps' initials inlaid in gold on the trigger guard. The stock would be an inch longer than usual, due to the size of the man who would be shooting it.

I had specified accuracy of one inch for a five-shot group at one hundred yards, tested at the factory. If a special order rifle would not perform to my standards, then all the beauty of it would be worthless in my opinion. This thought I conveyed forcefully to the custom shop at Winchester. No matter that Chaps couldn't hit his hat at forty paces, he was paying about five times as much for that .30-06 as he would for any common rifle off the store shelf. I wanted to see to it that his weapon was his pride, and was the envy of all who ever saw it or shot it. Nothing about this adventure would be second rate, and that included the food, horses, guns, and women, not in that order.

"Iver," I said one day while looking over this marvelous piece in the store, "we should spread the word about this rifle, and let everyone who is interested in guns get a look at it. It would be good for your business. For now, hand it down to me so I can adjust the trigger pull to something reasonable, like three-and-a-half pounds. I'll take the creep and back-lash out of it also, since the trigger performance is a large part of a gun's accuracy. It shouldn't take over half an hour, and I have my tools here."

"That's a fine idea," Iver replied. "Since half the town is already talking about this expedition of yours, I can end the rumors and tell everybody exactly what's happening. I'll never get another order like this again, either."

"Yeah, that's probably right, Iver, and besides, if this rifle ever decides to walk away with a stranger, it will be recognized by everybody in Montana."

The factories always set the trigger pull too stiff in order to save incompetents from accidents and to preclude any lawsuits. I opened the bolt with almost no effort and found the action to be as smooth as glass, with all the internal parts being hand polished, lapped, and very carefully fitted in compliance with my directions. The wood-to-metal fit was very tight, with no gaps anywhere, and the hand checkering at twenty-two lines per inch was done to perfection in a fleur-de-lis pattern. A lustrous blue finish on all exposed metal was the result of many hours of careful hand polishing. Neither Iver nor I had ever seen anything like it before. Chaps would appreciate the cosmetic qualities of this Winchester, but he could never get the best out of its great balance and performance. I would have given my eye teeth for that masterpiece. I couldn't get it out of my mind, but unlike Chaps, I did not have the likes of Teresa to distract me.

After lunch was over, Walt had to get back to his office, and Charlie retreated to lick his wounds. I talked Chaps into risking his neck riding over to Iver's store in my beat-up old pickup truck to purchase his new rifle.

"Herb, this old relic is likely to blow up at any minute," Chaps exclaimed, "and it has to be the roughest-riding vehicle I've ever been in."

"I think you're lacking in faith, Ed," I replied, laughing, "and besides, this is about like riding the horse that you'll be using, so you're getting good practice. Anyway, the smoothest ride you could find on the streets in this town is to fly over them."

"A railroad man has no use for airplanes," Chaps replied with a grin, "and if I have to associate with you very much I may have to get you a new truck just to keep us alive." I knew then that I might grow to like this devious man even if I could never trust him fully.

Chaps heaved his large bulk out of my truck after trying a couple times to get the door open. That did allow some time for the dust to settle, though. We were parked across the street from Iver's place, and Ed and I waded through that ankle-deep powder to reach Iver's wooden sidewalk. High-top boots were all that anybody ever wore around here. No merchant could see any reason to spend money on concrete, and there was still a lot of horse traffic on these streets anyway. When the fall rains started, the town became a sea of mud until freeze-up. After that blessing happened, nobody had to worry about mud or mosquitoes or dust for the next six months.

Iver knew immediately who Chaps was, and he reached for his key to unlock the closet where the new rifle was kept. Most of the townspeople had seen it, and Iver was taking no chances on getting it stolen.

"Howdy, gentlemen," Iver greeted us in a heavy Swedish accent, "I been waiting a long time to meet you, Mr. Ed."

"It is indeed a pleasure to meet you and to be here in this lovely country," Ed replied, while stamping the dust off his handmade Italian shoes. "Now, let me see this weapon that everyone in town has already approved of for me." He wrapped his huge hand around the pistol grip and turned to get into the light from the front windows. "Good Lord," Ed said, staring in admiration, "this rifle is a true work of art, like a great oil painting." He raised the rifle to his shoulder and sighted in on a dog lying in the shade of an apple tree across the street. "It comes to my shoulder by itself, as natural as if I was born with it. And just look at this walnut; fabulous."

"Work the bolt and then try the trigger pull," I suggested. "I believe you'll be surprised how smooth that action is. I set the trigger the way I like it, too, but could make any changes you want. Be sure that gun is unloaded."

Chaps tried the trigger a couple times, then sighted at the dog, and worked the bolt rapidly for several dry shots.

"This action is like a fine railroad watch," he commented, smiling at me, "but now comes the bad news. What is the price?" I doubted that Chaps would ever let the Winchester out of his possession now that he had seen it, regardless of the price. He took out a roll of greenbacks that he could barely reach around with those long fingers, and slowly counted out fourteen bills with One Hundred printed on each one. "Is this adequate?"

"Ya, tank you," Iver blurted out. His eyes grew larger each time a bill was laid in the lineup on his counter. He then reached into a box and produced the handmade saddle scabbard that I had ordered from Ray Holes Saddle Company in Grangeville, Idaho. It turned out to be a perfect fit to the rifle. The heavy top-grain leather was hand tooled with a wild rose design and was topped off with a cover that enclosed the buttstock when needed. Ed laid out two more bills from the roll, which didn't seem to be shrinking much even after the case of ammunition was paid for.

We proceeded to get everything loaded into the truck and then headed for the gravel pit. I had two sandbags on the shooting bench and I covered them with an old blanket to keep from scratching the beautifully finished gunstock. I fired the first three shots to check the rifle's zero, then made a few adjustments with the micrometer clicks on the Lyman sight. The next two shots printed touching each other and two inches high at one hundred yards. This would put the bullets exactly on center at two hundred. I figured rightly that Chaps could never hit a deer any farther than half that distance under hunting conditions.

I instructed Chaps to fire from the bench to gain confidence in the rifle, and to get used to the feel of it. After several fairly good shots, we changed to a sitting position, a well-used position in the mountains, and then finished with a bit of offhand practice. There were no more holes in the target, just lots of dust and powdered rock in the general vicinity, which didn't surprise me any.

"Offhand is for emergencies, at close quarters, with no chance for a rest," I explained, "And that style is generally to be avoided. You cannot hold on a target when your heart rate is way up and you're breathing heavy. Nobody wants to wound an animal and have it escape." We shot at different distances, at various angles, at rocks and cans, and I really developed a feel for that wonderful rifle. Its performance was every bit as good as I had hoped for, and I made a promise to thank the men who made it.

"Nice going, Ed," I commented as his shooting improved. "You seem to be getting the hang of it." Chaps was impressing me with his intellect and his ability to learn. I guessed that these qualities explained why he held the job he had.

"Well, it's been a long time since I had my .22 as a kid and did a little rabbit hunting. I wasn't too bad a shot then, but this is in a different league entirely. Thank you for the effort that you put into obtaining this truly fine piece. I like it immensely and will never sell it.

"I can see that about six months of shooting would be needed to really learn about the .30-06, but I could never match your skills. I'm going to practice as much as my schedule allows, and I will get Teresa involved too. She is a fine athlete, you know. Her tennis is quite good, she swims like a seal, and has taken riding lessons for years. She is going to surprise you on our hunt this fall."

"Ed, she has surprised me already," I said to myself, "and everyone else around here."

We returned to Chaps' palace in the heat of the afternoon. The long clear days this time of year forced the temperature into the high nineties in the valley, where any wind was rare. The hot weather was good, though, for making hay and growing a garden, which most families did. A dozen kids were making their voices heard as they cooled off in the shallows of the Kootenai River below the depot. I felt like jumping in with them, like old times, but instead joined Chaps for a lemonade in his sitting room.

"I already asked Walt to give you a few more months leave from your duties with the lumber company," Ed said, "and I invited him to join the hunt in October at any time he felt like it. Walt seemed to be delighted with this idea, and he was sure that you would be a whole lot happier out in the bush than you would be in town, anyway. You will be in my pay."

"You aren't far wrong with that assessment," I laughed, "but I always had trouble earning a living on a mountaintop before this." I was feeling at ease with Chaps by now. I had removed my boots at the door to keep from marking up the oriental rug that covered the floor an inch deep. New this morning, the boots now looked like they had been six months without a polish. The deep chair that Ed motioned me to was more than comfortable and I could easily have slept here in this cool, elegant, walnut-paneled room for the rest of the day.

"If it is okay with you," Ed continued, "I would like you to keep an eye on Charlie and Ingvar, to make sure that our spur is put where it belongs, and done quickly. Some of the track and ties from last winter's wreck can be salvaged for a low-use line like my spur, and the rest of the material will be made available out of Whitefish. All you have to do is tell Charlie to order it."

"After that is finished, you can complete setting up your camp, get the horses and mules together, and do whatever else you can think of to make this trip a success. You can correspond with me through Oscar on our telegraph."

Chaps was finished with me for the present. It took a lot of will power to force myself out of that European-made easy chair, but somehow I got it done. We shook hands, and said goodbye, with Ed sliding his carved walnut door closed behind me. I thanked him for the best lunch I ever ate. Teresa was waiting at the side door where my boots were, and before I could reach for them, she gave me a warm embrace, pressing her body against me with surprising strength, and then brushed my cheek with her lips. She flashed a knowing smile when she noticed the heat rising in my face and everywhere else.

"My lord," Teresa whispered while she still had her hands around my back, "Your body is solid as an oak. I'm never around anyone like you, but it would be nice." She was taking her time turning me loose, and I didn't want her to, but then I didn't need Chaps' wrath either.

Chapter 6

There was a lot of dust coming out of the corral, and I could hear Johnny's high-pitched voice: "Come on, you old outlaw, let's see what else you got under your black hide. Give it to me again if you're tough enough!" He was shouting at the big black gelding that was trying to throw him off without success. Both man and horse were covered with dust that was sticking to their sweat-soaked bodies, while both were determined to win this battle of wills and muscle. The horse swapped ends a couple times and jacknifed into the air, squealing in frustration as Johnny remained aboard.

The gelding finally determined that the creature on his back was going to stay there unless he scraped him off on the corral rails, and he made a couple of quick jumps angled toward the fence. Johnny sensed what was happening and immediately pulled the reins and a heavy halter rope to the left with both hands, using all the strength that he could muster. I could see the strain in Johnny's face as the black's neck bent into a U, and at the last second the horse turned away from the railing, sparing Johnny's right leg, while breaking the middle log with its rump.

The horse staggered and almost went down, but saved himself at the last second as Johnny let the pressure off the rope. Now its sides were heaving and the fight went out of him. Johnny urged him into a trot and stayed with it for a few minutes just to confirm who was boss. The horse was broke, and Johnny jumped off and remounted a couple times to make sure that there was no more bucking.

"This gelding sure was a hard case," Johnny said, managing a grin through his muddy face. "I think he would have tried to stomp me if he could have tossed me off, but I got lucky and changed his mind. I still have to give him another treatment whilst he is tired." Johnny picked up a couple grain sacks, tied them together end for end, and started flailing away at the black who was now tied to a heavy larch corral post.

The first few slaps brought an angry reaction as the black tried to turn his rump to his tormentor and deliver a kick to end it all. He failed at this and eventually quieted down, allowing the sacks to hit his face, under his belly, across the flanks, and between his legs.

"He figured I was going to hurt him, but now he knows better. A couple more times like this is all it will take to steady him down," Johnny was explaining. "Now hand me my pistol out of that leather bag, yonder, and we will teach this guy some more manners."

I handed over a short-barreled .22 revolver, which Johnny started firing into the air. The horse tried to break his halter rope during the first couple shots, but a half hitch around his nose with the rope soon taught him the folly of that move. After a box of .22 shells was used up, the black hardly paid attention to the shots. He was probably too tired to care anymore.

"Looks like we have ourselves another horse today, and with some use he will be a good one in the mountains. He learns fast, and he has a good build and a nice-looking head. He needs a lot of riding now, and some packing too. What I need now is a beer, and a chair in the shade."

"You are right on one count, Johnny," I said, "and I have a cool beer waiting for you in the truck, but you first have to jump into this pond here and clean up. After that I'm taking you to town so we can get our hay picked up and put under cover while we still have good weather. All it would take is one rainstorm and we'll be out of the guide business. I'll turn this black loose and you can get back to him in a week or so."

Johnny looked apprehensively at the pond, not moving, as I pointed my finger toward the water. Finally he slipped off his boots and hat and just sort of fell in, face first. At least the air in the pickup would be breathable on the way back to town.

We were going to need about five tons of hay and get it stored out of the weather where we could easily move it. Our summers this far north were quite short, so anyone being a bit late getting his crop in could end up with it being spoiled. Johnny Bates had agreed to help me after he finished breaking horses up in the Yaak Valley, where I found him this day. I needed to buy or rent some more saddle and pack stock for our hunt, so I put Johnny to work checking out likely looking prospects.

I had Buck, my saddle horse of many years, and a good pack mule of my own, but for what promised to be a major expedition we would need a dozen head of steady mountain animals. They would have to be alternated at times to rest up from some very tough days. I just wondered how my hunters would stand up to those same tough days without getting into condition beforehand.

Ed had hinted that there would be several visiting big-shots in the camp at times, which meant that I needed extra guides in addition to Johnny. The guides would have to be completely familiar with our hunting country if they were to be dependable in fog or snow, where visibility often was near zero. They had to know, also, how to hunt on those bright clear days when game would be in the lodgepole thickets, or on some dense north slopes until way after dark. Bull elk are especially difficult at any time, but in clear weather they become nocturnal.

The oldest bulls usually hole up in some narrow basin where there is a spring for drinking and wallowing. An area like this will be so thick with alders and willows that a man can barely penetrate it, much less shoot anything in there. A bull could stay for days on end in such a jungle, and hardly move a hundred yards. My guests would not likely see any of these elk, or even hear them bugle, as the mating season would be over. We would therefore concentrate on deer and black bear, where the odds were much better.

I needed to spend time training the guides and hiking them through the multiple canyons and over the ridges of Hornet Peak. This was a vast area, to say the least. Iver Iverson would no doubt be willing to guide, as he was a good hunter and liked being out for long periods of time. He had use for the extra income and would also recruit two more good men for us. Johnny's responsibilities were the care and training of our livestock. He had to make sure that the horses and mules were in shape, and gentle, as none of our guests would be experienced in riding rough country like this. We didn't need any mustangs. I figured that the days of sitting on a rail fence gleefully watching a dude get bucked off an unbroke outlaw were definitely a thing of the past. With a chef borrowed from Bill's cafe we now had a great crew secured.

Johnny and I found a hayfield that had just been put up with strong, wirebound bales of eighty pounds each. Two of these bales plus a light top-pack made a good load for a mule. A lot of loads like this would be hauled to the top of Hornet Peak. Any less was a waste of space, and any weight over two hundred pounds would cause a smart mule to lie down and refuse to move. It doesn't take one of these "Rocky Mountain canaries" very long to learn just how much he can handle during a tough day in the mountains.

After two days of heavy work in the ninety-degree heat, we had all the hay we needed for the camp plus some extra for the coming winter. It was difficult to imagine winter right now, while heat waves were radiating off the tarpaper roof of the hay shed and a shimmering mirage was blurring the trees at the far end of the field. My eyes were sore from dust and sweat mixed together, and my throat was dry as sandpaper. I could see that Johnny was in about the same shape, but he gave no sign of protest.

"Let's get up to the spur in the morning and find out how Charlie and his boys are doing," I said, while sitting down on a bale in the shade. "Maybe we can prod them along a bit. I doubt if they're hurrying the job any, as Charlie seemed mad as hell about being forced into this."

"Sounds like a winner to me," Johnny replied. "Maybe a ride on that speeder that Chaps gave us will cool us off some. I don't trust old Charlie none, either, and he could mess this job up good, the way he was acting."

"He is lucky not to be in jail," I was thinking out loud, "with the stealing that Chaps caught him at. Charlie doesn't seem to understand that Chaps is giving him a chance to work off thousands of dollars of graft over a few weekends instead of talking to the sheriff. I wonder what Ingvar is saying?"

We located the speeder parked behind the depot, empty of gas, and with a dead battery. This seemed strange, as everything had been ready to go when I looked it over a few days earlier. Johnny checked the oil and found that it was empty, with no sign of a drip on the ground.

"Somebody wants a little gas and oil real bad, or else they don't want us to use this speeder right now," I said. "Look this rig over carefully from top to bottom while I round up some gas and oil and a new battery. This has to be more than kids just fooling around. I think that someone is sending us a message—but why?" I didn't like trouble, but had never displayed fear of it either. What was it to be this time: women, money, booze, power?

I took my truck to the Texaco station and picked up a couple five-gallon cans of regular gas, a gallon of 30-weight oil and a new battery, all of which I charged to Chaps' account. I had to swing past my place to load in some plywood that Walt gave me for a floor and walls for the tent kitchen we would put up at the campsite. As an afterthought, I took my cased .270 along with a couple dozen cartridges. After all, if someone was going to cause me a lot of trouble, I could likely discourage him.

Most everybody in town had seen me win a lot of turkeys at rifle shoots, and more than one skeptic had seen me knock clay pigeons out of the air with this same .270 bolt-action Winchester. Perhaps a little show of backbone would prevent some major problems from developing. I had been around long enough to know that dogs, bears, and some men would take you down as soon as they saw you turn and run. I was neither dumb nor a coward, and I stayed out of trouble if at all possible. I also was aware that there were times when a man got crowded too much and had to take the proper steps.

Johnny and I loaded the plywood onto the speeder, filled up the gas tank and replaced the oil and the battery. The ten-horse motor would move us along at about thirty miles per hour on the level and about twenty on some of the grades on the Great Northern main line. Oscar gave us the schedule for all the train traffic in both directions for the next eighteen hours. We chose a two-hour time slot with no traffic, and took off for the hunting spur. Bill's chef fixed us up with a fried chicken lunch that we would eat on the way.

"This is the way to go," I thought. "The air feels cool when riding along in this open speeder. The lunch tastes good, the scenery along the Kootenai is outstanding, and here we are enjoying life on a smooth ride on Chaps' tracks while he is paying us to do it." I was relaxing, with the clacking rhythm of the rail joints on our wheels nearly putting me to sleep. I could not quite doze off, though, even with Johnny running the machine. Something was bothering me a little, but just what it was did not register for a long time. For the first half hour, we chugged along on fairly straight track, with just a few long bends following the course of the river. When we arrived opposite the angry water of Jennings rapids, the tracks quickly became a series of much sharper curves as the canyon closed in on us.

Suddenly it came to me. On a major S curve I heard a foreign noise from under the floor of the speeder, and I mentioned that to Johnny. On the straightaway, the noise disappeared, but returned again on the next bend, much louder now. It sounded like somebody using a hacksaw.

"Stop this buggy for a minute, Johnny. We need to look under the floor and find out what that noise is. It feels like we are swaying back and forth too much also, and there isn't any wind today."

Johnny pushed off the throttle and applied the handbrake, bringing us to a grinding halt on a straight section of track. We could see quite a way in both directions from here, which would give us time to get off the tracks in case an unscheduled freight came roaring down on us. Somehow, I didn't completely trust Oscar's timetable.

"Lookee here," Johnny exclaimed from under the speeder. "Somebody cut this axle in two right next to the bearing, on the inside, and then coated it with grease."

"Damn," I cussed, as I saw what Johnny was pointing at, "Some bastard is tryin' to kill us. This speeder is dangerous to run, but we can't stay here either." The axle had about two inches removed, allowing it to shift back and forth with the irregularities in the tracks. Sooner or later, with pressure at high speed on a curve, the axle would pull through the bearing and drop the speeder floor to the ties. Any passengers would be thrown onto the tracks and seriously injured, or killed if the speeder rolled over them. It was obvious what had been causing us to sway back and forth. It was also obvious that we had to get out of there, fast.

"Johnny, let's move this speeder along at about ten miles an hour. If we wreck, it likely won't hurt us too much, but we have a chance to get to the spur before the bearing gives way." I took a long look at my Ingersoll watch. "I think that we have time with a couple minutes to spare before the next freight is due up there. If it feels like the axle is coming off, hit the brake."

Our slow pace upriver had me worried. If we had to derail the speeder to free the main line for the next westbound freight, we would have to unload the plywood first. Our cargo made the speeder too heavy for two men to take it off the rails, while unloading it might take more time than we had. One could hear a freight when it was a couple miles away, but that gave scarce time to do what was needed to prevent being mangled. I was remembering Johanson, who was just returning to work after a long convalescence from his wintertime train wreck. Copying his experience wasn't in the plan.

Even with the breeze from our open air run trying to cool me off, I could feel a hot sweat over my whole body. Who was trying to get me killed, and why? I took a good look at my Winchester, lying on the stack of plywood. It had served me well in a good many scrapes with would-be thieves, toughs trying to flex their muscles, rogue bears in camp, and coyotes in the chicken yard. It wouldn't help me any now, though. I would be looking over my shoulder from here on if I wanted to stay healthy. We were getting close to the spur, but time was running out, and I nervously kept looking at my Ingersoll pocket watch.

This stretch of the Kootenai River was a long series of rapids with very deep swirling runs in between. The white foam, caused by the glacial water churning over huge boulders, floated in long fleecy strips, giving cover to numerous trout, which grew to huge proportions here. Many times I had drifted this same water in my handmade plywood rowboat, enjoying the great flyfishing. Always, the beauty of the place, with its green hills giving way to snowcaps, the rushing water being challenged by house-sized rocks, and the solitude, captured me as much as the fishing. I should have been watching a soaring pair of ospreys working to catch a meal for their young, but my mind was on the oncoming freight train.

"Do you hear it?" I asked Johnny, while pointing my hand up the tracks.

"Yeah, but I can see the switch leading to the spur, too. We can make it," he shouted back. Johnny hit the brakes, pushed in the throttle, and brought the speeder to a skidding stop. Sparks were flying from the steel wheels and I could smell the heat of burning metal as I piled off the deck and ran toward the switch. I grabbed the heavily weighted handle and used all the strength I could muster to turn it through the half circle and open the tracks to the spur. The throw was designed as a two-man job to prevent any accidental or malicious use of the switch. It felt as if I were lifting the back end of my truck until a heavy dose of adrenaline hit my muscles. The lever dropped on the back side of its arc as the rails opened with a screech from their friction on the steel pads beneath them.

I didn't have to tell Johnny to go for it. He hit the throttle, and as soon as the speeder was moving, he jumped off and helped me close the switch the instant the back wheels cleared the main line. I could feel the terrific strain in my back as we stepped away from the tracks and waved to the engineer of the westbound freight as it roared past. I could see the incredulous look on his face as he put his thumb and fingers into the okay signal and waved it at us. We walked over to where the speeder had come to a collision stop with Charlie's speeder and attached trailer. My knees went weak as I sat down and took the sweat from my eyes with a shirttail. Johnny had a crazy grin on his face. He always did like living on the edge.

Chapter 7

I took my rifle out of the case, loaded five rounds into the magazine and stuffed a dozen more into my pockets. I hid the case under a low-growing juniper, where nobody could find it. The sling had been detached, so I opened the swivels and carefully inserted their pins into the studs on the stock and locked them into place. The sling needed lengthening, so I used the old military system of pulling down on the outer leather and pushing up on the inner strap until the proper length was achieved. I then sat down, put my arm through the sling in the hasty position, and sighted on a raven across the river. I was steady as a rock and could have picked him out of the tree, "As easy as makin' duck soup," the way Iver would put it.

The section gang was out of sight behind a low ridge where we heard the bulldozers working. They would be smoothing up the roadbed by hand after the 'dozers finished with it, and then laying the ties at three-foot intervals. Eight men at a time would lift a rail off the flatcar with tongs, set it into place on the ties, and let the gandy dancers spike it down. Ingvar had a gauge for setting the exact distance between rails, insuring that the flanges on the cars' wheels would not bind or derail the train. Several lengths of track had been laid, in addition to the switch, and would soon receive four inches of crushed rock, tamped into place for stability. The new tracks now held our two speeders and a flatcar that was loaded with rail.

My thoughts turned back to our close encounter with a hundred tons of steam locomotive. This train was a good half an hour ahead of the schedule that Oscar gave me, which fact might easily have caused a wreck, or killed us. Oscar surely knew that trains will run late, but virtually never run more than a couple minutes early. Was this a rare clerical mistake? It didn't seem as though Oscar had any hard feelings toward me as he did for Charlie.

Charlie, now, was a different case. He was really burned up at Chaps for forcing him to choose between building the spur, or losing his job and facing embezzlement charges. He refused to recognize that Chaps was giving him an easy way out. He also had mouthed off in the Mint Bar about having an inside track with Chaps' woman, but he lost his cool when Ferd laid out his numerous shortcomings for him. "The only thing she would do for you is spit in your eye."

"I'll drink to that," Iver joked, along with uproarious laughter from the crowd at the bar.

"You son of a bitch," Charlie hissed at Ferd in a half-drunken slur. "You wouldn't know what to do with a woman if she wrote it out for you." With that, he took a big swing at Ferd, catching him in the face by surprise and knocking him back a step. That was the last thing he remembered until daylight the next morning. Ferd grabbed Charlie by both arms and pulled him halfway across the bar. He then laid a ham-sized fist across Charlie's nose with two hundred and forty pounds behind the punch. Charlie catapulted off the bar and hit the floor with his head bouncing in the sawdust, which absorbed the blood running down his face.

"Ferd, you better call Alice while I get this ladies' man home," Iver said, as he beckoned to two burly lumberjacks. They laid him in the back of Iver's truck for the trip across town, and then parked his limp form on a couch. Iver threw a hooked rug over Charlie before leaving.

Charlie's problems started way back when his hard-working dad was gone much of the time in the mining camps on Silver Butte Creek. They had a small place on Sheldon Flats, just above town, where a hay-field separated his house from that of his only close neighbors and their daughter, Mary Jane. She developed early, but also had a fine pair of legs, which gave her the speed she needed to outrun Charlie across the field after teasing him into utter frustration. He got to taking coins from his mother, sure that money would buy him what he wanted, but Mary Jane only tantalized him the more and ended up with the money any-way. Charlie grew up to be a bully and never forgot those early lessons from the fastest girl in school. He liked to throw his considerable weight around with little regard for anyone but himself till he met Ferd.

Maybe Charlie was going to cause a lot of trouble for Chaps, begin-ning with me. The cut-off axle on my speeder had to come from Charlie's twisted mind with Ingvar's help. The job could quickly be done with the right tools and a good knowledge of the way a speeder worked. I was thinking of a way to prove just who had tried to put me six feet under, and was coming up with a simple plan.

Chaps' shop foreman in Minneapolis had designed a lock for speeders after a couple hoboes had stolen one there and headed west with it. They made about fifty miles before an alert telegraph operator read a message, ran out to a switch, and shunted the speeder on to a siding where it crashed into a line of boxcars. Both hoboes ended up in the hospital and then went to jail. The lock consisted of a steel U bolt, an inch and a half thick with a very heavy ring welded to each end. The U bolt was to be passed through one of the speeder's wheels, and then locked with a special hardened padlock.

I now attached one of these U bolts to a front wheel of Charlie's speeder and put my own padlock on it. After pocketing the keys, I beckoned Johnny to follow me up the ridge. He gave me a savvy grin, fully understanding the plan. We found a deer trail going in our direction, took it to a point where we could observe the work going on, and concealed ourselves in a thicket of low snowberry bushes.

McRell, the long-time woods boss, donated some of his expertise for this project. He had the two bulldozers following the line of surveyor stakes that I had used to lay out the route, a two percent grade that ended on a small flat near my campsite. They were about finished, and one of them was piling brush for future burning. The second one was making an offloading ramp, which also might serve as a stop to keep Chaps' car from being pushed off the tracks.

The scene from the low ridge was a pleasant one. I could already imagine the corral full of horses and mules, shaded by some old-growth firs. We built a small runway from the corral to water, so the stock could drink at any time. I had marked out the cook tent and the sleeping tent locations with peeled lodgepole stakes that shone white in the afternoon sun. The picture windows on Chaps' custom-designed car would frame a green meadow backed by timbered foothills. Our white canvas tents set at the edge of the meadow with their thin wisps of wood smoke rising into the blue sky could create an inspiration for artists. All this was hidden from the main line, and sheltered from wind and noise by the ridge we sat on.

Charlie was sitting on a stump, typical for him, watching Ingvar and his crew cleaning up brush and leveling the roadbed. I planned on having the crew unload our plywood onto a rough sled of poles, and then drag it to the campsite with one of the cats. When that was done, my showdown with Charlie would begin. I couldn't wait to see his reaction when told that he was to ride my doctored up speeder back to the depot. The rest of the men could ride to town with Johanson, who was now on the evening passenger run, and would stop for a flagman.

Summer was moving along, and it was time to get the tent frames with their plywood floors constructed. I was going to do this after Charlie and his crew were gone, so I could enjoy some peace and quiet in the hills. It would take a few days, including some fishing and a lot of chopping for the mountain of firewood that was needed. Four of five big larch snags close by were a safety hazard, so one of the 'dozer operators was instructed to push them over and drag them to a woodpile site. Johnny and I had our work cut out for us but the weather was great for a campout and I was looking forward to it all. We had food for three days, and all the tools and camp gear we needed were stored in the hay shelter.

"Johnny, let's circle around the head end of the meadow and keep out of sight. I want to surprise Charlie by coming up behind him, and see his reaction to us. We can ease through that fir thicket behind the stump he's wearing out."

Johnny nodded his approval. "After thinkin' he got us wrecked or killed, the bastard will figger he's seein' ghosts. He may try to fight, though. Look what happened with Ferd."

"That was whiskey talking, and Ferd fixed him good. He's sober now, but I'll be ready for most anything. It will be a cold day when Charlie gets on top of me."

We crawled a few yards to the backside of the ridge before standing up. I worked the bolt of my .270 and quickly slipped a cartridge into the chamber in a move that was practiced to the point of reflex action. The rifle came to my shoulder and I had it pointing at a pine cone in hardly more than an eye flutter.

"My God, that was quick," Johnny said in admiration. "I've never seen you do that before, but I heard about it."

"Well," I smiled back, "There's been a lot of deer and varmints that never saw me make that move, either, and they're hanging on my wall." I pulled the safety on and started off along the ridge. We walked in silence for half an hour, avoiding any contact with the crew. I made sure that the sun was at our backs as we made the final approach through the fir thicket behind Charlie's stump. The tactic had always worked well while stalking game if the wind didn't mess it up.

Johnny stayed twenty yards behind me on the final approach, as any noise would be sure to alert Charlie. I crawled on my elbows and knees, gently removing any dry sticks that would crack with my weight on them. Finally, I eased up to the stump and slowly stood up about six feet behind Charlie, who was still unaware of my presence. My Winchester now was cradled inside my left elbow, my left hand on the forestock and my right hand on the pistol grip. From this practiced position, I was fast as greased lightning, according to some. Three of the crew were about thirty yards away, intent on their work.

I let the safety off with a metallic click. Charlie turned, and was stunned to see me. His eyes showed surprise, the pupils dilated. Then they narrowed, displaying obvious hate.

"Hello, Charlie," I said loudly enough for the crew to hear, "You seem surprised to see me alive."

"What the hell you doin' sneakin' up on a man like that. You could get yourself in trouble that way," he answered, a bit shaken. He was now looking at Johnny, who also stood up and approached us.

"You got that wrong, Charlie. You're the one in trouble, and you better start telling me about it, and quick." By now, the whole crew was listening. Charlie licked his lips, his eyes darting back and forth from Johnny to me. He had been whittling on a club off a fir tree while watching the rest of the crew work, and suddenly he backed up a couple steps, raised the club and started to hurl it at my head.

"No snake like you is gonna threaten me," Charlie yelled as the muscles in his right arm tensed for the throw that could crush my skull. No one saw my movement. It was like a shadow, a blur. The rifle came to my shoulder without effort and I pulled the trigger as the barrel lined up with my target. My bullet splintered the club, sending slivers of wood and lead into Charlie's neck and shoulder. He screamed, and clutched his left ear as the muzzle blast broke that eardrum. I worked the silk-smooth bolt and reloaded my rifle before the noise of the shot was gone.

Charlie fell back a step and went to his knees, cursing the day I was born. He transferred his sheath knife to his right and was going to bury it in my chest.

"Hold it, Charlie," I yelled, "Or I'll take your hand off this time!" I could see him grit his teeth, and he hesitated, thinking about it. "I don't want to shoot you to pieces, so maybe I'll just kill you. You just had your one chance, Charlie, so put it down." My Winchester held steady on his chest.

I could see the sweat roll down his face, running into his eyes. He shook his head, trying to clear his vision, but couldn't. He groaned as the knife slipped from his fist and dropped at his feet.

"Step aside, Charlie,' I ordered him, 'I don't want you to start thinking of that knife again." Charlie moved a couple steps. I dropped the muzzle a bit and blew the knife into two pieces, which disappeared into the grass. Charlie sat down, hands on his ears, the fight gone out of him, and lucky to be alive.

"Holy mackerel," Johnny exclaimed. "I wouldn't've believed it hadn't I been here watchin'! I never saw nothing till after I heard the shot."

"Well, I was a bit lucky, but Charlie was a whole lot luckier," I replied with a sigh of relief. "Let's get him and Ingvar out of here."

Chapter 8

McRell and his 'dozer crew were finished, and shut down. They had seen the incident, but did not have a clue as to why it happened. I took McRell aside and brought him up to date, beginning with Chaps' discovery that Charlie was padding his paychecks and Chaps' giving Charlie this opportunity to work it out. McRell was wondering why Charlie just sat around whittling while everybody else was working like a dog. When I told him about the speeder and our close call with the freight, he agreed that we should send Ingvar and Charlie back to Libby on that same machine. His crew would help get it done, and then join the section gang on the evening passenger train in a couple hours. He also gave orders to get my plywood delivered up to the campsite.

Ingvar and Charlie had walked over to the speeders, along with the crew, and were looking at their locked wheel with dismay. From force of long habit, I took two cartridges from my pocket and reloaded my rifle. The section gang took careful note of this and stood well aside as McRell and Johnny and I approached.

"Get aboard the front speeder," I ordered Ingvar and Charlie with a growl, "and head for home. The rest of you can flag down Johanson's train this evening and ride in with him."

"I ain't takin' your speeder, when I got my own sittin' right here," Charlie answered. "How come you got a lock on it, anyway?"

"I don't like the color of mine, anymore, so I'm trading you," I replied.

"I can't take that old relic, it'll never make it home. It ain't safe."

"How would you know that, Charlie," I asked.

"Uh, I can tell just by lookin' at it." Charlie was whining now.

"You two get on board and shove off, and no more screwing around," I commanded. I swung the muzzle of the rifle toward Charlie and added, "Or I'll burst your other eardrum. I am going to be in your office at eight on Thursday morning, and you both will be there or in jail. Got that?"

"Watch out you don't bust the front axle," Johnny said, laughing, "Or you could have an accident or a long walk." Ingvar had his hands over his face, and Charlie was cursing as the speeder moved onto the main line.

"I'll bet you can't do that again," McRell said, looking at me.

"What do you mean," I asked.

"This," he shouted, as he tossed his half-filled canteen in a long arc toward the meadow. He had held it by its shoulder straps and got a lot of power into the swing. My rifle came up like my right arm, and the instant the muzzle caught up with the canteen, I squeezed the trigger. The bullet hit about center at twenty-nine hundred feet a second, sending out water waves under great pressure. The canteen exploded, the water forming a mist that reflected a rainbow in the afternoon sun. There was a clatter as the remaining metal hit some rocks.

"Would you look at that!" McRell exclaimed. The rest of the crew were speechless.

A venerable old flyrod, too long unused, was waiting in its hard case back at camp. It was made with care by the craftsmen at Orvis, the split bamboo imported from China. I retrieved my rod, and after assembling it, I made my way to a spot on the river where a submerged gravel bar created a long riffle. The river rushed in a shallow torrent over the upper end of the gravel bar, aerating the water with millions of small bubbles, adding the oxygen so necessary for trout. The water gradually became deeper as it crossed the lower parts of the bar, and there is where I started casting.

The sounds given off by a river in late afternoon cannot be related to the noise one hears too much of in town. Water running over clean gravel gives off a quiet melody all its own. Combine that with a breeze rustling through the cottonwood and willow leaves, the calls of raven and meadowlark, and the splash of feeding trout, then nature performs its own symphony. I was deeply absorbed in this restful atmosphere, having endured far too much stress for one day, and not wishing to repeat it. It would take a couple hours of peaceful fishing to get my nerves settled down and to rebuild my appetite.

The last four inches of the gut leader I was using had been soaking in my mouth to become moist and pliant. Dry gut is brittle, and breaks easily. I removed the leader, which was about four-pound test, and tied on a number-twelve caddis, which was made from the tan hollow hair of last year's elk. While I let the ten feet of leader and a short length of line swirl around in the shallows, I teased a group of minnows that was determined to swallow the fly, but they could not quite take it in their mouths. "I'll be back for you in a couple of years," I was thinking.

Soon, the leader gained its maximum strength and pliability. I stripped off three long loops of line from the reel and started false casting until there was forty feet of line in the air. On my last cast, I angled the line upstream, let the leader roll out in a satisfying curl, and dropped the caddis into the feed line of bubbles. The leader and the fly were lightly treated with Mucillin, which kept them floating.

Three or four feet into the float, my fly disappeared, and I instantly raised the rod tip. My fly stayed where it was for a moment, and then took off across the river in a sizzling run, hooked to the jaw of a very wild cutthroat. I was forced to follow the fish downstream to keep from losing all my line, and by now I was in water over my waist. The cold water felt great after the hot sweaty day. Ten exciting minutes later, when I finally landed the fish, I dipped in all the way, taking the best bath I'd had in years.

The trout was a real beauty, a male of around four and a half pounds. Its sides flashed golden in the shallows, where I could see the brown spots along its glistening flanks. When I removed the hook to let him back into the river, there became visible the deep red streaks under his jaw that gave him the name of cutthroat.

"Go home, grandpa," I told him, "And father some more of your kind. I'm looking for a pan-sized pair for dinner." Too soon, the task was accomplished, and it was time to get the camp in order. We would not need a lantern, as the twilight seemed to last half the night this time of year along the Canadian border. The muted light and lengthening shadows of evening put me into a thoughtful mood after dinner was done, and our bedrolls were laid out on the thick grass. The crickets had started their chorus, the last sounds I heard until a pair of coyotes celebrated sunrise.

Our supply of firewood was becoming a long wall, laid on parallel poles to keep the bottom course dry. Already, it was home to a pair of pine squirrels, evident from the piles of dismembered cones lying atop the split larch. The cook-tent frame was taking shape as Johnny and I drove peeled and sharpened lodgepole uprights into the turf at four-foot intervals. We had first smoothed out the floor area with shovels and a rake, and had laid plywood sheets down, butted together in a twelve- by sixteen-foot floor. Plywood set on edge and nailed to the uprights created low walls, giving the finished tent a lot of extra headroom. The ridgepole was laid across X braces in the standard fashion and supported in the center by an upright, which also served as a place to hang a lantern and kitchen cookware. There would be a lot of wild stories told after dinner in this social center.

We spent a long time selecting the perfect ridgepole. It had to be thirty feet long, perfectly straight with minimum taper, and of manageable size for two men. We eventually found the right tree, growing in a dense thicket of tall, slender larch, where all the trees were competing with each other for sunlight. I cut off the limbs, sawed the best thirty feet out of it, and then sat astraddle, using an inherited drawknife to peel the bark. Hammer marks from its hand forging were still visible on the often-honed blade. The long overhang of the ridgepole would hold a tarp, forming a waterproof portico. Here was the place to barbecue steaks, hang raincoats, take a bath, and store wood for the cookstove. We had it a lot easier with the sleeping tents, erecting them with the speed of long practice.

This time, Johnny and I both lifted the switch handle and opened the tracks for the speeder. We pushed the speeder clear, and locked the switch behind us. It was another beautiful morning, but as we neared home, we could see a large cloud buildup looming over the Cabinet range, quite likely the preparations for an evening thunderstorm. Sometimes there were wondrous displays of chain lightning, bouncing off the high peaks, followed by a wind and a short but intense downpour. The sky usually cleared around midnight after these storms, and the resulting cool, clean-smelling air made sleep inevitable.

I was dreaming about these things when we spotted our speeder pulled off the tracks about five miles from town. The front end was damaged quite heavily, and a wheel was missing.

"There ain't any bodies here," Johnny observed, "But they sure had themselves a spill. I wonder if they was hurt any."

"Better them than us," I replied. "It's a miracle they got this far, with the condition that bearing was in. They had a good long walk to town, and I bet Ol' Charlie was crying all the way. If they weren't seriously injured, they must have been bounced around a lot. We were darn lucky to make it to the spur in one piece."

"You be careful when you go see Charlie in his office tomorrow," Johnny laughed, "'cause he's likely fixin' to run you through with a fountain pen."

"Or cut my throat with a ruler," I laughed in return.

At precisely eight o'clock Thursday morning, I stepped into the depot and nodded a greeting to Oscar. He motioned toward Charlie's office door and shook his head. I didn't bother to knock, but walked right in to find Ingvar and Charlie in a heated discussion.

"I didn't think it was right, and I don't know how you talked me into it," Ingvar was saying in his thick Norwegian accent.

"Shut up, you idiot," Charlie shouted at him.

"It's your turn to shut up, Charlie," I interrupted, pushing my fingers forcefully against his chest. "Just sit down and listen, if you expect to come out of here without handcuffs on. You two tried to get Johnny and me injured, or worse, killed, for no good reason. No one else could have booby-trapped that speeder, and nobody else would want to. I figure you are trying to mess up the whole hunting trip because Mr. Scharpe caught you cheating on the payroll, and I was the first on your list."

"I am sorry, Mr. Herb," Ingvar broke in. "Charlie paid me for some time I didn't work and then he said he would tell Mr.Chaps about it if I didn't fix up that speeder for a wreck. I don't want to hurt you, or anybody else, and I'm going to pay back the money I took."

"Ingvar, I could get you fired in about two minutes, but have decided not to do that. You will be responsible for finishing that spur, and doing a good job on the next two weekends. I won't say anymore about it, but I will check up on your work. You had better leave now."

"Thank you, Mr. Herb. I am a disgrace, but I know better now. You will see." Ingvar left, sad-faced, and smarter.

I turned back to Charlie. "As for you, you skunk, I never did anything to you to deserve what you did. You don't know how close Johnny and I came to getting run over by that freight. I also think that you somehow changed the schedule that Oscar handed me. I could get you arrested for attempted murder."

"You tried to kill me with that lousy rifle of yours, so you got nothing to snort about," Charlie replied in defiance. "Besides that, I got a bum ear now."

"Charlie, you are as dense as a rock," I told him while looking straight into his eyes. "You're lucky that I didn't blow your head off instead of shooting the club out of your hands. That was no accident, and I proved it in front of your whole crew with some shooting after you left. You owe me your life, for what it's worth."

"That damn Chaps, acts so high and mighty with his private car and that fancy woman. He wouldn't know what a day's work was, and he expects me to spend my own weekends building his crazy hunting spur."

"Wise up, Charlie," I said in a harsh voice. "Chaps gets more done for the railroad in an hour than you do in a month because he uses his brain, a habit you never acquired. He caught you stealing from the company and gave you another chance. I found out that you can take early retirement at the end of the year, and I'm going to let you work till December and then call it quits. I had Swenson over at the law office write a letter about what happened last weekend. He made two copies, one for Chaps and one for the sheriff in case something happens to me. Johnny Bates and McRell both signed it. No more bullshit from you, Charlie. Starting now, your luck has all run out!"

I could see the intense hatred in Charlie's eyes as I stalked out of the room.

Chapter 9

Sunshine at the end of September is getting a bit thin, but it feels good to sit in it and soak up the rays while the sky is a picture-book blue, the larches are turning gold, and the mule deer are still putting on fat. Buck and I had been making use of the perfect autumn weather by taking some time for ourselves to find a big old mossy-horned mule deer. It would be nice to put up my winter's meat while it was still tender and juicy. Then, too, I had a new high-ceilinged living room that I just added to my old house, and it needed a big deer mounted over the entrance.

The season opened early in the high country for trophy bucks, and I took my chances in the wilderness behind Sugarloaf Peak. On the north flank of the peak we found a spring and a small flat with just enough room for a mountain tent and a campfire. An old avalanche had stacked up firewood in a jumbled mess, but it was dry and close at hand. Buck had plenty of grass, as we were close to timberline, so I picketed him out during the night and tied him in the shade while I was hunting. My mule, Sally, just wandered around on her own, but would never leave camp with Buck around there. She hated bears, too, and would prevent any thieving black from raiding the camp.

From the surrounding ridges, I scanned a Canadian eternity to the north. I could see Glacier National Park cutting the skyline in the east, and could make out some distant peaks of Idaho, fading to a blue mist on the western horizon. Using my binoculars, I searched the deep canyons with their alpine lakes, and I studied a myriad distant open slopes, watching for color or movement. When game walked into view I focused my spotting scope on it to decide if it needed closer attention.

Pure white frost was turning to water as the sun moved from the peaks toward the creek bottoms. Droplets clinging to beargrass and huckleberry reflected the clear morning light, causing entire mountain-sides to sparkle like diamonds. Eventually, a very large buck moved into the scene, feeding, about a mile away. Several hundred yards of his backtrail were clearly visible where his legs had brushed frost off the bushes. It was still early enough in the morning that I might have time to close in on him before he holed up during the heat of the day. The buck was far better than the dozens of others I had spotted lately, so I gave him my undivided attention. I chose a route across the canyon after checking for wind drift with a handful of dust, and managed to stay out of sight and scent for the next half hour.

Old mossy horn was moving at a slow pace, into the wind, when I last saw him. He would stop at a particularly inviting bush or patch of bunch grass, take a dozen bites, and then move on. It seemed evident that he had a place in mind to bed down when his belly was full, and it was my plan to intercept him before he reached there. Planning and succeeding are two different things, as there are the variables of wind, difficult terrain, and remaining unseen. The area you are heading for never looks the same as it did from where you first viewed it, causing errors in approach. A mule deer can smell and see with the best, and many have been lost because the finish of the stalk failed in its needs to be out of sight and downwind.

None of this was far from my thoughts as I maneuvered through the brush and boulders of the canyon, trying to remain quiet while dealing with a pair of near-vertical slopes into and out of that deep hole. I sat on a smooth rock and slid the last six feet into the bottom, landing in a couple inches of water. Here was a good chance to peel off my extra shirt before the climb out of there, and to take a couple minutes for a very welcome drink. It's impossible to describe the perfect taste of that icy mountain dew.

There was no way to climb the opposite bank at that point, the brush being thick as dog hair. I started up the streambed, forcing branches out of the way and crouching under the largest ones. After about fifty yards of this I came to a narrow deer trail, covered with fresh tracks. I was grateful for the game that engineered this crossing, and used their trail to climb out of the jungle that choked the bottom.

It was time for a breather, and lucky for me that I took one. I heard a stick break, and some small rocks roll just ahead. By taking a half step at a time, with rifle ready, I covered the next hundred feet in complete silence, then waited, motionless. A branch moved, a dark spot appeared, and materialized into a deer's ear. Soon the head, without antlers showed, and a doe stepped into the trail, going uphill.

Things just seem to go right at times. If I had not worked up a good thirst and stopped for a drink, I would have walked right into that doe. One good look at me or a trace of wind would have sent her scurrying out of there, with the buck in tow. Hunting combines skill, knowledge, conditioning, and luck too. Sometimes, one can make his own luck, but chance always plays its role in the outcome. The longer I stood there, the more deer walked past, until I counted five does and three fawns, any of which could have ended the morning's hunt in one moment.

I was having problems in staying quiet so long, and breathed a big sigh of relief when the last of the herd moved on. As soon as I reached the edge of thick cover, I reached for my binoculars and spent five minutes searching for the buck. Several times I moved, until I found a glacial boulder to lean on while I studied the sidehill facing me. Finally I saw something, behind a mountain maple. A flash of sunshine reflecting from an ivory tipped antler caught my attention. The buck it belonged to was clipping off leaves and tender shoots, rocking the maple bush like a breeze when everything else was still.

There didn't appear to be any good route for a closer approach, and I knew it was going to be a difficult shot from this position. The buck finally showed his head, and I recognized him immediately. Four long knobby tines on each side, with additional brow tines of good length, proved him to be an old, mature mule deer. When he turned his head toward me, his antlers stretched past his shoulders in a very wide spread; a fine trophy indeed, most likely beyond his breeding days.

A long uphill shot, and one try was all I had. The obvious question was the exact range. I tried counting it off in 100-yard segments, coming up with 350 yards after several tries. Shooting at extended range requires some thought and good preparation, unlike instinctive shooting at close moving targets. My 130-grain .270 bullet dropped around twelve inches at three fifty. I laid the rifle across my daypack on the rock, and waited. The buck would have to be on my side of the bush, and broadside, or I wasn't going to shoot. He could just as easily move off, over the crest of the ridge and out of the territory.

Five minutes of tension seemed like five hours before my chance came. I laid the sight what looked like two inches over his shoulder and gently squeezed the trigger. The buck took off around the bush and disappeared. I marked the spot and quickly approached, finding blood on the bush. Forty yards down a slope lay my deer. He was a real beauty, hard earned, and worthy of a few minutes of contemplation. I sat down among dried sunflowers and green kinnikinnick, which blanketed the slope. In my mind, I thanked him for causing me to be in the mountains, for giving me meat for the winter, and for fathering a good many more deer like himself. In a short while, I had the cleaning chore done, and then I pulled the deer into some shade and covered it with brush to keep ravens and flies off of it.

"Lets go, Sally, we have a big job and not all that much time," I called to my mule when I finally returned to camp. I heard hoofbeats and got a few honks in reply. Buck was giving me several nickers just for good measure as he turned his head back to watch me emerge from the woods. Sally came trotting up, and put her nose into my pocket, where I had stashed an apple core. She loved the vigorous rub on her long ears too. Buck chewed noisily on a carrot that I handed him out of a canvas bag.

Sally didn't mind being saddled up with my well-used Decker pack saddle. Maybe she knew that after the work was over, we might be heading for home. I hung my rifle high in a big fir, took the spotting scope and binoculars out of my pack, and dropped in the axe. It would come in handy for making trail through the creek bottom and for cutting bone. We found the deer with no problem, but this huge buck was far too much for me to lift into the saddle alone. I finally halved it and managed to load one part on each side of the mule.

By mid-afternoon Sally and I were back at camp again. I ate whatever I could find in a hurry, and loaded the camp gear on Buck for the long walk out to the trailhead. Before leaving, I watered the animals and then carefully cleaned up my campsite. I figured it would be around midnight when we reached the truck, but the main trail was in reasonable shape, and it was a clear night.

A lone rifleman was leading his horse, while a mule loaded with a deer was following loose on a long mountain trail in the sparse light of a half moon. He heard no sounds other than the footfalls of his horse and mule. His ground-eating stride became automatic, his superbly conditioned body felt no fatigue. The dense forest stretching for miles in all directions showed no traces of civilization other than the thin strip of trail, leading ever lower from the high peaks into the valley of the Kootenai. What better time to reflect on the need for a good woman, on the plans for the Great Northern hunt, and on the future of a changing mountain man. What better time to reflect on the events of the past couple months?

I flipped up the light switch in the barn and opened the doors. The light streaming out added to the soft glow from the setting moon illuminating the trees. I unloaded Buck and Sally, put them into the pasture and watched them roll in the dust a couple times before shaking off and heading for their hay and water. The deer, I hoisted with a block and line, chained to a beam in the hay shed. It would cool nicely there under cover for several days.

By now I was thinking about the civilized joys of hot water streaming over my grubby body. I had a mud room built into the back entrance of my house so I could get cleaned up there sometimes without dragging my muddy boots and dirty clothes into the bedroom. I climbed into the shower and scrubbed down while singing a bad version of "Back in the Saddle Again." I toweled off, humming a quiet tune to set a mood for ten hours of sleep. It seemed like a good idea to down a little orange juice and some crackers, but when I reached into the fridge, there was an apple pie sitting there where none had been before. On the kitchen table was a nice bouquet of flowers, which had escaped frost next to the walls of my house.

Gerta, my German neighbor and hausfrau, sometimes came over to clean up my place and put a good home-cooked meal on the table. She must have been here today, expecting that I would get home about now. The flowers gave off a faint and delicious scent, but when I bent over the vase to get a better smell, it was not the same. I couldn't figure it out, but I was tired and sleepy and too full of pie to worry about small mysteries like this.

My towel found a place on the hook after an accurate toss in the general direction. I turned off the lights and headed for bed bare-skinned. When I turned back the covers, a trace of that delicious flower scent entered the room.

"What the hell is this," I thought, with a half-numb mind. My eyes still were not used to the dark, but I didn't have to see to realize finally that someone was in my bed. She was putting her arms around my neck, and pulling my lips into hers. I could feel her large soft breasts pushing against me, and her hands began a soothing caress, starting with my shoulders and working down.

"Teresa," I murmured, "I remember your perfume from the day of our luncheon. It should have come to me sooner, but I never dreamed that you would show up here." I kissed her fervently, and before she could reply, she opened her mouth, probing me deeply with her tongue.

"Are you glad I'm here?" she whispered, nuzzling my ear.

"Just try to leave, and you will see," I said a bit gruffly.

"My, but you sound threatening, you big bully," Teresa teased. "A big, big bully," she said in wonderment, after reaching her smooth hands around my rock-hard penis. "I have been thinking constantly about you and wondered how you would be after giving you that sexy hug."

"Disappointed?" was all I had time to ask as I took an erect nipple into my mouth, and held her other breast in my hand.

"You are a real man, with the body to go with it," Teresa whispered. "I've been waiting to get to know you better, and I'm tired of waiting." She rolled over on top of me and in a moment had me deep inside. She was on her knees, thrusting gently at first, gradually building in strength until she was completely taken with her burning passion. She was the most intense woman that I had ever been with, and my own control disappeared as she came in gasps and groans, and I emptied with heavy bursts into her.

Teresa smothered me with affection, her face perspiring. I pushed her hair back, and sat up a bit, alternating kisses to her breasts with ones to her mouth. She moved off slowly, curling up to me now in a sleepy manner.

"We have to talk in the morning," I said, "But tonight is for other things. You are so beautiful, and it's been such a long, long time."

A half hour later, I made love to her at a slower, gentler pace, wondering how a woman could get me so excited twice in a row, after the sort of day I had just finished. We slept until the sun was halfway toward noon. Our shower together in the morning turned into another loving encounter as we scrubbed and explored each other in daylight.

"How did you get here?" I asked over breakfast, "And where is Ed?" I was having trouble taking my eyes off her sculptured body, little of which she was hiding.

"My sister had her wedding in Portland, so I spent a week there helping out. Ed had to go to Chicago, where I am supposed to meet him in a few days. My exact schedule was too difficult to figure out, and I just had to see you."

"You've been on my mind a lot, too, Teresa, but I put off the possibility of ever getting together because I knew that you were taken."

"Ed has been good to me, generous for sure, but he is an intellectual, without much interest in me as a person. His business takes all his time, and this hunting trip will be the first time in several years that he is trying something else. Even that is more business than recreation, the way it seems."

"Surely he must take care of things in the bedroom," I mused. "With a person as desirable as you, how could it be otherwise?"

"I hate to say this, but I can't entice him very often, and when I do, it doesn't seem like love. I feel sorry for him in a lot of ways, but I want a companion as well as someone to discuss business with. He takes advantage of me with some of his business dealings, and I cannot continue like this. It would be fun to ski, or hike, or build a house, or ride horses together, and live for each other, but it won't happen. I'm convinced of that now. Money isn't everything."

"I know that to be a fact. I could never be happy sitting in a swivel chair forever, raking in the dough. It's a good feeling to be able to pay the bills, but there is so much of life outdoors that God put there for us, it seems a shame not to make use of it." I reached out to take Teresa's hand and guide her closer to where I was sitting. I put my face between her breasts and held it there for a moment, then I pulled her head lower and kissed her once more. "Where do we go from here," I asked.

Teresa thought carefully about an answer, and then her face lit up. "I have been here for a day and a half and already met your neighbor, Gerta. She is a real gem, and we hit it off right away. I told her that I wanted to do some things around here, so she just showed me where everything was, and left me alone. Do you know how long it's been since I weeded a flower garden, or baked a pie? I have been having a great time here, and it reminds me of a lot of things that I am missing. Gerta said you needed me around here."

"I wondered where that pie came from. You did a nice job."

"Thanks," Teresa flashed a big smile. "I sort of knew that a good pie would soften you up. With Richard around, I hardly have permission to walk through the kitchen, and at Ed's place in Minneapolis, he has gardeners, maids, and all that. I feel like an ornament."

"A great-looking ornament, but I get the point," I replied.

"I promised Ed that I would meet him in Chicago in time for a ceremony starting construction on the shopping area. He is a part owner of that, you know."

"No, I didn't know, but I'm not surprised. He was trying to give Walt a working over on the price of lumber, but we recovered most of that with the building of his hunting spur. He has treated me very well, but I get the feeling that he's a very tough businessman, and nobody to be fooled with."

"I want to be with you and get to know all about you, Herb. I felt it the minute you walked into Ed's car that day, but we will have to be careful for a while. I know that Ed could really hurt us if he wanted to."

"Yeah, he has the power, but I think he likes me at this point. He isn't ever going to dictate to me for long, though, even indirectly. We should take it easy, though, until after the hunting season, because the whole community is going to benefit from this big expedition. Take my phone number, and call once in a while when you get a good chance. I'd hate to lose contact," I laughed, as I put my arms around her. We didn't lose contact for quite some time.

I took Teresa to the train, and pecked her on the cheek as she climbed up the steps. I tasted the salt of tears.

Chapter 10

Ingvar and his crew did a fine job getting the spur finished without Charlie around. On the day before they were done, Oscar arranged to set out a flatcar, which Johnny and I loaded with hay. Johanson pushed it into the hunting spur on his morning passenger run to the east, and Ingvar's crew helped us stack the hay into the covered shelter. We had piled the tent canvas, stoves, cots, lanterns, and all the kitchen equipment on top of the hay, and Johnny and I had a great ride from town, sitting on the tents, with no worry about a sabotaged speeder.

Numerous trout could be seen feeding on a late hatch of tiny midges that swarmed above the slicks in the Kootenai. Before many hours passed, I would be making good use of this information, as I had several number-eighteen midge flies with me, and a new leader, tapered to nearly invisible half-pound test. For the first time, I wondered if I could teach a certain woman to handle a fly rod, as I gently slipped a slab-sided trout back into the water.

It took a couple days to set up the tents, put everything into usable order, and attend to all the details in making the camp comfortable. We put up tarps for shade and rain shelter. We spent half a day digging a pit for the outhouse that was carefully concealed in a distant thicket. Johnny proudly carved a half moon into a board for the door and nailed it into place with a flourish.

"Everything is gonna be high class around here," he grinned. "I even found an old oak seat that I sanded smooth to keep slivers out of your butt, and here is last year's Monkey Ward's catalog for our special customers."

I built a small dam in a narrow spot where our spring ran between some rocks. I laid a section of one-inch pipe in there and tamped some sod into place around it. The end of the pipe was about two feet off the ground, making it easy to fill a water bucket under it without stirring up any mud. My next job was to make a small corral around that part of the spring to keep horses or deer out of our water supply. They could do all the drinking they wanted down below. We saved the tops and bottoms of peach cans and nailed them into place on small trees to mark the trails to appropriate spots. No doubt some greenhorn would get lost at night while wandering around looking for relief.

"Let's test out the kitchen, Johnny," I urged him when my stomach started bouncing off my backbone. "I want to bake some biscuits and cook a couple trout. You can make up a salad with the greens we brought along. I even have a few Great Falls Select beers on some ice that I fetched out of the depot's ice house." Within a few minutes of lighting a fire, I closed the stack damper halfway and felt the old Monarch cook stove kicking out the terrific heat generated by dry larch firewood. I popped the biscuit dough into the oven along with the fish that I wanted to bake, put the kettle on for hot water, and lay back, holding a cold Great Falls. Could it get any better?

"Well, maybe it could," I mused, "If I knew for sure that Charlie had reformed. I gave him his chance, and Ingvar too, and Ingvar took it. Charlie, though, was pretty grim when he saw me put Teresa on the train. He could still be a big problem. That ornery old Scotchman is as mean as sin."

Our job was finished at the lower camp, but we would have to pack a small camp into the mountains as soon as we brought the horses and mules up for the month of hunting. More than once, a high camp had saved me a miserable night. All our canned goods we buried in canvas bags in a deep sand bank that was left by a retreating watercourse at the end of the last ice age. It was already the first of October and the nights were freezing hard. Cans easily rupture with the frost, letting the contents spoil. Just a foot of sand would prevent this until we could keep some heat in the cook tent overnight.

Johnny made a roof using some poles and heavy tarpaper to cover the large coal pile brought up for Chaps' cookstove, heaters, and hot water tank. Water for his needs would have to be hand carried to the fill spout on his private car, but Richard could hardly wait for the daily exercise, I thought, while observing that big water tank with a wicked grin.

We boarded the old speeder that Ingvar had repaired and left for us on the spur. It ran better than before, and even had a small windscreen added to ward off the freezing cold of open-air travel. A nice whitetail buck jumped across the tracks as we startled him on his way to water at the river.

"That buck is going to make some good camp meat," Johnny shouted above the noise of the speeder. "Maybe Chaps can shoot that one and not have to take a horse up the mountain. I doubt if he can make it, and anyway I don't like looking out for a guy who don't know much of anything."

"Chaps sure is no cowboy, but he is determined, and smart. I doubt if he'll be letting any of his guests get the better of him. You just be sure to take your time on the trail, and let him ride that gray draft horse. Nothing else you have will handle all the weight. I guess I'll be needed at our upper camp a lot of the time, so you just take care of our meal ticket, Johnny."

Johnny snorted at that. "He can't even mount up, and once he's up, how in the hell is he goin' to get off?"

"I figured that out a long time ago," I laughed. "You are going to have a pack mule with you at all times, in case one of these hunters accidentally gets a deer or a bear. Also, I'm getting Doc Mason to fix us up with a large emergency kit to keep on that mule. I told him to put in splints, bandages, cold medicine, hangover medicine, needles and stitching gut, and a lot of other stuff with directions on how to use it. It's likely going to cost us a couple hundred bucks. The last thing you put on that mule is going to be a folding stepladder after Chaps gets mounted, and the first thing you take off that mule is the ladder so's he can get down without breaking a leg."

"You gotta' be jokin'," Johnny retorted.

"No jokes, Johnny, and don't be laughing when you are doing your duty. Ol' Chaps may lean on you and bust your spine."

It was nearing quitting time when we pulled the speeder off the main line at Libby, so I hurried into the depot before Oscar left.

"Send a wire to Ed Scharpe," I told him, "and tell him that his spur is done, the camp and the horses are ready, and we have to know the exact day he is getting here. We need to buy fresh groceries, and eggs, and butter, and all that, and we will take the livestock to camp a couple days ahead of time. Get me an answer right away, because day after tomorrow I am taking Iver and his two guides up there for their training session. I may be gone all next week."

My mule deer buck was turning out to be better eating than I had hoped for. Some round steak cut into cubes and marinated in olive oil and a bit of lemon juice was soon spitted into kebobs along with green peppers, onion, mushrooms and tomatoes. Dry alder wood, burned down to blue-hot coals, cooked the meat with a delicious trace of smoky flavor. I ate about five kebabs and then filled the gaps with rye bread and a handful of ripe apricots. The phone rang while I was cramming down the last juicy apricot, and I answered with an unintelligible grunt.

"Herb, this is Teresa. It doesn't sound like you," she said.

"If you had your mouth full of venison and apricots, you wouldn't sound like me either," I answered after swallowing a few times. "I'm glad you called. This house is plumb vacant without you in it."

"I had a wonderful time at your place, and can't get it out of my mind. I miss you already and want to come back. Ed is planning on being there soon, but he is bringing too many people with him for the first hunt, so I will be along about the second week. Ed may have to leave camp for a few days at times, so that could work out okay.

"He is getting more demanding all the time and wants me to set up people for some of his power plays. I'm tired of seeing people taken advantage of and I don't want any more of it. Ed will never change, and you have reminded me of what it is like to live a decent life."

"I miss you, too, and don't intend to hide it for too long. I had Oscar send Ed a wire today to get his exact schedule to me. I expect an answer tomorrow, and then I'll be gone with the guides for most of the week."

"I have to run along now, and besides I am getting all choked up talking with you," Teresa said, as she blotted her eyes with a hankie.

"Yeah, I know exactly how it feels. Be good, and I'll save us a nice grassy spot on a mountaintop."

The wire from Chaps arrived the next morning about the time I stopped at the depot to inquire about it. Charlie handed it to me without so much as a greeting.

> For Herb the Chief Hunter. Received your communique. Glad your preparations are complete. I will arrive October 13, ready to hunt October 15. Please arrange to have my car spotted at spur on Oct. 14. Will have numerous guests at various times. Final hunting day November 15. Will have my private car there all month. Ask Walt to join me anytime.
>
> Ed Scharpe

I wasn't too crazy about having Charlie read my mail, but he would know most of the hunting details sooner or later anyway. Charlie was acting as grim as a hangman, and I sensed that he would never forgive me for putting him down in front of his old crew. His face turned beet red when I sat at his typewriter and poked out his orders to Johanson to spot Chaps' car on our spur on the fourteenth of October. I gave Oscar a copy and told him his life depended on remembering this. Let Johanson know several days ahead of time, also in writing. I took the third copy with me.

I wandered down the street to Iver's store, where we arranged for him to contact his two guides and meet me at the speeder the next morning. They would need their sleeping bags, extra clothes, and boots, which would be left in camp when we finished. If they forgot anything, they could bring it up in two weeks when our operation began. I intended for this week to be a backpack trip in order to get the guides into shape, and I didn't want to feed the horses at camp all that extra time.

A man on foot can go a lot of places that would endanger a horse, and I intended to show these guides every hole and brushpile in that part of the country. Ingvar let the word out that he was hiring a man to sit on the speeder all night with a shotgun. Needless to say, the speeder was in perfect condition when we headed out.

Some of the best game crossings were in saddles where two ridges came together, or where trails converged on a spring or an often used feeding area. These locations I had already marked with tin can lids or bottoms nailed to trees. I wrote Spot #1, and up to number six on the tin pieces with a black crayon. I intended to assign the guides their territory on a daily basis this way, and keep the hunters apart from each other. The areas would be hunted on alternate days, and would be rested much longer if any shooting took place. Each block had about seven square miles, enough space to keep stray bullets away or to keep excited dudes from shooting someone's hat off. My original blind was the easiest to get to by horse, and here is where Chaps would start his adventures.

The guides were instructed to do no shooting unless there was a wounded animal getting away, or some other real emergency. It was wise to find out how good they were with a rifle, though, and I had Iver bring along a lot of ammo for their weapons. The meadow surrounding our camp had a narrow opening where the spring came into it on the east end. Two towering pines stood opposite each other about a hundred feet apart. The one on the left was on a knob, some thirty feet above the meadow. I took a long section of old Forest Service phone line that I had found and strung it between the two trees on a long downhill slope. On the line, I suspended a smooth-running pulley with a heavy steel bracket that had two targets and a light rope attached to it. With the rope, I pulled the target setup to the top of the knob, laid myself down behind some rocks and then let go. The targets came into view at about ten miles an hour but were soon flying along at thirty. Iver and his boys were fifty yards out into the meadow from where they were to shoot as often as they could before the targets reached the lower tree.

The first few efforts were mostly misses, but eventually the guides learned to lead, and to follow through with their swing. When the scores seemed satisfactory, we practiced on targets nailed to stumps out to two hundred and fifty yards. By the end of the afternoon, everyone was a lot more proficient with his rifle than before, and we retreated to the cook tent.

"What's next, boss?" Iver asked, as I handed out huge helpings of venison stew and thick slices of Gerta's great rye bread loaded with butter.

"We start the backpacking tomorrow, and everyone is getting his chance to cook for the rest of us. We will make suggestions on how to improve the food. Also, we will go to all six Stops during the week, and explore all the best hunting sites and camping spots at each one. I don't want anyone getting lost with his hunter, and if it becomes necessary to spend a night out, I want all of you to know exactly what to do."

That week became one of the most enjoyable times I had spent in years. The guides were eager and they learned well. We made several successful stalks on whitetail and mule deer, and one bear. Several times, we jumped small groups of elk and could have put meat on the ground. We learned where the water holes were, where the brush was too thick to travel, and where our best chances were to make a small drive toward a waiting hunter. We were ready, our food was gone, and we headed for home. Anything that could be chewed up by mice or packrats was bundled and hung from the tent ridgepoles by heavy phone wire fashioned into long hooks.

Iver and the guides were going to help Johnny trail our dozen head of stock on the slow three-day trip to camp next week. The trip would well acquaint them with all the animals and with Johnny's ways of taking care of them. All that remained for now was for Chaps to show up on time, and I knew that nothing would ever stop him from that. I went through everything in my mind again, trying to find something that was undone, or overlooked, not wanting to make the smallest mistake. Something still nagged at me, and I wracked my brain trying to come up with it. It felt like the afternoon when our damaged speeder might have killed us.

Chapter 11

Charlie was getting into good graces again with Alice. She was not aware of all that had happened lately, and he told her a lie about his hearing problems. He was taking a long weekend before Chaps was due to arrive, and booked a room for the two of them at the expensive Davenport Hotel in Spokane. It had been quite some time for Charlie since he last bedded a woman, and Alice was available if he primed her a little. The hundred and fifty dollars in his pocket was going to help him relieve the pressure, and live it up for a couple days.

The Mint was Charlie's home away from home, but he had not dared go back there for weeks after Ferd knocked him off the bar with a hammerlike blow in the face. His ego finally took over, and he walked into the Mint one afternoon at quitting time and sat down at the poker table.

"Bring me a draft beer, Ferd," Charlie said as he laid a few coins on the table. "A man could die of thirst in this town, and I decided to come back to see that it don't happen."

"A man could die of something else, too, if he don't mend his ways," Ferd growled back as he roughly set a beer onto the table and scraped the coins into his hand.

"That's over with now, and I have time for some poker. My luck is changin'. I can feel it." Charlie started shuffling a deck of cards for a solitaire game, waiting for a few other players to show up. During the next two hours Charlie made some bad moves, but got lucky on two different pots and ended up the evening with a hundred and fifty bucks. The last pot had three good hands raising, and Charlie called when he ran out of money.

"I told you so," he shouted at Ferd, "I just won the best pot for the last year around here. Buy the boys a beer, and now I got to be goin'." It didn't take Charlie long to call Alice and invite her to Spokane. "Wouldn't that be somethin' if I could do this all the time," he was thinking, "But it sure takes the dough to keep a woman around."

The Davenport Hotel was designed after a high-class hotel in Europe where the owner had stayed a few times. The main dining room, called

"The Florentine Gardens," offered a vast menu of exotic dishes. The large dining area was divided by huge glass tanks, reaching from floor to ceiling, filled with tropical fish. Hundreds of fresh flowers from the hotel's own greenhouse were displayed in attractive vases on the dining tables, and this was fascinating to Alice, who had her own small flower business.

"Take me to dinner here, Charlie," Alice said, looking at him coyly, "and you won't be sorry. I want some of their fresh seafood that we never see in Montana and a nice bottle of good Italian wine."

"I guess I might be sorry when the bill comes," Charlie said as he looked at the menu and winced, "but we can get dressed up and come back in an hour. I wouldn't mind tryin' one of them fancy Italian dinners."

The route back to the elevators took them past some of the smart shops where guests could purchase the latest fashions. While Alice looked with envy at the various dresses and accessories, Charlie wandered into an exclusive art gallery. Some of the prices on paintings and bronzes shocked him, making him wonder how anyone could afford such things. It was then that he remembered the Charlie Russell painting in Chaps' car, and an original early Picasso that Chaps was very proud of. One Russell, or any of the early masterworks, would sell for enough to keep a man in clover for the rest of his life. What a waste to let one small picture hang on a wall, gathering dust, while he was breaking his back for the peanuts handed out by the railroad.

"May I help you with something today, Mister," Charlie was being asked by the art gallery owner. "My name is Blaise Pulaski. No American could ever pronounce my real last name, so I never use it."

"I'm lookin' for an original Charlie Russell, or maybe a good Picasso for my new house," Charlie replied, "but I don't see any here. What would be the price of something like that if you could find it."

Blaise raised his eyebrows, looking intently at Charlie. "My, but you have expensive tastes, but to own one of these masterworks would fulfill a life's dream for anyone who loves the best. They would be very costly, a quarter of a million dollars each, possibly, or more if we have to find them at an auction where no one knows what the final bid will be. Sometimes one can wait for years or a lifetime to even have a chance to bid on a Russell. Picasso painted more, and perhaps I could locate something in Europe when I go next month on my annual buying trip."

"Europe is a big place," Charlie said, "so how do you find what you want in all them foreign countries."

"I was born in Hungary, and learned to speak many languages. My father was interested in art and sent me to an art school in Budapest. When the communists took over, we left, but I go back to other countries regularly. I have reliable sources that do much searching for me.

One never knows what will become available in Europe, where war has destroyed people's fortunes and changed everything. Displaced royalty will sell things at times."

Blaise was a very sharp trader and businessman, and he was quick to suspect something wrong about Charlie. There were the clothes, not well tailored nor made from any expensive fabric. There was Charlie's speech, obviously not cultured, and his manners did not fit those of a man who was normally interested in world-class fine art. Blaise did vividly remember one weatherbeaten miner who looked like he hadn't been in civilization for years. The old codger came in and bought one hundred thousand dollars worth of art in a single afternoon, paying in cash. That was the quickest trip Blaise ever made to the bank, and he was going to string along with this scraggly customer for a while longer, just to play it safe.

"What would you say if I told you I knew where two paintings like this are sittin' around right now. I could get them over here and you could just hand me the half million, minus a little commission for handling."

"What? Do you mean that you own these two paintings and wish to sell them?" Blaise was wide-eyed and nearly speechless.

"Not exactly, but I can get 'em to you, and then you sell 'em. Sellin' paintings is your business, ain't it?"

Blaise was doing a lot of quick thinking, something that he had become good at during his dealings with postwar opportunists. Many of these people had found precious art objects in bombed-out ruins, had no way of knowing who the owners were, and desperately needed money. It just figured that there would be traffic in these objects in a straight line toward the money source, or North America. Mostly, few questions were asked.

"Did you say your name was Charlie?" Blaise asked. "Yes? Well, Mr. Charlie, you should know that in the United States and in prewar Europe, all these famous paintings had a list of owners, going back a hundred years or even to the original owner. This is still true here, but in Europe, that chain of known owners has been broken by the war. I understand that reputable art dealers are starting the process all over again. It prevents the sale of stolen art because the new buyer will check with the last owner to see if he actually sold the painting or not."

"You tellin' me that you would turn down a chance to sell a good Russell once in a lifetime?" Charlie asked.

Blaise was quickly going over all the possibilities in his mind, and would need some time to think this over. "Come back in the morning. We will do some more talking then, but you must not discuss this with anyone. Also, be prepared to answer many questions, as this can be a very, ah, delicate business. Good day to you. I must close my shop now."

Keeping up a front that he deemed necessary in his business was costing Blaise a lot of money. Good-looking women, shown off at the right places, custom-tailored clothing, and bribery all added up to a large budget deficit. Blaise figured that one or two big sales would set him up forever, and he could then dispense with all but one of his lady friends and still live the good life. Maybe his Mercedes could go, too, but that would be a small sacrifice. He wouldn't need it in Mexico, where he would live when things became too hot for him around here. Maybe he and Charlie were alike in some ways, but he figured that he could out-maneuver Charlie any day.

It was time to call his contacts in Seattle and San Francisco, and maybe a buyer from San Diego. Actually, the farther from home, the better. He knew that Charlie must have stumbled upon these paintings somewhere that did not have much security. Charlie was not sophis-ticated enough to pull a complex job in a modern gallery, and maybe he would settle for a lot less than the paintings were worth. "I have to insulate myself from this bum."

Long after midnight, Blaise finally came up with a workable plan. It was too risky to handle hot art personally, so he would become a middle-man. He could collect fifty grand in advance, held by a third party until Charlie delivered the goods to an art expert who would pay him what-ever they agreed upon. An additional ten thousand would be paid directly to Blaise in cash before the caper commenced. All he had to do was to find a buyer who would not show the paintings anywhere for many years. Some people were like that, he knew. They would look at the paintings in their own home once in a while, and then replace them in a safe. He, himself, might even move to sunny Guadalajara, where no one could ever trace him.

Charlie ordered dinner and a bottle of Italian wine. Alice was enjoying her seafood and hardly noticed that the wine was gone by the time she had one small glass. She was on her first big night out in a very long time, and she was going to make the most of it. Later, she admitted, she would have to satisfy her escort, unpleasant as it was at times. Why could she never find a man with real class who cared for her? Charlie was having visions of the big money he might come into now, and the high living and sexy young goddesses he would enjoy in Florida. To hell with Chaps, and Ferd and all of Montana.

Chapter 12

Chaps' private car was gently pushed into place on the siding behind the depot. One of the section gang immediately filled up its water tanks, while another replenished the coal bunker. They then proceeded to wash all the windows with soapy water and clean towels. The coal smoke and dust from the trip west had made a dirty mess of Chaps' new paint job when the train went through some light rain, so the entire outside of the car was hosed down until it sparkled. This car was going to be in tip-top shape to receive guests.

Richard had another of his noteworthy meals planned for the evening. Chaps invited the mayor, police chief, fire captain, and at my suggestion, Ferd, from the Mint Bar. Walt and I were to attend also, for the festivities marking the opening of the now-famous hunt. None of the guests other than Walt and I had ever been inside a private railway car before, much less eaten a gourmet meal there.

Ferd surprised everyone with a display of polished manners totally unlike anything we had seen around him in the past. His parents came over from England because they were looking for land of their own, and more personal freedom, blessings denied them in the old country. Ferd had been taught the old country respect for his "Betters." He had also learned table manners, where no cursing was allowed, and where a nap-kin, instead of a shirt sleeve, was used on the face. He had long ago given up most of this, as his life in the new world revolved around log-ging, hunting, bar keeping, and raising horses. He wasn't against a bit of poaching now and again, either. When he arrived in Chaps' dining room, I could see a transformation take place in the man, like his youth was returning. An old boar grizzly turned into a cub. He was all smiles.

Ferd regaled us with his remembrances of a frustrated youth in England, where he was sometimes successful in poaching pheasants from a neighboring duke's estate. There was no way that he could hunt legally, as no public lands existed, and the average citizen could never obtain permission to shoot anything. He dreamed of moving to Africa, but his dreams were fulfilled when he arrived in Montana where his father took up a homestead on one hundred sixty acres of hay and pastureland. Ferd's meager savings were quickly turned into a used .300 Savage Model 99 rifle. With this weapon, he soon began supplying the family with meat, and he spent weeks roaming the country by himself or with a brother and a new horse.

Listening to this made me feel lucky to be born here. My grandparents came over from Denmark for the same reasons of freedom and opportunity. They first went to Germany, escaped the Kaiser's call to join his army and rule the world, and then took the jump to New York, Minnesota, and ultimately Montana. Wood, water, and mountains are what they sought, and found, along with more freedom than they knew existed anywhere.

I also grew up roaming the hills with a fish pole, or sometimes a worn-out rifle of nondescript character. My camp was two thin blankets for sleeping, and a canvas to string up between a couple trees to fend off the rain and reflect heat. A great deal of cooking was done in an old lard pail with a wire handle, hung over a small fire. We had never heard of nesting, stainless steel cookware, or miniature, gas-fired camp stoves. Ferd and I had a great time comparing notes. Chaps asked endless questions, keeping us occupied for hours. He was fascinated by what he was hearing on this special evening.

The mayor told how Libby was started during its own small gold strike. Early trappers explored the vast area and named many of the streams and mountains, often after their own families. Prospectors, followed by pack strings of mules, found the old Kootenai Indian trails along the river. They used these trails as the one possible route into the seemingly endless mountains and timberlands. No covered wagons ever penetrated Northwestern Montana, the terrain making it impossible for even the most persistent wagonmaster to reach the territory. Some prospector found gold nuggets in the upper reaches of Libby Creek, and his activities started a rush that brought frustrated miners and Chinese coolies from the worked-over fields of California. Most of the survivors left poorer than when they arrived.

Some of the Chinese miners who worked themselves half to death were able to resist the usual temptations of saloons and whorehouses. They saved their gold for the inevitable trip back to California and family. When rumors of this started floating around the gold camp, it created enmity between the "rich yellow thieves" and their European counterparts.

"No Chinaman is going to steal our gold and get away with it, and we're goin' to put a stop to it right now," a burly miner grumbled. He hadn't hit good paydirt for months, and could use a good stake before heading back south and out of this endless wilderness. "The first thing you know, they'll try to take over the whole country."

With this sentiment running high, the six or seven remaining Chinese were rounded up and escorted down to the Kootenai, twenty miles away. There they were lashed to log rafts and sent to their deaths through the wild rapids and falls downstream from the settlement of Libby. That section of river became known as the Chinese Rapids and later was so marked on the area maps.

Eight months of winter, twenty feet of snow, isolation and starvation, ended most newcomers' dreams of getting rich in the high country of the Cabinet Mountains. Exorbitant prices were charged for tools, food staples like flour, rice, and beans, and guns and ammunition. Everything was brought in by pack mule on a two-week trip from the nearest supply area in Washington, except during the long winters when nothing moved at all.

It was late in coming, but in 1903, the Great Northern pioneered a railway through the Rockies, building an expensive line over Marias Pass into Flathead country, and from there over Haskill Pass into the Kootenai. Mr. Jim Hill was the driving force behind the building of the Great Northern. Chaps knew about this man, but did not know the history of the railroad in the Libby area.

Jim Hill paid Scandinavian immigrants their passage and transportation to Eastern Montana to start grain farms and stock ranches. He figured that they were willing enough to endure the privations and winter weather in northeastern Montana. They then would use his railway to move their products to market. Hill was also aware of the vast timber resources of the mountain areas to the west of the prairie and he determined to push his line all the way to the Pacific Ocean. The mines supplied income for the Great Northern, but timber outfits became the major shipper between the Blackfoot Indian reservation at Browning, and Seattle on the Pacific coast.

Walt was a major customer for Chaps, and had done numerous favors for the railroad as well, including the wintertime emergency help during the big wreck. The two men were becoming good friends, and this hunt would cement a personal relationship that an adventure in the wilds could bring about. Walt told about how his father had arrived in America at Ellis Island, penniless, and unable to speak English. He worked at a market selling vegetables and fruit in New York, until he learned the language and saved enough money to head west. He taught school, started a hardware store in Minnesota, eventually moved into lumber, and finally migrated to Montana to go into the sawmill business. Physical labor was a necessary part of growing up in Libby, regardless of the family background.

Chaps, having grown up in affluence in New Orleans, could not relate to this sort of childhood. He did, to his credit, convey his respect for the hunting abilities and woodsy knowledge of his guests at the dinner party. He had not heeded my warnings about getting himself into good shape, though, and by now he knew he was going to suffer some on this expedition. What was routine for Johnny and me would become an ordeal for Chaps before it was all over.

Ed was fascinated by my accounts of tracking cougar for two or three days on snowshoes, sleeping out on the trail, eventually bagging the cat, or coming home empty-handed and out of food. He was sincerely pondering the fact that a common man from the mountains around Libby could do things with ease that he had never even dreamed about. Ed was determined to learn, though, and I had no doubt that he would remember things from one hunt to the next, and continually improve himself. He did practice with his new rifle until he could hit a deer-sized target about half the time, and with some luck, maybe that half would come while he shot at his first game.

We ate Richard's memorable dinner, course after course, until it was impossible to eat any more. The stories kept getting better as we downed a few beers and tasted some excellent wine. Our cop, called Blue by everyone because that was the color clothing he ever wore, grew up in a water-oriented family. His father was a boatbuilder, doing beautiful work with thin strips of clear cedar, molding them into exquisitely designed canoes, and sometimes rowboats for the fishing lakes and rivers nearby. Blue's grand-father had been the captain of the *North Star*, the sidewheel steamer that plied the Kootenai between Fort Steele, B. C., and Jennings Rapids, the southern end of navigation in Montana.

Heavy mining machinery that was needed in the Libby area could never be packed in by mules, and building a wagon road to Libby at that time was far too expensive for consideration. Fort Steele, an old Royal Canadian Mounted Police outpost on the upper Kootenai in British Columbia, was made accessible from the prairie by a new and very rough wagon trail over Crowsnest Pass, using the ancient Indian trails from buffalo country. The idea to open up northwestern Montana by river steamer soon followed, and a company was formed to finance the construction of the *North Star*, a shallow draft vessel, using wood for fuel.

Eventually, a coal deposit was discovered in Canada that supplied enough cheap fuel for the steamer. Coal took up less room and created a hotter fire than wood, as the railroads had discovered long before. Passenger and freight business for the steamboat thrived for a time, until another boat was built by some competitors. The new boatmen claimed faster service, using this reason to attempt a takeover of all the *North Star's* customers.

The gauntlet was taken up, with races on the river being common, and dangerous. Eventually, the inevitable happened. The *North Star* hit a rock on a narrow bend while attempting to cross in front of the other boat, the *Northern Lights*. The *North Star* was mortally wounded, with a hole in the hull below waterline, and it sank in the swift current. The *Northern Lights* had overstressed its boiler, which made it unsafe to operate and too expensive to repair.

Surveyors for Jim Hill were in the vicinity, and eventually found a route into Libby for their Great Northern Railway, which soon put to rest any thoughts of more river commerce. The anchor of the North Star was placed on a concrete pad in our schoolyard, where it rested for decades. The ferry terminal at Jennings Rapids was turned into a farmhouse, not far from the new tracks. The railroad's coming brought progress to the isolated mountain towns in Idaho and Montana, and allowed wintertime travel where it had previously been difficult or virtually impossible. The economy built rapidly as lumber and ore started moving east, but everything has its price. The area was held in a somewhat benevolent colonialism, subject to the whims or goodwill of the railroad's regional supervisors. The availability of empty cars was the key, and the supervisors parlayed this knowledge into great personal fortunes. They were the greatest "poker players" of the times.

Walt was aware of all the politics relating to the welfare of his company, and the area in general. He was also a gifted diplomat, and used his talent to massage Chaps' great ego without Chaps really knowing it. It was Walt who subtly infused Chaps' mind with the idea of a big-time hunt in the area, and now the hunt was coming to fruition. The immediate expenditures in Libby were a benefit to the whole town, but the long-term goodwill and ensuing business had immeasurable consequences.

The first to step off the evening train were two brothers, Don and Scott Kronberg, heirs to a huge building supply company with outlets covering five states in the Midwest. Their company was a major supplier to the Chicago shopping area that Chaps was involved with. They had purchased lumber from Walt at times in the past, but had never visited Montana. This was a perfect time for Walt to cement a relationship with a conglomerate that controlled much of the building trade in the nation's heartland. A steady demand from this company would go far in smoothing out the humps and dips in Walt's operations, a problem that had bankrupted many mills in the past.

Walt seemed eager to share time and pleasure with these two, and he gave me a good but unneeded lecture on how to treat them. He had his secretary meet the two train-weary hunters at the depot and escort them to the hotel. They would need to be rested and prepared to ride in Chaps' car to the hunting spur the next morning. My job was to check out their equipment to be sure they would stay comfortable during the hunt, and to supply what they were missing. I would have them test their rifles at the campsite.

Don and Scott were as different as day and night. Scott was the thoughtful type, pleasant, and reserved. His forte was keeping the accounts straight, a very important function in any business, but totally boring to Don. Scott had never been much of an athlete, but did fancy a little hunting sometimes, doing his bit with rabbits and pheasants in Ohio. Don was a large, solidly built man, and a former college football player. He displayed an outgoing aggressive personality that attracted me to him right off. He was quick with a joke, and seemed to love life in the outdoors. Neither man had the proper woolens, so I hauled them over to Iver's place and outfitted them with Malone pants and Filson wool coats, two of the best investments for a fall hunt in the mountains.

It was time for Johanson to push Chaps' car upriver with Don and Scott aboard. Richard was preparing a monstrous brunch, as no one had eaten breakfast before train time. Chaps would have a good visit with his guests during the prolonged meal. I was going to follow on my speeder, accompanied by the cook from Bill's cafe. I took my saddle and duffel bag out from the front of my truck and laid them on the speeder, but kept my rifle with me. I found Cookie ready to go at his home, and we went to work loading the speeder to the limit with fresh supplies. Johnny and the guides would help us unload and store everything in the cook tent when we hit camp. Hopefully they had arrived the previous evening and had the horses and mules well taken care of.

The depot in Libby was filled with curiosity seekers and goodwill wishers. Nothing escaped these curious railway buffs. We answered lots of questions, and finally started up the tracks, following the train in the crisp October air. Johanson leaned on the whistle chain, causing a shrill blast to echo back and forth between the mountainsides, announcing the beginning of a now-famous hunt. A high plume of smoke from the laboring engine shaded us from the morning sun. I was chewing on one of Richard's fresh cinnamon rolls, while hugely enjoying this rare moment. Charlie didn't wave, but gave us a sour look as we cleared the siding and rolled onto the main line. What was he thinking about now, I wondered?

Chapter 13

Five a.m. was a bit early for the hunters after enjoying an evening of dinner, cocktails and tall stories in Chaps' car. The two hunters were sleeping in the tent, on hard beds, in cold air with no bathroom handy. They would sleep better after a few nights of this, and a few days of tough going in the mountains. Our cook had a good solid breakfast ready by the time I rolled Don and Scott out of the sack, and we all sat down to coffee and hotcakes after washing up with ice water. There was light showing from the private car, and smoke rising from the cookstove. Ed would be ready.

A couple days earlier, Johnny thought that he could bring the horses around the face of Tony Mountain and into the mouth of the Fisher River where it joined the Kootenai. This route would save him a whole day's travel. The sheer sidehills and thick brush he encountered finally forced him to take the alternate route that I had explored up Johnson Creek. This small scenic stream entered the Kootenai at the southern base of Tony Mountain. It ran steeply from a canyon that turned north after a couple miles, cutting a vast hole into the side of the mountain. At the head of the canyon was a saddle that remarkably had a spring flowing for fifty feet or so before disappearing into loose gravel. It was possible to get horses to the saddle by following the left side of the canyon, where there were no cliffs. Huge ponderosas and ancient firs covered the ridge, leaving the ground open enough for horse travel, and providing shade for a lush growth of bunchgrass. Johnny camped at the spring after an exhausting day.

An old mountain man and local legend, Bob Bakker, had told me of this route long ago when we were tracking a cougar together in the general area. Bob was out training a pack of hounds for Teddy Roosevelt's African safari. The Redbones had cut a fresh cat track that led them across the saddle and down People's Creek to the Fisher River on the north side of Tony Mountain. The Fisher could be forded here, Bakker said, and then followed downstream to the Kootenai. From there it was a slow but much easier trip to the hunting spur. I asked Bob if he ever caught up with that cat, but he told me that the cougar must have stayed in the water for a mile or two because he could never pick up the tracks again. The old tom must have been an ancestor of the smart one we were trying to put up a tree, but never managed to during thirty grueling miles.

Johnny and Iver and the two guides breathed a major sigh of relief when they finally crossed the Fisher. The horses and mules needed rest and a half day on good graze. It took the crew a short while with everyone cooperating to strip the saddles off the horses, rub them down, and ground hitch them with halter ropes in the tall grass. Long narrow flats above the river made for great campsites and excellent feed. The river had deposited silt over the centuries to a depth of twenty or thirty feet on these benches. With some irrigation, a man could likely grow most anything here if he could keep the game away from his crops. Iver unlimbered his fly rod to provide some trout, and Johnny picked up his .22 rifle, hoping to put a few ruffed grouse into the pot.

The black gelding that came from the Yaak was becoming Johnny's favorite mount. It was learning rapidly and had a good natural athletic ability, which paid off in dangerous footing. Blackie was tough and willing to go the limit. He was never introduced to bears, though, until this day, when a centuries-old, inborn fear put him on the alert the second he saw the big chocolate-colored form approaching. Blackie instantly turned to face this unknown intruder. He swiveled his ears forward, stomping his front foot and snorting with increasing volume until the rest of the herd noticed the bear. A shift in the breeze brought the primordial scent of a predator to Blackie's nose, and he bolted, taking the rest of the horses with him. They ran up the riverbank, bucking and farting as they crashed through the underbrush toward safety.

"Hold on there," Iver shouted, as the herd galloped past him in a cloud of dust. He caught the halter rope of the last horse as it hesitated before jumping a pile of driftwood logs. Iver was pulled off his feet, but he held on and brought the horse to a halt after being dragged through the grass. Johnny came running over, cursing the luck, and horses and bears in general. One tough mule, Sally, had refused to run, but turned her backside to the bear and tried without luck to plant a hoof on his nose. The bear had seen enough, and decided to find more pleasant surroundings, without the strange braying sound that hurt his ears. He splashed across the river on the run, throwing spray all over his glossy coat. The old boar quickly disappeared into the reddish-tipped alder thickets on an impossible slope of Tony Mountain.

Johnny jumped onto the horse that Iver was holding and took off bareback to head the herd back to camp. He returned within the hour with a now very subdued remuda.

"We had better make camp here," Johnny said, "I think the stock is all tired, and I need a chicken dinner. If Herb had been here, we would be sleeping on a bear rug tonight, eating steaks, and using fresh bear grease on our boots. I never seen anybody shoot like that in my life." He now told Iver and the guides of the incident involving Charlie, thinking it would be good for everyone to know what had happened. He still did not trust Charlie, figuring that maybe he would try again to ruin this hunt for everyone. The crew should know what to expect.

Johnny loaded his .22 and started upriver on a brushy bank that was both shady and damp, a fine place for a crop of ripe snowberries. There would be plenty of ruffed grouse feeding in those thickets, waiting to be treed and taken for a hungry crew. Iver was having a great time with his fly rod, supplying a second course for dinner. No one had fished these holes for years, it seemed, as the trout fought each other for his #10 Western Bee. Beans and bacon were sure getting tiresome.

Anticipation is a large part of any hunt, and this one was to be no different. Scott and Don were full of talk about the coming adventures in an environment unlike anything they had known before. What is the difference between an elk track and a moose track was a discussion that took much of the time at breakfast. How far away can one shoot at a deer without making a bad shot or missing it. What do you do when your horse falls with you, and how do you find your way to camp when the fog rolls in or it is snowing too hard to see. What rifle and caliber are the best in this part of the world. Nobody can answer all these questions, but we tried. Some of the answers were a bit wild and were the mainstay of jokes among the guides for the next week.

Johnny had all the horses and mules saddled except mine. I preferred to take care of my own chores, doing it to my own satisfaction. I saddled up Buck, put on the breast collar, and put his tail through the crupper. We were going into some very steep country today, and I wanted that saddle to stay put. I tightened up the cinch after waiting for wise old Buck to exhale. He never did like a snug cinch. After sliding my rifle into the scabbard, I put my foot into the stirrup and swung up. Halfway into the seat, the saddle slipped sideways on me, and I fell into the dirt on my left shoulder. Buck took a jump away from me before settling down as he had been trained to do.

"What the hell is this," I shouted, as I rolled away from the horse with a sharp pain going through my shoulder. "I just tightened that cinch!" I reached out and took hold of Buck's reins as I got to my feet. Johnny rushed across the corral when he saw what was happening and slid my rifle out of the scabbard before it fell and was trampled. I never kept a round in the chamber while the rifle was on a horse or in my truck, a safety precaution I learned as a young boy. The saddle was now hanging along Buck's ribs, held there by the breast collar and the crupper.

"Damn," I exclaimed, "That could have been a bad accident. Let's get that saddle off and see what happened." I was rubbing a very sore shoulder.

"Your latigo must have broke," Johnny observed, "But I never saw that happen before." He took the breast collar and crupper off, and the saddle hit the ground. There was just enough daylight now to see things up close, so I dropped the reins and examined the latigo, which holds the cinch on the horse's right side. A horseman seldom looks at the latigo, once it is adjusted to the horse he is riding, and my saddle had not been on any animal but Buck for a very long time. The tug strap is on the left side, where the cinch is always tightened, and can be observed every time the saddle is used. Johnny lifted the right stirrup leathers and peered at the latigo where it normally passes through a flat steel or bronze ring.

"Good God, look at this," Johnny said, as he pointed to the strap. "Some son of a bitch cut this latigo and then punched a couple holes in each end and tied it up again with some thin cord. No wonder the saddle came off. Lucky for you it didn't happen someplace else 'cuz you could've got yourself killed. We have extra straps in the hay shed. I know right where I put 'em."

"The one time this could have happened is when my saddle was on the speeder and we were hauling supplies." I was thinking out loud. "It's a good thing I never leave my rifle sitting around, or it would be messed up too. How long would it take somebody to do this, Johnny?"

"About two minutes or less, if he was ready."

"Charlie, you are going to meet your maker one of these days," I mumbled.

Chaps came striding over, having not yet climbed the stepladder to his saddle. "What is going on, anyway," he wanted to know.

"It's a long story, and we'll get into that later," I answered thoughtfully. Breaking into a smile now, I added, "I've heard that we have a date with an old mule deer buck on top of Hornet Peak. I'd hate to disappoint him."

Johnny had the folding stepladder set near the left side of a big gray gelding. This horse was part Percheron draft horse, plumb gentle, built to handle heavy loads. His head was tied close to the center snubbing post in the corral, so that he couldn't move much when someone wanted to climb aboard. Chaps sort of waddled up the ladder and unceremoniously plopped himself into the saddle while the rest of us breathed a sigh of relief. The gray gave a moan, like he was ready to collapse, but I figured him for a real actor. After a couple hours of climbing, he would have plenty of good excuses to moan, considering the load on his back. Johnny slid Chaps' new rifle very carefully into its scabbard after checking to see that it was unloaded. We weren't looking for any shooting accidents on this hunt.

Chaps' ladder was folded and lashed to a pack mule along with the lunches for the day, foul-weather clothing, and our emergency gear. If we saw a deer that required a quick dismount, we would clearly be out of luck unless Don or Scott could move quickly enough. The Doc had made up a compact but complete first aid package, which I placed into a rubberized bag and included with the food for easy access.

My own personal equipment, besides my rifle, was always with me in a small backpack. It included the elements of a young lifetime of learning things the hard way. I never went hunting anywhere now without a hand axe, knife, sharpening stone, waterproof match case, area map, compass, fire starter, rope, dried food, and reserve ammunition. Warm gloves and a small flashlight with extra batteries completed the essentials. I would add my lunch to the backpack if I intended to leave the pack mule for any length of time. It had always been my contention that a hand axe was more essential than a knife. It could be used to blaze a trail, to quarter an animal or gut it if necessary, to chop small firewood, make a shelter, cut and trim tent poles, and for a hundred other uses, depending on the imagination.

Interestingly enough, the Kootenai Indians had learned the same things with their use of the tomahawk during their centuries of isolation in these mountains. Many ancient pines still showed the marks of the crude stone axes, made before steel ever found its way into the northern Rockies.

Johnny led off, clucking to his black, with Don and Scott right behind. Chaps was next, followed closely by me and then the two guides, each leading a pack animal. My shoulder was hurting, but I considered it lucky not to have a separation or a broken bone. All in all, the crew had to feel relieved to be on the trail at last.

Shooting light was still a ways off, leaving the ink-black heavens dappled with stars too numerous to imagine. There was no fog or clouds, just a few frost crystals floating down as the cold night air froze what moisture there was in it. Distant peaks downriver were becoming visible, with their alpine larches picking up the first light. The larches appeared luminescent, like candles through a frosted window. Dawn traded with the night for this view, as the stars were slowly fading out.

There was an occasional whiff of our woodsmoke in the air as we started up the mountain. It brought back memories of other hunts in other years, mostly pleasant, but some were memories of downright survival, too. This was a new time, now, with new people, and for me, some major responsibilities. My hunters were green, and completely under my jurisdiction, a fact that I didn't take lightly. I was always able to relax when finally under way to some distant peak, with Buck as my companion. It was a perfect time to think about my life's ambitions, or to put some meaning to what had already happened. Trailwise old Buck, who could see like a cat in the dark, who had an easy, steady walk, could put me into a mindframe where my best ideas took form.

It was too early to look for game, my stomach was satisfied for the moment, but my shoulder ached. Thinking about Charlie put me into a bad mood, so I brought up a vision of Teresa. She could massage my shoulder anytime, and bring the pain to an end with her soft, caring manner. And then there was something about her voice that had a bit of music in it. I wondered if she could sing. My mother had a beautiful clear soprano voice, and she entertained our family on many occasions when we had troubles. Always she managed to bring about a new set of smiles to replace the tears. Could I be blessed again with such music? Could I truly love this woman?

It was a privilege to be here, but privilege brings responsibility with it. I was leading the greatest hunt of my life. Nothing was spared in the way of horses, food, or equipment. I had been hired to do what I liked best in the world, for the entire summer and fall. I was being paid more than I ever earned before, and now I had thoughts about taking up with my benefactor's lady friend. What had happened between us last month was a very bright spot, a time to be remembered and cherished, a time of intense feeling and satisfaction. I hadn't instigated it, and could not have prevented it from happening. It was as if the whole process was meant to be.

Perhaps Teresa was being used unfairly by Chaps, who could not love her even though he did show care and respect. Maybe she was too strong a person to continue life like that, living on easy street, but never truly happy. I was hoping that was the case, but now I had Chaps under my wing, and it would be my moral undoing if I ever let anything happen to him.

Buck kept his even pace, rocking me into deep thought, my eyes nearly oblivious to the gathering daylight. I would do my very best, knowing that now I was the real commander of Chaps' fate while he was in my mountains, regardless of the power he had when grasping a telephone or a telegraph key. I was planning just how to gently get this across to him when Johnny stopped the procession to let the horses blow. Steam rising from our resting animals curled slowly downhill with the cold morning draft, sinking into the canyon below.

We made it to within a half mile of Stop One, the blind I had built for Chaps to spend some time in ambush. From here on to the blind was mostly level going, so we tied up the horses and proceeded quietly on foot. Johnny unlashed the stepladder, helped Chaps dismount, and then loosened the big gray's cinch. Gray had done a fine job, and deserved a good rest. He would be rewarded with a bit of oats after he cooled off for a while.

Scott and his guide started out for Stop Five, leading their horses in a roundabout way to keep from disturbing Chaps' hunting area. Iver was to stay with Chaps, while Johnny and the other guide might make a drive later on, through a nearby ravine. This would be a way to run a deer or two out of the dense cover below, and hopefully they would follow one of the well-used trails past the blind. I took Don with me toward Stop Three, which was about a mile and a half up the center of the three ridges leading to Hornet Peak, and two hours of hard walking from here.

Back at the corral, it had occurred to me that Don seemed to know his way around horses, even though he never mentioned anything about it. He was not in the best of shape for climbing at this altitude, though, so we stopped regularly to take a breather. There was enough daylight now to use my binoculars, so I always picked the edge of an open glade to stop for a good look and a little whispered conversation. Don's father was a very severe old German, believing that his kids should stay at home and work hard at the family business. Don thought that a certain amount of exploring around was an enlightening experience, so he took off for Wyoming the year he finished college, and got a job punching cows on a large ranch. He didn't do any hunting there, but learned his horsemanship by a year in the saddle.

When the chance for this mountain hunt came up, Don never hesitated to accept. He had been having some medical problems the past couple years, so he determined to get back into shape and get away from stress as much as possible. I guessed he was never meant to be cooped up in an office, but that is where his livelihood was, and he had a family to care for. The longer we walked, the slower he became. Don's labored breathing and a very heavy sweat on his face causing me a bit of concern.

"Let's stop here for an hour or so," I suggested when we came to an outcrop of rock which offered a great view of the sidehill before us. There was a deep ravine directly below. "We are plenty early enough to see game feeding along here before they head into cover for a midday snooze."

"I didn't have any idea just how bad a shape I'm in until I tried keeping up with you this morning." Don replied. "You're not even breathing hard, and it looks like you're still bone dry. I find myself wishing for your lifestyle, and to hell with the big money."

"There is always a trade-off, Don, but living in these mountains sure has been good for me. I made that decision when I got out of the service. I even went to college in Missoula, where I could hunt on weekends instead of sitting in a bleacher seat watching football and drinking booze. I ate elk steaks while my buddies were living on macaroni and white bread."

We had hardly hidden ourselves among the rocks when I detected a musky scent floating down on the cold draft from our left. On still, frosty mornings, the heavy air sinks to the valley bottoms before it rises again after the sun warms it up enough. One has to realize this in order to keep the wind in his favor. I laid my hand on Don's arm, pointing to my nose and looking uphill.

"I smell elk," I whispered. "Be very quiet and don't move. We may get lucky right here. Put a cartridge into your chamber. Easy now." We had been seeing a lot of fairly fresh elk sign for the past half hour, and I guessed it came from the same bunch the guides and I jumped near here during our exploring trip. There had been no shooting or tracking, so luckily they stayed in the area. Elk will often move many miles upon the slightest provocation, successfully losing hunters and other predators this way.

"I can't smell anything," Don whispered back, as he loaded his rifle and slid on the safety. After doing the same, I put my fingers to my lips and nodded my head uphill again. The complete silence was broken by a pair of ravens as they talked to each other with low throaty voices. They were riding the air currents high over us, hardly moving their wings as they looked for their breakfast with the sharpest of eyes. Nothing escaped them, and I wondered if they could see the elk that I had caught scent of. Oh, to soar like that!

Dried sunflower leaves and bunchgrass stalks remained motionless, still covered with patches of last night's frost. There was soil here instead of the usual preponderance of rock, and the grass was luxuriant. Bunchgrass dries on the stem into a very nutritious hay, light in color and sweet to the taste. Elk will come from miles around to feed in areas such as this, as was evidenced by their numerous tracks. No air movement was discernible except for the telltale vapor from our breath, which drifted slowly downhill into the ravine. Even the ravens became quiet now, as they moved off through a perfectly blue and cloudless sky.

Directly in front of us was a barren mound of freshly turned earth, the night's workings of a pocket gopher. As I looked across the open ridge, I could see a lot more of these mounds, created by the rodents as they ate grass roots from below, and tilled the soil at the same time. A large, sharply outlined elk track was clearly imprinted in the near mound, with a series of small tracks beside it. A cow and calf elk had stood before dawn, not twenty feet away from where we were now waiting, while the calf was obviously drinking its breakfast.

Across the opening, the forest took on a new beginning. Immense old yellow pines stood in the forefront, sixty feet up to the first branch, and spreading out from there with limbs the size of a man's body. Pine squirrels had harvested a vast crop of cones, dropping them in a wide circle around the base of the ancient sentinels. It was very difficult to walk quietly among the dried cones, and many an elk and mule deer had been saved by a hunter crunching one of these noisy seed pods under a heavy boot. Next in line were a lot of old growth firs, creating shade for the needs of young larch, and the browse that wintering game survived on, like mountain maple. The many colors before us formed nature's fall mosaic. Green, brown, gold, and black and white blended into an eye-pleasing pattern beneath the blue sky. I never tired of absorbing scenes such as this that an artist would be hard pressed to duplicate.

Elk like to move a lot while feeding, and I was counting on that fact now, hoping that this herd was feeding in a circle. That would bring them back through the open ridge before us where we might get lucky. The herd would soon head into the ravine for water and the day's shelter. It would be next to impossible to get a shot when they were in those alder jungles along the stream below us, and Don was surely in no condition to try.

The sun peeked above the mountain directly east from us, causing the trees to cast their stretched-out shadows along our hillside. Soon the warmth of the morning would change the air flow, and any elk above us would catch our scent and never come into the clearing. It was time for something to happen, or we would be back to deer hunting. As if on cue, a very excited squirrel commenced a rapid scolding from the ridgetop above us. I gave Don a little elbow push to alert him, and noticed his right hand squeezing the grip of his rifle until his knuckles were white. I wriggled my fingers at him as a sign to relax, and caught a thin smile in his eyes.

Squirrels have bedeviled me since my first day in the woods, and seemingly before that. My dog and I used to hunt them around our homestead, but all this small boy ever got was a lot of sassy chatter as the squirrel would climb just above our reach and then torment us. My dog was a real jumper, and he would launch himself skyward to within six inches of the pesky varmint, with jaws snapping, but he never got a hair off a squirrel's tail.

I was hearing a repetition of this when I caught a glimpse of movement. It was as if a puff of smoke, thinned out by distance, had found its way to the edge of our opening before dissipating. My eyes were riveted on that spot for several long minutes, until I had to blink. There was not a sound, even in the pine cones, as a cow and calf elk appeared among them, seemingly without motion. This magic had often been worked on me in the past, when after I had glassed an empty area ten times, there would stand a deer or other animal in plain view.

Don responded by trying to raise his rifle when I squeezed his arm and moved my head in the direction of the old pines. I pushed the rifle down and indicated that he wait. Soon another cow and calf appeared, walked into a grassy spot and took a few bites, often raising their heads to look around. Things were really getting exciting now, as more and more elk walked in on us, until about twenty were in sight, and more coming. There could be no bigger thrill for a beginning hunter than to have an entire herd of grand animals such as the elk appear out of nowhere to stand in plain view. Once in a while, a wise old cow would stretch her neck and put her nose straight up into the air to test the wind. One small whiff of man scent was all that it took to spook such game into a wild gallop through the timber. We were lucky that our tracks were on the opposite side of the clearing from where they entered.

Now we could hear the faint mewing sound of the cows talking to their young. Sometimes I had used this sound to stop a suspicious bull in his tracks for long enough to get a better look or a shot. Don was on the verge of losing control.

"A bunch as big as this has to have a spike bull with them," I whispered, "And that is what we want." Sometimes a cow will be barren for a year and will not chase her calf away after weaning it. These male calves grow spike antlers after their first season and will hang around with the cows where an older bull goes off alone. The last cow appeared like a vapor floating out of the dense cover, with a large spike by her side. The grass they walked into was belly deep, hiding any motion from their legs.

"As soon as he is clear from the others, and broadside, take him directly behind the front shoulder," I instructed Don as I took my hand away from his rear sight. "Rest your elbows on this rock and gently squeeze the trigger. He will be two hundred and fifty yards."

Don's breath was coming in short bursts, with excitement about to render him incapable. Buck fever was certain to ruin the day, so I said, "Now," as the spike moved into the clear. The shot came and I saw the bull flinch, but then heard the alarming plop of the bullet striking too far back.

"Oh no, not a gut shot," I thought to myself as the bull instantly turned back toward the dark timber. There was but one chance to end it on a proper note, so I leaned forward onto my knees and swung my .270 with the racing bull. There was a small slot between the trees that he would have to clear before disappearing. When I saw his head flash into view in the opening, I was ready, and fired as he vanished, the recoil taking my eyes away from such a small target. The rest of the herd was gone with a clattering of rocks into the canyon below. Nobody would get another look at them for days.

"Let's get up there, Don, and see what happened. We may have a long tough job ahead of us, or we may be lucky. I suspect your shot was too far back, and that could make a big problem." A wounded elk can go for miles through the worst terrain imaginable, and I knew that Don would never be able to follow me on a difficult track. Don had yet to reload, but I said nothing, as he was still too excited to be safe while following behind me.

I marked the place in my mind where the spike had gone into the trees, and walked a straight line to that point. It would be there where running tracks in damp earth would be visible, and perhaps I could spot some blood. Large patches of moss were overturned by running hooves, with dirt from beneath scattered about the trail. Twenty yards into the dark timber lay a tan and chocolate form, with two nearly yard long spikes pointing uphill. There was no blood except where the bull lay with a broken neck from my shot. The hole that Don had put into him was sealed with tallow, a common occurrence with elk, making a scant blood trail nearly impossible to follow.

"Here he is, Don, and what a beauty," I called down to my laboring friend. "You have just taken your first elk. A lot of people hunt them for years and never fire a shot."

"Damn, but that was exciting," Don wheezed, completely out of breath. "I won't be forgetting this day for a long time. I've never seen such a beautiful sight as that wild herd of cows and calves feeding along in front of us. I guess I didn't do so well with the shooting, though, did I?"

"You were just a bit excited, is all. I knew that the odds were all with us that a spike would be running with a bunch as big as this one. The old bulls like their solitude, and after the rut, they disappear into the thickest cover there is that has any feed and water. They might stay there till winter drives them down if nobody gets close enough to jump them. Your chances for a shot at one of the old monarchs are about zero until we get two feet of snow."

"You sure made a terrific shot on my running bull, Herb. I would never have thought it possible, but then you are continually surprising me. I can't tell you how much this day means to me, and I sure do miss the West. The way our whole expedition is organized, and the way the crew looks up to you really impresses me as much as your hunting and shooting abilities."

"Thanks a lot, Don, but I feel a bit embarrassed. I'm doing what Chaps is paying me for, but I have to say I like this sort of thing and work hard at it. There is one guy, though, named Charlie, who isn't exactly a brother to me, and he is the one who operated on my saddle. He also tried to take my head off with a club, one afternoon, and I shot it out of his hands."

"My God, he is lucky to be alive," Don replied.

"That's what I tried to tell him, but somehow he isn't listening. Three times now, he has been after me, and the next time will likely end with somebody getting hurt or killed. It all started when he got caught cheating the Great Northern on his commissions."

"Well, Herb, I'd put my money on you, but I hope it never comes to that. In the meantime, I want to tell you that I need a good man in my business, and I am making you a standing offer of a job with a great deal more than you could be making now. My health is not good, and I need someone like you to take a load off my back." Don sat down, easing up against a tree, looking like he was exhausted.

"You sure know how to make a man feel good," I smiled, "But I guess I'd need every other month off to get into the hills to keep away from all that traffic and noise back East. I will keep this in mind, though, and thanks. Right now, we have ourselves a real job to do, and you can help."

I started in on the bull by rolling him onto his back and keeping him there by tying a rope from a hind leg to the nearest tree. I made the first cut, and then split his brisket and pelvis with my hand axe. Opening him this way made the job much easier, and before long I was finished with the chore. The liver and heart and tongue went into a meat bag and into my backpack. There was a downed tree just below me, and I managed to wrestle the bull over the top of it, where air could circulate completely around the animal and cool it out.

"You look tired out, Don, and I think it best if you wait here till I can get back with a couple horses and a mule. You can ride from here, and we will take this elk off the mountain today and hang it in camp. Maybe I can find Johnny to help me. In the meantime, here is the lunch and some water. Please stay right in this spot so I can find you again, or we might be in trouble. I am going to cut some fir boughs to cover the elk, and you can use one of them to keep the flies away. Those blowflies will be here within the hour when it warms up a bit more, and they can purely ruin this great meat. I guess you know that a spike elk is the prize eating of any game in the country."

I opened a can of King Oscar sardines and put the lot on a piece of bread. In no time I finished that, took some water and a fresh cookie, and headed for Chaps' blind at Stop One. I looked back once, and got a weak wave in return. I was far more concerned about Don than I dared to let on.

Sweat was running down my face, and my undershirt was wet. It seemed to me that the sooner I could get back with some help, the better. I paused to take off my light wool shirt and stuff it into a loop on my backpack, and nearly jumped out of my skin when a shot broke the silence.

"That had to be Chaps," I thought, but I didn't figure I had made such good time getting here. Another shot echoed around the hills, and I aimed right for it, slowing down now, not wanting to be looked at through a rifle sight. A horse nickered at me, and there was Buck, looking in my direction, obviously having smelled me and recognized the scent. The rest of our stock was tied up in the surrounding trees facing the direction of the shots.

I cupped my hands together and blew hard between my thumbs, creating a two-note whistle. I tried once more, and was relieved to hear Johnny's whistle in return. It isn't prudent to walk into a blind unannounced, no matter who is in it. Johnny and the guide had made a drive, after Chaps ran out of patience waiting. Iver tried to tell him that he would get his chance before noon, but like an unquestioned big-time boss, he wanted action on demand. Johnny and his partner made a long circle, coming back uphill, one on each side of the ravine. They jumped a very large whitetail buck that went steaming up a game trail, right past Chaps as I had planned so long ago.

Chaps missed the first shot at thirty yards, probably out of surprise at seeing a great whitetail virtually on top of him. He missed the second shot as the five-pointer turned to the right and angled down another trail, which he doubtless knew would put him out of danger in a few jumps.

"I see what you meant by telling me to practice," a chagrined Chaps drawled in greeting. His New Orleans accent tended to come on strong when he was excited. "I did shoot some, but obviously not enough. Then, again, I never dreamed you boys could put a monster buck like that one into my lap. I swear I could hear him breathing, and I admit I became rattled. Who would ever believe that a deer could do that to a man."

"We call it buck fever, around here, but don't worry, you'll get over it in fifteen or twenty years," I joked. Everybody had a good laugh at that, and I knew there would be many repeats of the day's events told at dinners across the country. "Don had a bit of the same trouble, but with different results," I went on. "We had twenty elk walk out in front of us, just as pretty as a picture. Don was getting awfully excited, so I told him to take a rest across a boulder in front of us and knock off a spike bull. He gut shot it, but I managed to put the spike down as he ran through a slot in the trees."

"How far away was it?" Johnny wanted to know.

"About two hundred and fifty yards, running like a bat out of hell."

"Where d'ja hit 'im?"

"Broke his neck. Plain luck."

"Doubt that," Johnny finished the conversation.

"I hate to tell you this," I said to Chaps and the crew, "but Don does not look well to me, and I think we have to get him down to camp immediately. We need a horse for him, and a couple pack animals for the elk. Iver, you are in charge of Ed, here, and I suggest that you hunt around this ridge for a while and then head on down the mountain. Take this meat sack with you and give it to the cook. Tell him that I like boiled tongue with some chili sauce on it. If Ed shoots a deer, put it on your saddle, and lead the horse to camp. Ed will follow on the gray. Scott and his partner can handle their own hunt. Let's get going."

The horses had been resting all morning, so we pushed them some on the way back to Don and his elk. When we arrived, Don was still sitting on the log with his back resting on a large limb. He didn't seem to have the energy to stand up and greet us, which worried me a lot, as he was a friendly and very outgoing man. We tied up in some shade, and then loosened the cinches.

"Nice goin', Don," the guide said in greeting, shaking hands. "You got yourself a great animal, here. I bet your friends in Ohio are goin' to beat a path to your door for a barbecue."

"Thanks a lot," Don replied, while managing a slight grin. "This morning was an experience of a lifetime. I think that all the activity and excitement has me drained, though." Don was fascinated by the guide's slick knifework as he started removing the spike's lower legs. When that was done, preparation was made to halve the animal. A knife cut was made separating the third and fourth ribs on both sides of the spine, and then the guide used an axe to cut through the spine, effectively making two parts of equal weight. We removed the head, saving the spike antlers for Don as a memento of his first and successful elk hunt.

A short raucous call perked up my ears about the same time that a shadow flickered across our work. I looked up to see a pretty bird, larger than a robin, sitting on the log next to me, obviously unafraid of anything we were doing. His blending of grays and blacks was very attractive, and combined with his saucy demeanor, made him an instant friend. I cut off a bit of fat and tossed it in his direction, but another Canada jay beat him to it, and immediately flew it off to a nearby tree. Soon an entire flock of these birds was entertaining us, arriving from nowhere by some unknown signal. Before long, four or five ravens were circling above the trees, calling to their buddies, but waiting for us to leave before dropping down to investigate the situation. By the day's end, nothing but a few bones would remain here.

My shoulder was still so sore from my fall off the turning saddle that I had no desire to swing an axe. Johnny and I held the elk's rib cage open while the guide carefully chopped the spine lengthwise. He eventually finished with four separate quarters after running his knife lengthwise through the hide. I laid out the four canvas tarps that my mule Sally had been carrying, and we mantied up[1] the four quarters of elk in those, to keep the meat clean during the long trip off Hornet Mountain.

The front quarters were loaded on Sally, hide side to the horse, leg down. I used a relatively simple basket hitch to secure the nearly square bundles. The hind quarters were loaded on the second mule who also would be carrying Chaps' stepladder, which Iver was leaving behind. These long, cylindrical shapes required a barrel hitch consisting of a loop of rope passed through the front ring of the Decker pack saddle, around the heavy end of the bundle, and then duplicated with the back ring of the saddle and the shank of the rear quarter. The lash rope was tied off to a cinch ring on each side of the mule.

Our pack animals had carried lots of bloody meat in the past, as well as noisy objects like stovepipes and tools. They had seen about everything, and now remained very patient during the whole packing process. I was in a hurry to get going and thanked the stars that I wasn't fighting an ornery, skittish pack string that wanted to bolt off through the timber at the smell of something wild. Don appeared to be getting weaker, and needed help mounting up. His own horse, a red roan, was gentle

[1]To mantie up a bundle of camp goods, or clothing and sleeping bags, meat, or anything else that needs four-legged transportation is an art form when done properly. Done less well than that, it is a catastrophe waiting around the next bad spot in the trail.

A mantie comprises a heavy canvas tarp about eight feet square, the cargo to be placed on it, and twenty-five feet of three-eighths-inch manila rope to lash it up with. The end result must be a cylinder about thirty inches in diameter, four feet long, with the eventual bottom end somewhat heavier than the top. This is to ensure proper balance once the load is secured to the pack saddle. The canvas is carefully tossed into the air to land without wrinkles on a flat, grassy area. The selected cargo is divided into two parts of equal weight and bulk, to make a proper load for the mule, whose duty it is to deliver it twenty miles up the trail in usable condition. Eighty pounds per side is about proper for a large and well-conditioned mule to handle during a long day. If the climbing is to be very severe, or if the trail is narrow and in poor condition, the loads must be proportioned accordingly.

Once the cargo is placed in a line with two opposing corners of the canvas mantie, the ends are pulled tightly across each other. The sides are then folded across the middle to make a waterproof container. One end of the rope is passed through a small braided loop on the other end, forming a large noose. This is placed around the mantie end for end, and pulled as tightly as possible by a strong man. The rope, without any knots, is then passed around the cylinder at the top, the middle, and the bottom, each loop interlaced with another and pulled as tightly as possible before tying off. The end result must be two identical manties that have no chance of coming apart at the wrong time and spooking a pack horse or mule over a bank, or worse.

I saw a pack fall apart in the middle of the Flathead River, pulling the mule off balance and nearly drowning him. I was lucky enough to get a rope on that jack and pull him into shallow water with my saddle horse, where I could get the upside-down saddle off a frantic animal. If one learns the hard way, he's not likely to forget it. These day I can safely pack eggs, Coleman lanterns with glass covers, or most anything else that makes life a bit better on some mountaintop.

enough, but I had watched him walking all morning with a stiff-legged sort of gait that would be very tough on Don through the long downhill ride. "Buck, old boy, you are going to have to do me a big favor today," I gently spoke to my partner of many years. Buck lowered his head to me, as if in understanding, but in reality he was urging me to rub him behind the ears, a treatment he would stand still for until my hands were numb. Buck nuzzled me with his nose until he found half an apple in my pocket that he was sure would be there. I kept talking to him as I took a pick and cleaned the hardened mud from Buck's hoofs. He was going to need all the traction he could get. "You are going to take Don off Hornet Peak, no matter that he is in bad shape. Just take it easy, and give him a wide berth around the big trees." Buck nickered in response while Johnny gave Don a hand up into the saddle.

"Lead off, Don, we have to get out of here before dark. Just let Buck have his head, as he knows we're heading home, and his pace will be the best for you. Johnny will stay right on your tail to keep his eyes on things while the rest of us pull the mules off these ridges. See you in the cook tent."

Buck was born to a fine mare owned by Johnny's brother. The sire was an American Saddler, owned by the U.S. Forest Service, and probably the best stud in northwestern Montana. The Forest Service was bent on upgrading its own stock, but for a few dollars would take care of local mares of good quality. When Buck was a spindly two-year-old, I was in need of a very good horse, and willing to pay for it. Johnny and I had talked of this numerous times when on our endless hunting trips, and he mentioned that this buckskin colt had more promise than any horse he had ever seen in this part of the country.

Johnny's brother, Luke, was raising a large family, but had plenty of horses to go around. He was horse poor, as the saying went, and needed money, so I finally was able to close a deal on Buck. Luke's kids were already riding the horse three at a time with no problems. He had been broke gentle, never allowed any antics, but never beaten or mistreated in any way. He already knew more at two years of age than most horses ever learned in a lifetime. He had a gentle, quiet nature about him, which belied his stamina and speed. I left him with Luke's kids until winter, when I brought him to my place to get acquainted with me and to learn where his home was from then on.

When he was three, he was plenty strong enough to take me most places I wanted to go, but I took it easy with him. Soon he could pack, too, and he would swing his body around the old trees on the trail without touching the wide manties. He learned about hobbles, picket ropes, gun-fire, electric fences, trucks, and trails. Once on a trail, he never forgot it. There were times when we would be riding past a place where we had spent a night some years before, and Buck would veer off the trail and stop by the same tree he had been tied to. Riding most horses off a mountain with their stiff-legged gait is like sitting in the rear of a pick-up truck on a washboard gravel road. You just know that your insides are going to be jolted every few seconds. Riding Buck downhill could put you to sleep.

Don managed to stay upright in the saddle for the first hour, but then Johnny noticed him slumping over, and slipping off the right side. Buck sensed the problem and stopped, with his rider head down on the trail and his right boot caught in the stirrup.

"Whoa, Buck, hold it right there," Johnny shouted as he cleared his saddle and ran past Buck, grabbing the reins before the horse decided to move. His quick action and Buck's good sense probably saved Don from being dragged to death. "Stand still, boy, while I get this boot unhitched." Johnny kept soothing Buck as he tried to lift two hundred pounds of man high enough to free his leg. It wasn't working, but some quick thinking put Johnny into the idea of untying the laces. With that done, Don slid the rest of the way onto the steep hillside and rolled halfway under Buck. The boot hit the dirt behind him.

Blackie had never seen anything like this before, and he didn't like it. The trail was too narrow to pass, so he turned and started back the way he had just come, no doubt hoping that Buck would follow him. Johnny dropped Buck's reins, effectively ground hitching him, and took off after the black. It was imperative that he salvage his ride.

"Whoa, Blackie, you spooky devil," Johnny called after him without effect. There was a slender chance of catching that horse, and that meant a sprint through the timber above the trail until he passed him. The black, true to form, would stay ahead of anyone or anything following him until he reached the morning's tie-up area. Johnny spotted an open lane between some old-growth timber and sprinted through there until he was completely winded before turning back to the horse trail. He made it just in time as the black came trotting up to him, all sweated into a nervous lather.

"You and me will be learnin' some new manners real soon," Johnny scolded his mount. "We got to get back down there and look after Don." He was now talking to himself. "I hope Buck didn't step on him or take off too."

Buck turned his head back along his right side until he could see the form lying under him. He remembered Luke's kids crawling around under his belly, pulling his tail, and sliding off his rear end. He very carefully maneuvered his hind feet around the obstacle, and then quietly searched out a bit of bunch grass, avoiding stepping on the dragging reins.

"My God, but you are some horse," Johnny said to Buck as he returned with the black. "I knew it right off when you were born." He tied Blackie to a tree with a stout halter rope while figuring out how to get his partner back to camp. "I doubt if I can tie him into the saddle even if I could get him up there. Maybe I can bring him around." With that, he opened a canteen and poured some cold water onto Don's forehead.

Don's eyes fluttered open as his pulse strengthened. It was hard to know whether the cold water or just lying flat on the ground helped him regain consciousness. He looked at Johnny and asked in a quiet voice what had happened to him.

"You must have fainted, and I saw you slip off the saddle, but your foot was caught in the stirrup. Lucky for you that Buck didn't take off and drag you down the trail. I had to take your boot off to get you clear."

"Oh, yeah, I notice my right foot getting cold. I hate to tell you this, but I have been going to a doctor lately and he tells me that I have a heart problem. He thought it would get better if I started exercising again and got away from the job more. Maybe I should have done it sooner."

"Let me help you sit up and maybe you can get back onto Buck, here. We can't stay where we are, and you need a bed tonight, for sure. I wish Herb was here, but he couldn't get them wide-loaded mules through this thick timber, so he took the long ways around." Johnny took his hat off and let his sweat-soaked red hair fall down to his shoulders. He wiped his face with a bandanna, thinking how lucky he was not to have a dead hunter on his hands.

"I'm not dizzy anymore," Don observed after drinking from the canteen. "I am sort of weak, though. Let's get going again if you can help me mount up."

"There's a flat rock right above you, and I can lead Buck right up to it. Put your arm around my shoulder and we'll stand you up there. You can just slide into the saddle while I hold the horse steady." Johnny led Buck up alongside the boulder, and Don put his hands on the saddle horn and eased himself aboard.

"Hang on there for a minute, Don, while I get Blackie going. If you start feelin' faint again, just stop and let me know. If you fall off again, you might not be so lucky. Buck knows his way down, so just let him have his head."

The temperature was falling back into the freezing range as the sun set behind the Cabinet Mountains in the southwest. A few flame-hued larch needles were falling from the lighted treetops into the deep shadows of dusk on the forest floor. A horse nickered from the corral, and Buck answered him as he stepped into the clearing at camp.

"I thought we took the long way around," I said as I greeted the late-comers, "but I didn't see your tracks coming down the lower part of the trail where I cut into it. I figured you got sidetracked by a big rack of antlers or something."

"I almost took the very longest way around," Don said slowly as I helped him out of the saddle. "If it weren't for Johnny and Buck taking good care of me, I wouldn't be here now, or ever. How much do you want for that horse?"

"How can a man sell one of his own family," was my reply. I smiled as Johnny and Don recounted what had happened. "Let's get you into the cook tent and then into the sack. I think I hear Scott comin' down the hill now, too." Don was exhausted, and would hunt no more, but he was home.

Dinner was a mixture of fine food and guarded conversation. Everyone was worried about Don's health, and probably thought that there was more to his problems than a fainting spell. Johnny took me aside to fill me in on the details, talking with a great deal more emotion than I had ever seen from him before.

"Don didn't look healthy when we first started out," he said. "When he slumped down and went off the horse, I figured he was dead. A lot of horses would have dragged him to death anyway, but Buck just stopped and looked back to see what was happening. It was a good thing he did, 'cause Don had his boot caught in the stirrup, and you know what that means."

"Yeah, I know, all right, and I think we should keep him close to camp from now on. Maybe do some fishing, or sit on a stand and wait for a whitetail deer. There is no way I would be responsible for taking him back up that trail. Anyway, he has his first elk and that is really something!"

"I've been forgettin' my prayers for some time now," Johnny said softly, his eyes looking down at his feet, "but I did a mighty lot of prayin' whilst I was holdin' his head on my lap. Maybe it did some good, and I think I saw a miracle up there. Ma used to tell me about miracles, but I never was too sure about it then."

Richard and our camp cook put their heads together and came up with a great meal. They taught each other a lot of things, and were becoming good friends. Chaps was the life of the party, and he really let his hair down. His account of the buck that gave him the tremors was hilarious, and he took his ribbing in good humor. Don was the hero of the day, having shot his first big game and then surviving what we suspected was a small heart attack. He managed to walk over to see his elk quarters hanging on the pole, and stood there for a long time without saying a word.

Finally he looked away and turned toward me. "I have wanted to get back into the mountains for years now, but my family and my work seemed to take up all my time. I know that my health is not good, and today really made me think about how lucky I am. When you signaled that you smelled those elk, I thought to myself that you were just trying to make me feel good, like there really was game around there. Then I made that poor shot, and knew it, too. It looked to me that a wounded elk was going to get plumb away, which would have turned a great day into a disaster for me. I don't think that I'll ever see the kind of shooting again, either, that you did up there, and I want you to know how thankful I am that you instantly finished the job. How did you know where that bull was going, and when to pull the trigger?"

"I guess it has to do with experience, a bit of practice, and some luck, too."

Don Looked at me intently for a few moments, then shifted his gaze down to his feet while deep in thought. Finally he broke the silence, speaking slowly with some difficulty. "I would like my son to have you for a guide next year for at least three weeks if you can arrange it. He thinks he knows it all, but he would have a real eye-opener around here. He is strong, but a smart-ass, and not a bit humble. Run his tail off, too, and perhaps you can make a true man of him, something he is taking too long to do for himself. I may not be around long enough to wear down his rough edges."

"That's quite a compliment, Don," I replied, "but I hope you can come back with him. You could have your strength back by then if you work at it."

Don raised his eyes to me once more. As if in prophecy he spoke softly, "I have gained nothing but respect for you this week, Herb, and I want to give you a 'word to the wise' while I am still able. Keep your eyes open around Ed Scharpe. He can take you to the cleaners if he figures there is something in it for himself. The man can be ruthless at times, a characteristic I've discovered the hard way."

"Thanks for the advice, Don. I'm generally very careful where I spread my money and my friendship, and Chaps had me fooled for a while. He can't hide it all on a trip like this, though, and I have read a few danger signals in his actions. I have other problems too, with Charlie, and also my feelings for Teresa, including both apprehension and affection. I'm not sure how to proceed in either case, but I doubt if I have long to wait for things to happen."

"Ah, Teresa, a real gem." Don sighed as he looked at me with arched eyebrows. "She doesn't deserve what Scharpe puts her through sometimes. If you can catch her . . . " His voice trailed off. Don was aboard the Eastbound a few days later, but our hunt with Chaps was far from over. Tomorrow would be a memorable day.

Don stayed close to the tent and tried a bit of fishing during the day. He was in no shape to go anywhere, but he did seem a bit stronger at breakfast. He urged Scott to try for a good buck one more time, and I suggested that Scott take a guide and spend a night or two in the mountaintop camp. That would put them into prime country right at daylight and also save a lot of travel. A couple days in spike camp proved to be the right move, and an overjoyed Scott came out of there with a fine mule deer buck.

The wild stories would go on for years, told in his Ohio gun room under the mounted trophy. The rest of the crew had their orders to prepare the elk meat for shipment east, and then go scouting for more game. Walt was coming to camp in a day or two, and I wanted some action for him.

At Christmastime, a package arrived from Don, containing the best wool mackinaw I had ever seen. The card read, "How can I thank you enough for getting this city boy back into the mountains one more great time? I have looked forward to this opportunity for half a lifetime, and getting my elk was the frosting that really wasn't needed on the cake. Stay warm, *both* of you! Don."

Shortly after New Year, a letter arrived from the same address. Sadly, this time it was signed by Don's wife. "Dear Herb, You made my husband a very happy man. All he could talk about was you and the hunting experience. I am very distressed at the loss of Don, and I hate to give you the news that he died of a heart attack on New Year's Day. God bless you. Corrine Kronberg."

I didn't feel like taking this message standing up, so I sat by the window, staring out at three feet of clean snow, sparkling in the clear, twenty-below-zero sunshine. Don knew it was his time, and he went happy and without suffering. He did not know that Chaps was in a power play to get a part ownership in the Chicago shopping center, and that Kronberg Lumber was being used to launder some of the shipments from Montana. Chaps evidently had a rare thought of compassion when he invited Scott and Don on this trip, but it seemed that he always had other reasons also for being a nice guy.

A jet black raven landed in the tree by my window. He was the lone dark spot on a sea of white, but a survivor of maybe forty winters and counting. How could he manage in these harsh elements with his food covered by deep snow, the temperature dropping off the mark at night, while his main asset was an almond-sized brain? I pondered this while thinking that Don had a sharp mind, a fine warm home and a loving family, and he hardly lasted till midlife.

The raven glided off effortlessly as I picked up my pen and prepared to carry out Don's wish for his son. Maybe I could make a survivor out of him, turn the boy into a man who was straight, tough and compassionate, a credit to his family.

Chapter 14

Daylight found me riding Buck once more, leading Chaps on his gray along a level bench facing the Kootenai River. Sally was plodding along behind us, untied, and lightly loaded with our lunch, some meat sacks, and the stepladder. Chaps was far too tired and sore to attempt the trip to Hornet Peak again, so we would spend the day looking for a low-country buck, without much riding and little walking. It would also be a good time to plumb the depths of this man's mind and see if I could figure out his plans for the future, including Teresa.

Two main game trails came together in an open grassy area overlooking the river. Buck never hesitated. He just automatically turned onto a heavily used deer trail and followed it like he was reading my mind. Presently he stopped, put his nose down and snorted at a faint trail joining our route.

"What is it, old boy," I asked him softly after I dismounted and dropped the reins. Buck stood like a statue, pointing his ears along an obscure trail that barely had the grass bent down. I followed it back into some ancient fir trees, where the grass gave way to bare ground. Imprinted in the loose soil as plain as day were numerous tracks of a large black bear.

"Whoa, now," I said to myself, "this is really fresh, and if Buck smelled it, that bear is around here yet. I bet it's the same one that jumped our horses the other day. He is just smart enough not to walk in the game trail and scare all the deer out of here, but he wants some fresh meat and knows where to get it. This is a good ambush spot, too, as he has the deer between himself and the river, with a bit of open ground to run on."

"No deer can outrun a bear in the first rush," I explained to Chaps as I helped him off the big gray. "This is a perfect place to do a reverse ambush, and thanks to Buck, we found ourselves a project for the day. We should stash these horses and Sally, find ourselves a good hide downwind of here, and try for a bear rug. What do you say?"

"How do you know this bear is still around here? He could be miles away," Chaps was asking.

"I'm quite sure he hasn't made a kill yet. If he had, we could smell it. We have been coming into the wind for some time, and a dead animal is more than hard to ignore. He has a bit of grass and clover on this bench to keep him in light rations for a couple days, and water is close enough that we can hear it. Don't shoot any deer unless I give you a signal. We won't likely see any big buck, since the rut hasn't really started, but who knows. That bear has a five-inch-wide foot, meaning he is a real oldtimer, and big enough to handle 'most anything he comes across. His tracks are fresh, from early morning."

Chaps looked at me a bit apprehensively as we took our seats on a mossy log. Part of the deer trail was in view, and we had a good look at most of the clearing in front of us. We were concealed by a thicket of small firs, growing where our fallen log had disturbed the soil. I now had the big man in my own element and was going to make the best of it, remembering what Don had told me.

I took a chance with my first whispered question. "How did you come to get an interest in the Chicago shopping center, Ed?"

"What?" Ed sucked in his breath as he turned toward me in surprise, accidentally swinging the muzzle of that beautiful Winchester in my direction. I reached out a hand and pushed the gun away. "Oh, sorry old boy," he said, his face turning beet red as he lay the rifle across his lap in the opposite direction. "You caught me thinking about bears instead of business. What made you ask me that?"

I could see my advantage at the moment, and answered, "It took me a while, but I just put two and two together. There's a better than usual grain harvest going on, but the mill has all the boxcars it can use, which has been rare for this time of year. There's other things I've noticed too, like the way Charlie was acting around Teresa, scared to death of her, and you too."

Ed looked me straight in the eyes. "You are a lot smarter than I would have thought. You know how it is, a little squeeze here and there puts the profit on the books. Sometimes a person gets too soft and then others take advantage. I could use a man like you on my staff. It's plain that you learn fast, and seem to be able to act on your own. It looks like you don't have any real ties here." Ed became thoughtful for a few minutes. "The money could be much better too," he finally added.

I frowned a bit and looked straight back at him. "This is the second offer for a job in as many days, and I am flattered. The first one would be to help a friend, which would be temporary at best, and this job of yours I guess would eventually make me a lot of enemies along with the big paychecks. Charlie already tried to kill me, and somehow I sense that Teresa isn't all that happy either. I like the wide-open spaces, and when I am working for Walt I seem to be able to do pretty much what I want, as long as it benefits his company."

"You sensed that about Teresa? And what's this about Charlie?"

"I will tell you about Charlie, shortly, but Teresa strikes me as being a lot deeper than meets the eye. I suspect a woman like that, with a brain to go along with her other rare assets, wants to be proud of her own accomplishments. I bet she would welcome a real love in her life, with a home of her own."

Chaps looked down now. "I have bought her the best of everything, but I cannot make her smile much."

"It takes more than that, Ed. Money won't buy love, even if it does bring an easy lifestyle along with a sense of power over people."

Chaps' eyebrows rose a bit and his forehead wrinkled while he thought that over. I heard Buck paw at the base of the tree where he was tied a hundred yards behind us, and I motioned Chaps to silence. Sally gave a short half-hearted bray, which really got my attention, as she rarely did that without a good reason. At the edge of the clearing, a very nervous whitetail doe appeared, stopping nearly every step to lift her head and test the wind. I could see her ears swivel back and forth while she stood motionless, wondering if it was safe to get her morning drink from the river. The deer was a bundle of nerves, a perfect picture of grace and energy, ready to explode.

Something was bothering the doe a lot, but she wasn't able to figure it out exactly. Somehow she had caught a trace of bear scent but wasn't quite sure where it came from. I guessed that Buck and Sally caught more than a trace of the same scent and were letting us know about it. A slight movement in the tall grass went unnoticed by the deer, but I touched Chaps' forearm while taking a good grip on my old .270 Winchester.

Chapter 15

It was 1956, in Hungary. Blaise Pulaski was worn out, fed up with the labor camp, and ready to try his long-planned escape. The communists had put him to work along with the rest of the people in his village, making shell casings for their 105 mm howitzers. It was slave labor, twelve hours a day, with a wretched, stinking shelter to sleep in, and not enough food to maintain his health. The choice was imminent: escape and risk being shot, or die of starvation and brutality while making munitions for the enemy.

Blaise was educated in an art school before his country was overrun by the Nazis. Now the communists, backed by Russian military power, had taken over, and things were as bad or worse than before. Blaise never did make the money he thought he deserved from his own paintings, and he was always on the lookout for a fast deal. His training in art history and considerable skill with the palette and brush led him to the work of restoring war-damaged paintings and copying those that were impossible to repair.

One each of Degas, Monet, Renoir, and Picasso oils that Blaise had meticulously researched as missing were now in his possession, very skillfully reproduced over a period of several years before the communist takeover. Every discernible flaw in the canvas, every permanent smudge, even the difficult-to-copy signatures were done to virtual perfection. Ancient canvas, made on an antique loom, and discovered by accident in a visit to an obscure art shop, proved to be indistinguishable from that used by the masters. The chosen paintings were small, the exact size of the originals, and easy to conceal in the lining of an overcoat. Everyone had cast-off military overcoats, a drab but reasonably warm garment generally available with a small bribe. Anyone wearing one was automatically considered part of the mainstream, the same as all the rest of the workers, toiling for the glory of the motherland. Hanging on a nail above his wood plank bunk, in plain sight of the secret police, was the ticket to freedom in Canada. Freedom, the brightest inextinguishable flame in human experience.

Sundays were a day off to hand-wash what clothes there were, and to take a cold-water bath. The one recreation allowed was soccer, but only a few of the hungry workers had energy for it. The rest mostly looked on, and cheered for their favorite players. An extra ration of food was dispensed to the players, who sat at a separate table during the evening meal. Blaise was the best player because he worked at it, knowing that being in relatively good condition was the surest way to outclimb the guards and make it to freedom through Austria, across Switzerland and into France. He was still losing weight on a diet planned to keep people too weak to run away.

Blaise knew that one Sunday night would be his time of escape, after he had eaten enough to gain his maximum strength. He saved several sausages and some bread over several weeks to eat during his flight to the Austrian border. It was going to be a grueling walk for a man with no mountaineering gear, no boots, and no down clothing, sleeping bag or backpack. The time must be late summer when the snow was gone from the several passes that were navigable over the peaks into Austria. The weather had to be clear, also, as rain would bring on hypothermia and death in the high-elevation cold as surely as a bullet.

This evening the skies were clear, he had extra food of sorts, and his nerve was up. Things were never going to get any better, just more difficult. His so-called equipment was the soccer shoes, which had cleated soles, and the overcoat with four rare canvasses in its lining. Somehow he would turn his small forgeries into money, the universal lubricant.

Nobody knew of this planned escape, as the last time a group had tried it, too many things went wrong with the elaborate plans. Several people were shot to death, while the rest spent a long and miserable time in prison before being dragged back to work. One athletic man, determined, moving at his maximum speed with nobody else to worry about, could possibly make it. He would need close to a half hour start, the time interval between patrols along the base of the mountains where they jutted up sharply from the farms and woodlots below.

After putting on both his shirts, Blaise pulled his patched-up pants on over his soccer shorts. His good socks went on first, covered by his pair of worn-out ones, and then the soccer shoes. He used a piece of light rope to tie the overcoat into a roll with the sausages and bread inside and fasten it around his waist. He had no water bottle and would be forced to do without, but anticipating this, he drank all the extra water he could hold during the evening meal. It would have to do. No one was watching as he stepped into the black night.

It was the lunar period of a half moon, which would rise around midnight and give him some light for the second half of his climb, the most dangerous part. The mountains became steeper as one neared the top, with slopes turning into cliffs, and ravines turning into chutes. Blaise had studied the possibilities from the soccer field, and knew that two of the chutes were filled with brush nearly to the top. The one slightly to the north looked more dense, and that was where he would climb to freedom.

Right now, he had to get through the woods to the base of the mountains without being seen. He forced himself to take his time, moving quietly, and stopping frequently to plan his route. Finally, the noise of a patrol drifted downwind. He froze for what seemed like ten minutes before getting up and moving as quickly as possible to the first steep rise out of the valley. He had to quarter to the right and cross some logged-off areas before entering the ravine he had chosen. It was lucky for him that the moon was still down, as the area was nearly devoid of cover. A searchlight and a skilled rifleman could end this escape before it really started.

Out of breath, and counting his blessings so far, Blaise made it into the ravine, where he washed the sweat out of his eyes with a bit of polluted water. He was going to need whatever vision he could manage to climb out of here without injuring himself or falling to his death. Domestic goats were allowed to browse in the lower part of this ravine, and Blaise could smell them. They had to have trails to get around in here, he figured, and soon he found one leading uphill. The trail went as far as the last water, where the brush closed in like a wall.

"Well, I sure as hell never liked goats before, and I can't hardly swallow that tough meat, but they really helped me out tonight. I've come farther by now than I thought I could, and maybe I still have a chance." Blaise was talking softly to himself, trying to keep up his confidence. Climbing now was mostly on hands and knees, the brush being so thick that a man could not stand up in it and walk at all. Two hours of this had Blaise exhausted; his hands were bloody, and his knees ached. He had to take a short rest, no matter if someone was on his trail or not. At least he was out of rifle range from below, and hidden for the moment.

It was getting colder now, and he stopped sweating. He reached the end of the thick brush and broke into a steeper area of grass, rocks and ferns. At least he could stand up now, but the cover was gone and the ravine had turned into an avalanche chute. A few remaining bushes were his best handholds other than sharp rocks. Several times he dislodged rocks that tumbled into the void below, noisily crashing their way into the thickets that finally stopped them.

"I'll be lucky if I don't follow one of those boulders off this mountain," Blaise was thinking as he took a break. The moon was rising now, which made it easier to see, and his timing was just right. Nobody could climb the rest of this route in the dark without getting killed. Nobody in his right mind would do it anyway, unless he craved freedom more than anything else. An excited dog barked at something down in the flat, but Blaise didn't think much about it until somewhat later when the same barking came from the bottom of the ravine.

"I knew they would find my trail eventually," Blaise said, talking to himself as usual, "and now is when I try to win the game in the second half." An hour later, the exhausted climber could hear the dog again, still in the thickets, where his handler was having the same problems that Blaise had. Perhaps his motivation in continuing was less than that of the one being pursued, as the dog and his handler never broke out of the brush into the ferns.

"No one has escaped this way before, but a couple guys were killed falling off the cliffs," the handler said to his partner with the rifle. "If this one stays alive after he falls, he is going to be sorry. When the factory boss gets hold of him . . . . Better he breaks his neck." With that, the two sat down to await results, like spiders knowing that an insect would hit the web at any moment.

The weather had been dry for weeks, which was unusual in these mountains, but it was good fortune for Blaise, as the rocks he depended on for footing were somewhat more stable than usual, and not slippery with rain. Bit by bit, he inched his way upward, feeling for any slight foothold to take the strain off his hands. A few tough bushes gave him fingerholds in some of the worst spots, while rocks breaking off under his feet sent cold fear through his body. Finally, Blaise arrived at the moment of truth. He was exhausted. With daylight approaching, the sky was turning brighter, leaving him exposed on the bare face of the chute. There was a hundred yards to go, most of it nearly vertical, but the rock here was solid.

Blaise hardly had any feeling left in his hands, and his legs were cramping up. He knew he didn't have much time to finish the climb or he would die in the attempt. He looked around for the next handhold and spotted a dull gleam in the half-light. It turned out to be a piton, left by some climber many years ago when climbing was legal and popular here. Looking past the piton, Blaise could see more steel driven into the cracks, forming a stairway that a novice mountaineer could master if he but had his equipment. Guides must have used this route to take visitors to the peak at one time, and just left their pitons and spikes there.

With renewed determination, Blaise finished the climb, using the old route, bloodying his hands again, enduring painful cramps, and finally pulling himself over the top into some long grass. He passed out for a time, completely done in, awakening when the morning sun found his face. He was freezing cold in his wet shirts, so he unrolled his overcoat and put it on. He ate a sausage and a piece of bread, stood up on wobbly legs and headed across the ridge.

Underfoot, he noticed a bronze marker, the border between Hungary and Austria. As he stepped on it, Blaise threw his head back and laughed until his sides ached. He was thinking what the boss would do to the dog handler and the rifleman when he found out about the escape. How nice if they would just shoot the boss and follow the same path out of servility. His elation was quickly tempered by his urgent need for water, and he knew that the route to the nearest road was a long way to walk in his weakened state. Still, the euphoria of escape into a western country lifted his spirits. At three o'clock in the afternoon, he stepped onto a road, completely done in, and was soon picked up by the Austrian police.

It took two weeks of interrogation, paperwork, confinement in a courtyard, and sympathy from a lot of officials before he was declared a political refugee and given a new passport. Blaise headed for France and a new life, making it to Canada, and eventually to the U.S.A. He sold his forged paintings in Paris, after making a lot of contacts in the art world there. Those contacts would come in handy in the years to follow. His French and English were fluent by now, too, which was part of the plan. He had money for a few years and was going to make up for lost time.

Blaise was gaining weight, his good looks and easy smile returned, and he was living a nice life with the help of a few women, the good food and wine, and his art interests. He was never completely satisfied, though, maybe from his early and hard experiences, thinking that he had missed a lot in life and wanted more. One really good coup was what he needed to set himself up in luxury. He was confident that he could out-maneuver Charlie with little effort.

Chapter 16

The nervous whitetail doe took a step or two toward us, looking ahead for anything suspicious. That turned out to be her fatal mistake. The old boar picked his place and time perfectly, and with a rush of incredible speed from the blind side was on top of the deer before she could run a couple steps. The bear knocked the doe down, then turned like a flash, grabbed her by the neck and quickly broke her spine with a vicious shake.

"Hit him now, Ed," I shouted above the noise of the bear's growling, and the thrashing around of the deer. "Shoot him right through the shoulder." The dust was flying everywhere when Chaps shot, but I could see where the bullet kicked up another spurt of dust on a boulder just beyond the bear. "You missed him high," I yelled at a highly excited Chaps as he was fumbling with his rifle. "He's going to leave. Shoot again!"

The big black wasn't paying any attention to us, being preoccupied with his fresh kill, but the crack of the bullet going past his head caused him to look up in time to see the puff of dust from a pulverized rock just beyond him. This was an obvious danger that the old battler didn't understand. He had beaten up on numerous others of his kind, had run cougars off their fresh kills, and backed down a surly bull moose when passage on a narrow trail was in contention. Now he could see nothing to fight, but the sound of thunder hurt his ears and chips of rock in his face maddened him. The bear let out an angry roar, turned directly toward us and came on with a blinding burst of speed.

The roar turned Chaps' nerves into jelly. He was unable to find his rifle's bolt handle and didn't get the piece reloaded. I scarcely had time to think, but could have put one bullet into that broad glistening chest as he ate up the distance between us. I hesitated as it flashed through my mind that I had already finished off an elk after another man's poor shot, and I didn't want to take any more game for someone else. The look of surprise and deadly fear clouded Ed's face as he dropped his rifle into his lap and threw his arms up in a desperate attempt at self-defense while I was screaming, "SHOOT!"

Five hundred pounds of clawed and fanged predator, moving like one of Chaps' Great Northern freights, hurtled over the log we were using for cover and hit Chaps in the chest. Chaps shouted something unintelligible as he was knocked flat on his back. The bear left several long claw marks on Chaps' chest, ripping through a jacket and shirt, ending with a bloody gash across the side of his neck. A hind foot landed on the rifle, probably saving Chaps' manhood, but leaving three claw marks in that beautiful walnut stock. Chaps fell hard into the bushes, and I heard a loud whoosh as the wind went out of his lungs. If the bear had been intent on finishing the job, he would have stopped and I would have killed him. As it was, he disappeared as quickly as he had run at us, no doubt wanting to leave this cursed territory well behind.

The bear's retreat took him directly toward Sally and the horses. Buck had no use for bears, but Sally hated them, and when she heard the old bruin roar, she broke her halter rope and prepared for battle. The bear burst into the small opening where Buck and the gray were still tied, but when both horses started to squeal and dance around, he altered directions and headed straight for Sally. My feisty old mule swapped ends quicker than a striking rattler and laid a pair of shod hoofs across that bear's ribs as he dashed past and disappeared for good.

Sally kept braying and bucking as she worked her way toward us, finally quieting down as I ran over and caught the remains of her halter rope. I lifted a back hoof out of suspicion, and found a clump of black fur stuck under the steel shoe. At least one of our gang had good aim, the way it seemed to me. Chaps was slowly regaining his composure as I took the ever-present first aid kit out of Sally's pack and poured a liberal dose of disinfectant across Ed's chest and neck.

"Gawd a Mighty, that hurts," Ed cussed, as he clutched at his chest. He was coming around, now, getting his eyes focused and his brain in gear. Maybe it was the sharp smell of iodine mixed with rubbing alcohol that focused his mind, but whatever it was, it started him thinking and asking questions. "Man, that was close, and I thought I was done for. Why in God's name didn't you shoot him, Herb?"

"I could have, I guess, but he was your bear, and the best one that I've seen anywhere for years. I bet he's smart enough by now to die of old age, especially after Sally educated him. I'm sure he's the same one that the boys and Sally saw on the trip up here, by the way they described him. If he'd attacked you, he'd be lying here dead now, and you can count on that."

Chaps thought that over for a while without saying much, so I handed him the tuft of shiny, prime, bear hair that I took off of Sally's right hind shoe. It was still attached to a small piece of hide. "You can keep this souvenir, and buy Sally a drink or a bucket of oats next time you get the chance! She made a direct hit for you."

"Let's get the hell out of here." Chaps was talking to himself. "These damn bears and whitetail bucks have a southern hex on me."

"I think you should be settled down now, with all the action of the past couple days. Things will start changing shortly." I wasn't so sure of that, but what else was there to say? I had just seen some of the best hunting scenes ever, but with a man like Chaps around, who could tell what else was coming up. I gathered up the horses, threw a loop of the gray's halter rope over Buck's saddle horn, and let Sally trail along untied, as usual.

"Lead on, Ed, and we'll follow just behind. Head upriver slowly, load up that rifle, and keep your eyes open. There's a lot of good whitetails on this bench."

"I thought this rifle was loaded," Ed replied skeptically. I looked at him without saying a word and shook my head no. Ed reached for the bolt handle, finding it easily this time, and yanked the action open. An empty casing flipped across the trail, landing in some tall grass. Here was a story told without words, but I could see what the big man was thinking, and I couldn't hold back a good laugh.

"You crazy old mountain man, you could have gotten me killed. I had a bear on my chest, and you knew my barrel was empty." Chaps was getting himself worked up again, but this time I knew he wasn't completely serious.

"Loosen up a little, now, Ed," I cautioned in reply. "You had a good chance and you missed, but the second time you could never have hit him even if the rifle was loaded. Any way you look at it, that bear had your number. Most of 'em don't act that way, but this old boy is smart, and wilder than a March hare. I knew he wasn't wounded, which makes a big difference, and with an empty barrel, you weren't going to turn him into a killer. Besides, I was sittin' there, cool as a cucumber, ready to handle things. Right?"

"Get lost, you son of a bitch," was the answer, but this time there was a broad smile on Chaps' face. "If you ever tell anybody about this, I'll have you drawn and quartered."

About a mile up the bench, we jumped a nice three-point buck. He ran across a gully and up the hillside a short way before stopping for a last look. Chaps raised his custom-made .30-06 and dropped the whitetail in its tracks. When the echo died away, everything turned to absolute quiet. No jays called, no squirrels chattered; hardly a breath of air stirred. Buck was motionless, his eyes riveted on the deer, and Chaps just stood there transfixed, with all the adrenaline gone from his body. After a time, he slowly turned his head toward me where I could see his eyes sparkle and a widening grin light up his face. Maybe Chaps was becoming a hunter.

I returned the grin while shaking my head in utter disbelief. Buck led us over to the three-pointer all on his own. He knew that Sally had a job waiting for her now.

The great boar had earned his own deer, and he was welcome to it if he wanted to return to feed in the light of the half moon. I guessed he had the brass for it.

Chapter 17

Teresa Parker was born in Vermont of a comely Italian mother and a strapping Yankee father named Clayborn Parker. Parker was a fine athlete in the days when the best would starve if they depended on sport for their living. He had a keen eye and a good sense of proportion and balance, traits that led him into photography. He would often leave home with sixty pounds of camping equipment and photography gear in his backpack and roam the surrounding hills for days in search of good pictures.

Parker was not a loner. He cherished his weekends, when Teresa could accompany him in the search for an award-winning photo of a whitetail buck, or a pair of beautiful wood ducks with their young fuzz-balls trailing in the ripples behind. Sometimes he would do still-lifes, concentrating on fall colors in the hardwoods, or patiently retaking a scene of some small pond with the reflection of birches in the foreground, highlighted by a snowy hill in the distance. Clayborn sold enough of his work, which he also turned into greeting and Christmas cards, to make a decent living, but he always kept trying for the jackpot. He wanted pictures in national magazines, which would give him fame and credibility and make him a fortune.

Teresa always preferred her swimming lessons to playing with dolls and toys. When she was big enough for her first bicycle, she badgered her father until he finally broke down and bought two of them, preferring to be with her on long rides, always with a camera handy. Teresa was becoming an especially pretty young girl, a tomboyish sort with her father's athletic body and her mother's sultry European features. The older boys at school started pestering her, being a bit young yet to know exactly why, but Teresa taunted them, and then always outran the fastest of the lot. By the time she was in the eighth grade, she could beat all but one of the boys on their high school tennis team, while also doing honors work in class.

Like most fathers, Clayborn was very proud and very protective of his daughter. He kept thinking of her as a grade school girl while she was becoming a woman in front of his eyes. One afternoon in late September, the colors were coming on in the beeches and maples, which meant picture time. The afternoon was unusually warm as the two started for an abandoned farm about ten miles down an old country road. Clayborn worked up a sweat and had to stop to take off his jacket. Teresa parked her bike along a rail fence, took off a warm sweater, and shook her silken brown hair out of her eyes. It was at that moment when Clayborn woke up to the fact that here was a beautiful woman, already full-breasted, lean in body, with an innocent, tanned, outdoor look just made for a portrait.

"This has got to be my lucky day, Tessie. I must have been blind for the last couple years! Just sit up on the rail fence next to your bike and lay your hands back on the top rail. Yeah. Try moving to your left a bit so that old crimson maple in the field will make a background. Perfect. Now turn your head to the side. Great. Now let's get an entire profile. Tip your head back to get a bit more light."

Clayborn shot a couple rolls of film, using all the expertise he had, putting Teresa into a dozen different poses, shooting at many angles and distances until the light started to fade.

"You were great, Tessie," he complimented her, "A natural model. Why didn't I tumble to this before now," he mused. "I don't want to spoil you, but you have turned into a lovely young lady, which I am sure the boys at school have discovered, too. It's way past time for me to give you a lecture on honor, prevention, and self-defense."

"I pretty much know what you're talking about, Dad," Teresa answered seriously, "but I'm not embarrassed to listen."

"Okay, let's get into it then," Clay replied. "By the way, this photo session has to be a winner. I can tell it inside me. Everything is natural, the sun is out, we have fall colors, you are on a bike ride in the woods, and your pictures are going to be spread across the country. Let's get on home with this film. I can't wait to develop it and show the results to your mom and little sister."

Parker took a dozen of the pictures he liked best and walked confidently into a large advertising agency in Stowe. The first lady he talked to thought the pictures weren't bad, but not great, but said to wait a minute until Bill Blake could take a look. Blake was somewhat impressed with the photography, but wanted a sexy look, much more skin and curves exposed. If Parker could come back with something like that, he would take another look at the model, but he had his own photographers. Clay stood up to his full height, looked Blake right in the eye and told him to go straight to perdition. A few months later, a chastened Blake was on the phone, desperately trying to contact Clayborn Parker. He never received a reply.

The next agency that Parker visited was much smaller, dealing in more local ads, and struggling to stay ahead of its creditors. Ms. Fulton, a very astute and independent soul, took a long look at the dozen enlargements without saying a word. She motioned Parker to sit down while she was pondering the possibilities presenting themselves. They needed some new local talent badly, but their search had never come close to uncovering this gem.

"What a lovely young girl," Ms. Fulton finally said softly, looking up at Parker. "Where on earth did you find her? We have had contests for a year now, but this one has never surfaced."

"I know about your contests, but this is my own daughter, and I thought she was too young until now. We've been teaching her the humble art of becoming a lady."

Ms. Fulton seemed surprised by that, raising her eyebrows. "Now that is a refreshing difference," she commented, "and it comes through in the pictures. When do I get to meet Miss . . . ?"

"Her name is Teresa Parker, and she will be here at three p.m. tomorrow, if that is okay with you. She is still in high school, but will graduate shortly at the head of her class."

"I'm eagerly looking forward to this meeting, Mr. Parker," Ms. Fulton said earnestly. "I could put your obvious talents to work also, if you have the time." She knew instinctively that father and daughter were close, and if her first impression was right, she could leverage this opportunity into the big time.

It happened fast, the first ads being sensational. Calls started coming in to the Fulton Agency, including one from the Great Northern Railway out of Minneapolis. They were looking for traffic on their passenger route to Glacier National Park and the Pacific Northwest as far as Portland, Oregon. It was in Portland, near Mount Hood, where the photography would take place. Clayborn Parker was to be the photographer, since he had proven himself in the outdoors, and would he like to take his family with him for the summer?

The move proved to be permanent and quite lucrative. Clayborn Parker worked a lot with his daughter, although other photographers were clamoring for their chance and some were granted the favor. The Great Northern Railway was highly pleased with their investment with the Fulton Agency, and continued using Teresa as their model. By the second year, the advertisements were a proven success. The agency's prices, naturally, greatly escalated, which drew the attention of Ed "Chaps" Scharpe.

Chaps liked to keep track of things personally, and when an important or expensive matter was under consideration, he often brushed aside his aides and looked at the proposition first-hand. One afternoon while waiting for the evening run east out of Portland, he made a visit to the Fulton Agency's office, a visit that changed his life.

Teresa was being featured in tennis clothes, doing a series of advertisements for a national sporting goods company. There was no one behind the reception desk as Chaps entered the office, but hearing voices in the next room, he stepped into the studio. He was stopped in his tracks by the beauty of what he saw, drawing in a deep breath and holding it for a long moment.

What would it be like to possess an alluring creature such as the scantily clad one before him? His mind was already racing ahead. He had his extensive, priceless art collection, but here was something alive, sensuous, something useful perhaps. Ed's eyes moved from the model's overflowing bra to her slender, curving hips, and back again. Maybe he had at last found the answer to his many personal problems. Chaps would turn on the charm and find out.

Clayborn Parker wasn't doing a lot of outdoor work lately. He was tired and irritable, not inspired as he had generally been with the outdoors. His family started to worry about him, finally talking him into having a complete physical done. The results were not heartening, the doctor having found a virulent cancer. Within six months, Parker was dead, leaving a devastated family behind. Teresa was deeply affected, since her father had been a close friend as well as a talented career advisor. She felt an emotional void in her life, and tried to forget it with more and more work, but it was not the same.

By this time, Chaps was having trouble staying away from the agency and from Teresa. He started in by giving her sound financial advice, at which he was an expert. Later, he turned his efforts into a full-scale courtship and finally convinced Teresa to become his traveling secretary, with romance on the side. Nobody guessed that Chaps had a wife in the deep south whom he had not slept with in years, a woman who cared less for a relationship than she did for position. They rarely saw each other, but divorce was a thorny problem in Catholic New Orleans.

Teresa was always impressed with Chaps, but also carried some nagging reservations about their arrangement. Other men she had dated were more athletic, some were wealthy, most were not sincere, but Chaps was for her an enigma. She had certain romantic notions at times, which usually ended in frustration, but there were never any harsh words. Chaps always seemed to come up with an expensive gift to smooth things over, but Teresa was not one to be bought off for long. The power plays he made against other businessmen bothered her also, as did the continual presence of servants, cooks, and maids. Her first trip to Montana was a real breath of fresh air in several ways, which she decided to test a lot further.

A certain mountain man caught her imagination, and reminded her of a childhood in outdoors Vermont. Those were her best memories: the skiing, hiking, bike rides, and tennis. Her father had taught her well the love of the outdoors, but now she had been away from it too long. Suddenly, Teresa was brought back to all this by the appearance of an unusual, self-assured woodsman at her luncheon. His blonde, sun-bleached hair was somewhat in disarray, topping off a solid athletic body. His steady, blue eyes, of Nordic origin, seemed to drill right through her until they crinkled into a friendly smile. She sensed an intense, inner warmth which was all new to her and nearly impossible to conceal.

Teresa felt the warm glow reach her face as she watched this articulate man who apparently was equally at home in the mountains or in a board meeting. She wondered what he was really like, and decided to take the chance whenever it arrived, and find out. Her hopes for the sort of life she really wanted were going nowhere at this point, and she was dreaming of a change, of taking charge of her own life for once. A small, remote spot amongst the frosted peaks in northern Montana was changing a lot of lives these days, of people from the far ends of society, and from several continents.

Chapter 18

Walt was hunting for a few days with Johnny Bates and Iver, two of the best men in the country to have along if one wanted to fill the meat house or bring home a wall-hanger buck. Chaps was overjoyed with his first deer, and decided to take a few days in Minneapolis to catch up on business. He would accompany Scott and Don that far, having plenty of time to talk over the exciting days of the hunt. I was happy that Don managed to catch several large trout, and while he was telling me about it, I gave him some clues about Chaps' trials with the huge old bear. There would be a lot of teasing and red faces on the trip east, but that ribald humor generated plenty of fine memories. Sadly, that was the last that any of us ever saw of Don.

Charlie was more than busy these days, planning the ultimate caper to set himself up for his retirement. Resentment over his self-caused problems still boiled up in his mind, while an ulcer from too much booze was doing a job on his stomach. He couldn't even concentrate on Alice anymore, either, which finally led her to give him the axe. No matter, he would find a couple of young maidens in Florida, sexier, and more lively than Alice. Money would buy him anything, and he would have it soon, he swore.

On his days off, Charlie kept looking for just the right man to do his dirty work for him. He needed someone reasonably bright, mostly broke, and physically able to cover a lot of ground. Lars Anderson walked into the depot as if on cue, asking for Ed Scharpe. Charlie overheard the conversation between the big rawboned Swede and Oscar, and his ears perked up like those of a good watchdog.

Lars had inherited his wheat and cattle operation from his grandfather, who came over from Sweden and homesteaded with the help of Jim Hill, the founder of the Great Northern Railway. Hill's offer to pay the travel expenses of Nordic immigrants wanting to settle along his new railway in Montana and the Dakotas was an instant success. When Lars' grandpa heard about the chance to gain a farm with a lot of hard work but little money, he jumped at the chance. Never mind the brutal Montana climate and the privations that went with it. He could handle that, and would ship his grain and livestock from his remote homestead to market on the railroad, according to plan. It was good for everyone until Chaps came along.

Chaps had been in close contact for over a year with the Interstate Commerce Commission. He had convinced the commissioners that the freight rates from the prairie states were too low, and he now had won the authority for the Great Northern to levy a substantial increase for transporting wheat and cattle. Chaps' calculating mind told him that now was a good time to make a lot of extra money for the company, as excess grain was overflowing the elevators, and the farmers needed their paychecks. It was risky leaving the huge pyramids of wheat piled up in the open prairie, and what was more, the sheep and cattle had used up their graze and needed to be sent to the packing houses. It took too much hay to winter any big herds.

Much of the high-protein wheat from Montana was sold in Italy for the world's best pasta, but the set price was contracted far in advance. Any increase in shipping costs came out of the ranchers' pockets, while the cattlemen closer to Chicago or New York also had an edge over the Montanans in the auction barns, with less freight to worry about.

Lars grew up working for his grandpa, in the fields and chasing cattle from the time he could sit a horse or a tractor seat. It wasn't until he made it into high school, which he attended for one year, that his family home finally got a few electric lights. The well had an old windmill to pump water for the stock, but domestic water was raised by hand with an antique pitcher pump in the kitchen sink. The outdoor john was a real pain in twenty-below-zero weather, and bad enough the rest of the time. Cooking and heating were done with coal that he dug by hand from an exposed seam in a deep ravine that ran through a corner of his land. The drafty house was always too hot during summer, and in winter it was already too cold for comfort by the time dinner dishes were put away and the fire was burning down.

Early frost, drought, dry wind, blizzards, low prices, unsure markets, and a lot of other problems put down all but the most stubborn and hardy of the ranchers in these high plains. Those who were left were not about to sit still for any tycoon squeezing them to death in the first good profit year of the decade.

Lars was trying to find Chaps after rumors of the sudden and unfair rate increase came from his local grange. Lars was first going to plead his case with Chaps, face to face, and if that was unsuccessful, he was determined to find any other way to get enough money to pay off the family's mortgage as well as the tax bill. It would be good for once to have some money for seed, and for a herd of spring yearlings, too. He was sick of being in debt, and now that he finally had the harvest to pull him out, he was in no mood to see his one opportunity disappear.

Talk of a major hunting expedition near Libby was running all along the tracks from Seattle to Chicago, and even down to New Orleans. Wild stories and exaggerations became the order of the day, but everyone knew that Chaps was involved, which was why Lars hopped a ride to Libby. What better way to get a job done than to face it head on, or man to man, as he had done all his life. Lars was big, strong, and fearless. He was smart enough even with minimal schooling to know what he had to do to keep his property, and he was going to do it now, one way or another. Lars was a very determined man, a man with whom Charlie might have a quiet talk.

Oscar tipped his chair back while readjusting his visor and putting down a lined paper tablet.

"My God," he thought out loud, "this is going to raise Cain all along the Hi-line." The telegraph spoke of a notice from Minneapolis headquarters, signed off by Ed Scharpe. It detailed an immediate and substantial increase in freight rates on grain and livestock coming out of the Montana-Dakota prairies. Ed had these growers over a barrel and he was going to push them to the limit, never mind that many of his customers would be insolvent after the end-of-the-year sales.

One thing he overlooked, though, was the survival-at-any-cost attitude of the people who found new lives in this harsh and lonely place. They were prepared to fight politically or personally for their land, remembering the royal elite from the old country that controlled all the farms and the people who worked them. No one could be anything without property in the eyes of these Nordic pioneers, and neither Scharpe nor crooked bankers were going to remove them from it at this time or in the future. Lars' mindset was molded in bronze, and his brow developed a deep furrow like his newly ploughed barley field when Charlie read to him the new regulations.

Lars had a pretty, statuesque wife, fair of skin and blessed with a mop of red hair. She could outwork a lot of men around the farm and often did when she wasn't looking after the two towheaded rascals she was raising. These kids had their own ponies, and often followed Lars all over the ranch, and far beyond, like Vikings of old on trips of adventure. The land meant everything to this family, and all the other people that settled there with them. The possibility that his kids might not be able to take over the place someday was unthinkable. Lars loved his family, and he hated being away from home. He would do for them what had to be done.

"Let's wander over to the Mint Bar, Lars," Charlie said, "and I'll ante up for a couple beers." Nobody could hear a conversation in that place, and Charlie knew he had the man he needed. All he had to figure out was a cheap way to get the job done, and then send Lars off to his ranch, where no one would think of looking for an accomplice.

"Hey, Ferd, slide a couple draft Budweisers down the bar," Charlie demanded, "And don't push off any of that Great Falls Select alkali water on us."

"You got a big mouth, Charlie, that needs closin' again like I did for you a while back," Ferd replied, as he skillfully propelled the two beers down the polished hardwood. "Slide your money over here before I decide to come and get it!"

"You can't talk to me like that, you old bear," Charlie crowed. "You got to show some respect."

"The respect you're gonna find in here is from this bung starter when it bounces off your skull," Ferd replied, his face starting to flush. Ferd moved his massive forearm toward the counter behind the bar, where he grabbed the bung starter with a huge fist. He raised his hand as high as he could reach, and then dropped the heavy oaken mallet onto the bar for emphasis.

For once, the barroom quieted down enough for everyone to hear Charlie's labored breathing. Charlie was just now beginning to remember how he landed on his back the last time he insulted Ferd, and this business with Lars was too important to spoil by getting crushed with a bung starter. What a gorilla Ferd was, he thought. All muscle and no brain. Charlie took the beers to a battered table in the back of the dimly lit room, and sat down, motioning Lars to pull up a chair next to him.

"Now listen up, Lars." Charlie started talking in a barely audible voice. "I can't go through this with you again, and we are runnin' out of time. Ed Scharpe's private car is spotted on its own siding a couple hours' travel upriver, where his bunch is doin' a lot of deer hunting, if that's what you want to call it. He has this fancy lady with him some of the time, plus a full-time cook. Then there's a bunch of high-priced paintings hangin' on the walls that he likely hooked somebody out of. A couple of those would set all of us up for life if we can get 'em out of that car and out of the country. Old Chaps has got himself enough money to buy a whole truckload of them paintings, and here we set with nothin' in our pockets." Charlie looked furtively around before lowering his voice to a whisper. "It ain't fair, and it's time somebody did somethin' about it."

The plan was for Charlie to create a diversion up at the camp. Lars would grab the artwork when the car was empty and disappear with it into the woods for a week. At that time, Charlie would come get the paintings and Lars could head out with his share of the money and get lost in the endless country of eastern Montana. If details of the plan were changed, they would discuss it in a couple days.

"I do it for two t'ousand dollar," Lars whispered back. "Dat's vat I need to pay my tax and mortgage. Not vun dime less, ya? Ve heard about dis freight deal from our grange, but dey couldn't do nodding for helping us. And Charlie, I ain't goin' to shoot nobody, neither."

Charlie choked when he heard Lars' price, but kept his mouth shut. Lars could plan on paying his taxes, Charlie would retire with a good bank account somewhere, and Chaps would threaten his insurance company with cancellation of the railroad's account if they didn't pay him off. Simple but smart plans like this one had less chance of going wrong. Charlie was congratulating himself already, and soon would figure a way to get his payment back from Lars, too. No point in letting a dumb Swede run off with that kind of money.

Now it was time to contact Blaise and set up the time and place for exchange of greenbacks and art, with a few antiques thrown in. Charlie was patting himself on the back for coming up with the idea of getting even with Chaps while lining his own pockets. Wouldn't that damned Chaps have a fit when he found his private car stripped and had no way to prove who did it! Maybe some of Teresa's jewelry was stashed in there, too.

He was salivating at the idea of trading a night in bed with a luscious and grateful woman for a fortune in recovered jewelry. Charlie's jeans were stretching a bit with these thoughts in mind, when a loud crack and a shock wave hit his table. Charlie turned just in time to see Ferd raise the oaken bung starter again, and this time aim at his head.

"What the hell you doin, Ferd," Charlie yelled as he recoiled from impending disaster, his eyes widened with fear. "You could kill me with that thing."

"You guessed it, Charlie," Ferd growled. "When two coyotes like you get your heads together, you got to be plottin' something ag'in my friend Herb, and I aim to see that you don't get no place with that idea. Besides, the two lousy beers you bought was an hour ago, and I got people waitin' for this table." With that, Ferd brought the mallet crashing down on the heavy fir planks, exactly where Charlie's fingers were a split second before. Lars and Charlie disappeared through the back door like smoke in a stiff wind. It was time to leave, anyway, and to contact Blaise in Spokane.

Chapter 19

Walt and Johnny were seeing lots of game while Iver handled the horses. In fact they were seeing too much game, so much so that Johnny figured something was wrong. Deer were everywhere, feeding, moving through the open grassy areas like it was the middle of the night, and not even running when they were practically stepped on. Walt could have shot a dozen grouse also, in the past hour, but was going to use this great opportunity to take the best buck of his hunting career.

The weather had been crisp, but not really cold, with sunny days and freezing nights. It was just the kind of weather that was all too rare in the fall around here, but a smart one counted his blessings. By noon-time, Walt and Johnny had looked at nearly a hundred deer, which surprisingly were all headed down slope. Walt finally located the buck he wanted, and made a fine stalk. One shot at under a hundred yards put him in possession of a great five-point mule deer. The massive buck had a good thirty-inch spread on his antlers, with long heavy tines arching high up in beautiful symmetry. The buck would dress out at three hundred pounds, which meant that it would have to be cut in half before the horses could handle it, and then there was the delicate work of caping it out for a shoulder mount. This trophy was far too good to waste, and Walt knew that he would never see the likes of this heavy, barrel-chested monarch again.

Iver heard the shot, and managed to find the two hunters as they were cleaning out the deer. He tied up the horses and threw a lariat over a man-sized branch of an old Douglas fir tree. With an axe, he cut a gambrel stick from a stout branch and wedged it between the bone and main tendon on both hind legs of the buck, above the knee. When Walt finished gutting, he took the rope and tied it to the center of the stick. Iver led a horse down to the end of the rope and put a clove hitch around the saddle horn.

"Let's go, old boy," he urged the horse as they started uphill, raising the deer off the ground. Iver led his horse around another tree a couple times, then unhitched the rope from the saddle and tied it off. Now they could skin and cape the buck, split it in two, and keep everything clean before sacking the meat.

"Walt, you have about the best mule deer that ever came out of this country," Johnny praised him. "There is no way we could have handled this one without the horses, but we have to get with it if we expect to get home tonight." The three men were so caught up with the success of the day's hunt that a dramatic weather change caught them by surprise. The sun disappeared behind an angry cloud formation, and the calm afternoon became blustery, with the temperature starting to plummet.

Before the deer was fully processed and ready for packing out, a blizzard was in the making, with visibility almost zero. An icy wind was now driving the snow parallel to the ground and plastering the west side of the tree trunks.

"We got to get out of here now, or we won't make it back to camp," Iver said. "It would take us till after dark on a good day, but with the horses all loaded down we might be out half the night."

"I don't like the idea of ridin' in this blizzard," Johnny shouted above the wind. "We can't see a thing. I want to get us into the timber and find our upper camp. At least we have a tent and some dry wood over there. We left a couple bales of hay and some grub, too, and we have us plenty of fresh meat to go with it. Herb will figure out what we're up to." The wind whipped the words away.

Johnny led his horse down the ridge and away from the open grassy slopes where the wind cut through his clothes like a knife. Iver followed, with his horse also loaded with half the deer, while Walt rode in their tracks. One miserable hour later, Johnny's horse whinnied, and pulled off to the right. Johnny was wise enough to take the hint, and within minutes walked up to the tent. The horse remembered the place from when he was there with Scott, which was very lucky. Finding the tent saved the three hunters from a bad or maybe fatal experience. Hypothermia was stalking Johnny already, as his clothing wasn't good enough for this kind of storm.

Iver knew the symptoms from spending his early years in Sweden. He took Johnny inside, peeled off their frozen outer clothes, and crawled into a sleeping bag with him.

"Walt," Iver shouted, "Get the fire going in the stove here, and put some snow in a pan for hot water. We got to get some hot soup down Johnny or he won't warm up quick enough. Tie the horses up behind some of the thick fir trees, out of the wind, and throw out a bale of hay. I'll trade off with you then, and get the meat unloaded. We'd better leave the saddle blankets on those horses to help keep 'em warm.

Walt brushed the ice crystals off his whiskers and eyebrows, then took off his hat and pounded the crusted snow off of it. He found some of the pitchy kindling and dry wood that we put up while building the spike camp, and made a small cone of it in the center of the stove's fire box. One match out of his waterproof case, struck on the stove door, was all it took to get a blaze started. A few dry fir sticks soon built into a hot fire with the draft wide open, turning the stove top near the stack a cherry red.

It didn't take long to make a pot of hot water and get a package of dried soup boiling. Johnny responded to that, and within an hour he was out of danger. The wind and heavy snow continued most of the night, and twice, Iver had to pound on the canvas from inside to bounce the snow off and reduce the weight on the tent. Shortly before daylight, the blizzard moved out to the east, leaving two feet of snow behind. A jet black sky above glittered with brilliant stars shining everywhere. The temperature in camp on that mountaintop bench dropped to twenty degrees below zero. The air was dead calm, making it easy to hear the horses chewing the last of their hay. The boys ate soup and deer tenderloin for breakfast. Johnny allowed as how he had probably seen his second miracle on one hunting trip, while he put his left hand on Iver's shoulder and shook hands with his right. He wouldn't forget this, ever.

"No wonder we saw so many deer yesterday," Walt said while he and Johnny were brushing the horses down. "Every one of them knew this storm was coming, and they were all headed for cover down below."

"Yeah, them deer was a lot smarter than us, gettin' out of here early," Johnny replied, as the long stream of tobacco juice he spat disappeared into the powder snow. "Let's get outta here ourselves, as Herb will be wonderin' about us by tonight. I ain't complainin' to him any more about puttin' up these high camps."

"I can also think of someone a hell of a lot better than you to spend time with in a sleeping bag," Walt said with a grin.

"Yeah, and I bet Herb can too," Johnny replied softly, turning toward Walt. Then Johnny slowly grinned back. Maybe he had gazed into a ball made of ice crystals, seeing a young maiden inside.

The lower country was alive with deer, and the trio crossed a lot of elk and moose tracks on the way down. Iver managed to shoot a pair of fat old dry does out of a group of mule deer. They were feeding on bunch grass on a windblown south slope and never heard him approach. Iver and Johnny had their winter's meat aboard their horses, and Walt had his great trophy lashed down in plain sight as he led the procession into camp at dusk. Anybody would be proud of that one, earned the hard way.

The welcoming committee consisted of Buck, who pranced up to Walt and nuzzled his arm, looking for an apple or some other favor. Sally would never willingly be far from Buck, and she appeared out of the trees to join the crowd. She was always glad to see somebody who could lay out some hay and alfalfa pellets.

"Something's wrong here," Walt exclaimed. "Nobody's around."

"Yeah, it ain't right that Buck and Sally are runnin' loose, either," Johnny answered. "Looks like the rest of the stock is gone, too."

"Here's a bunch of man tracks," Iver shouted from the corral where he was going to unload his horse. "Somebody opened the gate and run 'em all off."

"Let me take a good look at this," Johnny said, while hurrying over to the corral. This new snow will let us do some trackin', and that's just what I intend to do. I don't recognize any of these footprints. Look at this here boot track, the tread is almost smooth. Nobody in our camp would wear boots like that in the snow. A man would be fallin' down every time he set foot on a side slope."

"Do you think somebody is rustling our pack animals?" Walt asked Johnny.

"I doubt it," was the reply. "Nobody would want to herd this bunch all the way over Tony Mountain to get away from us. Besides that, there's three feet of snow on top by now, and anybody rustlin' is lookin' for easier pickin's than this. I got a good idea who's up to this deviltry, and he'll be eatin' more than trackin' snow when I catch him. All I need is a bite to eat and some warmer clothes, and I'm gone. God help that son of a bitch when I catch him for runnin' my horses off thisaway."

Johnny was a born horseman. He worked his animals hard and knew how to get the best out of them, but he always treated them right. They were his family, his life. He would do what he had to do now. Johnny loaded a backpack with some oats and pellets, put in a bridle, saddle blanket, and some rope, along with food, fire-starting pitch sticks, hand axe, and a few candles and a flashlight.

Iver knew that Johnny would go for days, if needed, to get his horses and mules back, and he didn't say a word when he shook Johnny's right hand and placed his own .357 Smith and Wesson in Johnny's left. With a wink, he forked over half a box of shells.

It was getting dark early these days in the long Montana winter. Johnny had slow going for a while, but the horses were still together after a couple of miles. They made a trail that was easy to follow in the fresh snow, even though he could barely see under dim starlight. After an hour of dark, the moon came out, casting its glow across the snow like a huge Chinese lantern at Halloween. The pines threw long black shadows across the landscape, creating a mosaic pattern of intricate beauty where they blended among thin shadows cast by bare alders and mountain maples.

The single sound that Johnny heard was a lone coyote calling to the moon. Four inches of powder snow muffled his footsteps, allowing him to walk right up to a lone bull moose who was feeding on the maple twigs. He stopped when suddenly close enough to hear large molars grinding up the sweet-tasting maple shoots. They stared at each other until Johnny said, "Hey, bull, time to move over. I got to get along here." The bull's eyes widened, and Johnny pulled out the .357, not wanting to get himself trampled.

An almost indiscernible upriver draft carried a man scent to the old bull, who grunted once, then wheeled around and legged it into some heavy timber. He ran without a sound, like a ghost. "I wish I could move like that," Johnny muttered aloud. He watched, fascinated, as a thousand pounds of animal glided across the moonscape, to be swallowed up by dark shadows in a timbered creek bottom.

"This is as good a place as any to so do some figurin'." Johnny was still talking to himself. "It's been awhile since there was any man tracks in the trail, so that means this varmint caught up a horse and is ridin' it now. Also, a pair of tracks made a big swing away from the trail awhile back, and they ain't joined up with us again. That means to me that Buck got tired of bein' herded away by some stranger, and he took Sally with him back to camp. It would take a hell of a man to keep that horse separated from Herb for very long."

Johnny was thinking hard, but was having difficulty making sense out of the whole caper. The trail was heading north, upriver, with no place to go except Eureka. It was a good week's travel to Eureka under present conditions, but there were no pack saddles missing, no grub gone, and no way to pack horse feed. It just wasn't reasonable, he mused, that someone would go to all this trouble to move our horses so far out of camp and then let them starve. "They had to be meetin' somebody upriver a ways," he concluded, "and I'm goin' to join that meetin'!"

When it came to tracking horses, Johnny was with the best. He spent a lot of time at it, and could pretty much think like a horse by now. Sometimes a pack string wandered a long ways from camp during a night's feeding, and Johnny would forget the tracks and just head to the spot where he figured they ought to be. He was right most of the time, too, unless a moose or a bear got involved. His black was still with this rustled bunch, and he knew its tracks as well as he did his own. The black was starting to wander out of the trail, like he was looking for a way to leave the bunch and head back to the camp. Twice, the rustler took his mount after the black and managed to push him back into line.

"This guy knows his business," Johnny said to himself, "And he wants my black because that horse is the best of the bunch, by far. He is a-goin' to try ridin' him, and that's where he makes a bad mistake. I'm gettin' my horse back right soon, now."

Nobody had ever successfully been on the black except Johnny, who broke him that hot summer day up the Yaak Valley. The black understood Johnny and learned to trust him, but anyone else who climbed aboard this horse ended up flat on his back, and wondering where his brains had gone for trying that dumb stunt.

Sometime during the past ice age, the Kootenai River was dammed up in this place by a huge rock fall, brought down from the mountains by an avalanche. Enough silt was then deposited to create a beautiful bench in the midst of the canyon. The rich topsoil now nurtured an open forest of ancient trees. Ponderosa pines, larches, and firs grew to immense dimensions here, spaced as in a park, with deep grass beneath them. Bright moonlight reflecting off the new snow lit up the landscape like it was early morning, lending an enchantment to the place that was not lost on Johnny.

The black was getting hungry, and Johnny knew he would leave the bunch now and move downwind a ways before stopping to paw the snow off the grass and fill his belly. Johnny left the trail and headed toward the distant ridge which bordered the flat. He crossed numerous elk tracks, scraped out areas where the elk had found bunch grass and the beds they rested in before heading back to cover. It wasn't long before he cut a horse track that he instantly recognized. He followed the black's trail for about ten minutes and came to a large opening in the pines where the horse had obviously been feeding a short time before.

A single man track came back from the north, and as Johnny studied the flat-soled print, the answer came to him like a shock. "This is a winter moccasin! What in creation is this Kootenai Indian doin' by rustlin' our stock thisaway? Somebody had to put him up to it, and who else but Charlie would think up a scheme like this?" Alex Black Deer caught up with Johnny's horse a quarter mile from where Johnny now stood.

Alex had a vision as a young man, in which a large black deer saved his life from drowning. He had been in his canoe, spearing whitefish to be dried or smoked for the winter. A sudden whirlwind appeared from the far end of the backwater where his canoe was anchored with a heavy stone. The whirlwind gathered force as it approached him, picking up drops of water that turned into a spinning mist. It created a rushing sound, as if a waterfall were in its center, causing Alex to look up in great fear, hearing the waterfall speak to him.

The mist sparkled in the fall sunshine, turning into all the beautiful colors of the rainbow, but the center of the whirlwind was black. The closer the whirlwind came to Alex, the more frightened he became. His breath came in short gasps, and his eyes turned glassy with fear, very unusual for Alex, as he was admired for his bravery. Signs from the spirit world were an altogether different matter, having little to do with bravery. He stood transfixed in the stern of his canoe, watching the black waterfall change shape to become a large, dark-colored deer with huge palmated antlers, like those of a moose.

"Hunter of moose," the deer called to him, "You are a respected member of your tribe. You are to become a leader, a provider for your people. Your totem is black. It will bring you good fortune. Paint an antler on each of your cheeks. You must remember this sign, and I will help you when your people need game for food or skins, and fish for the long winter. Go now, and return to your teepee to be with your young woman. Tell her, but no one else of your vision."

The deer with the moose antlers started whirling in the same direction as the waterspout, coming always closer until Alex was enveloped by it. The sun disappeared and it became as night in the canoe. Alex was dizzy from watching the spinning deer, and he fell from the stern of the canoe, hitting his head on the gunnel. He nearly passed out, but vaguely remembered being carried to shore on the smooth, palmated moose antlers and left on a sandy beach.

The sun was setting when Alex fully regained his senses. He looked around for his canoe, which he saw grounded just below him, and marveled that it was low in the water from a full load of fish. Weekeena, his woman, whom he would rename Morning Star, was overjoyed at the sight of all the fish, the best catch that Alex had ever made. Morning Star gave a flawless birth to their son in the dark of that very night. Alex took the name of Black Deer, and from that day on, would never shoot another moose.

Alex Black Deer soon developed the best nighttime vision of anyone in his tribe. He usually hunted at night when game was not so cautious. On his special days, he painted two black antlers on his cheeks, never forgetting the gift of his vision. Life was not always easy for Alex Black Deer, but he managed to raise his son well, and to provide for his wife. Things were a bit tough right now, which was why he dropped in on Charlie to see about a few days' work on the section crew.

Charlie immediately saw his chance, and convinced Alex Black Deer that the black horse in the hunting camp was destined to be his. After all, black was his totem, wasn't it? All that was expected of him was to perform the task of herding the camp's horses to a siding upriver where they were needed. This service would greatly please the big boss of the railroad, and now he would receive a token fifty dollars in advance. He should take the black horse with him back to Canada for the winter.

Alex was not a thief, which explained the fact that he took nothing from the camp, but that fact sure kept Johnny perplexed. The tracks of winter elkhide moccasins and a tall black horse came together in the loose snow. The snow held the story like an open book, which Johnny was reading with great interest as the tracks turned north again, toward Canada.

Alex Black Deer had a way with animals, and horses were no exception. He led Johnny's horse with a rawhide chin bridle that also served as a halter when necessary. Upon finding just the right two trees, Alex led the black between them until the horse's front shoulders were wedged rather tightly, restricting his motion. There in the snow was written what happened next.

Alex mounted up, backed the black out of the trees and turned him upriver. The black didn't like it, and he plainly did a lot of prancing around, but no serious bucking yet. "This isn't as bad as I expected," Alex thought to himself, as he entered a patch of young firs, but his good fortune ended about then.

The old bull moose that had turned away from Johnny hours before made his way rapidly to this feeding area, which he had known of for years. He had been undecided about what to do with a motionless, strange looking, two-legged creature, and at once his hunger overcame his curiosity. He backed off one other time a few years earlier from a huge, evil-tempered black bear that was determined to have a narrow trail to himself. He was unnerved by an aggressive display of fangs and claws, and the raised hair along the bear's back. That would not happen again since he now had attained his full growth of eleven hundred pounds of muscle and antler and bone. He learned to enforce his will on anything in the forest, and particularly now that he felt the urges of breeding coming on, he was going to have his way. Johnny was lucky that night, but not Alex Black Deer, who rode his horse right into the thicket that hid the great bull.

The bull moose didn't know whether he was going to have sex or a fight when he heard the four-legged animal approach, but he was alert, hungry and ready for anything. His sensitive nose registered instantly that here was no cow moose. He gave a loud grunt just before he charged. The horse didn't need any lessons to know what that grunt meant, and he was not about to fight any bull of these massive proportions. He just wanted to get out of there, without that Indian on his back. The big black tensed his muscles, dropped his head down by his knees and rocketed straight up into the air, kicking viciously at the moose with his hind legs. Several times he launched himself, twisting right and left before he came down squealing with fright, farting and bucking like a champion.

Alex flew off, crashed against a tree with enough force to crack two ribs, and lay in the snow until the cold on his face revived him. His black totem was standing before him, looking down to see if there was any threat there. Finally satisfied, the old bull shredded a limber sapling with his antlers, then turned and disappeared into the night. Blackie trotted back the way he came, stopping abruptly when he heard a familiar whistle. He was back with Johnny, the one man he trusted, and was glad of it.

Alex found the first horse he had been riding, where he left him tied to a tree. He painfully mounted up, and made tracks out of there with several of Johnny's pack string following him. The moose had not injured him, but had given him a message. No free black horse, which seemed unfair to Alex Black Deer, but his guardian likely saved him considerable misery, as horse thieving was dealt with severely in Montana. He would do what his totem wanted.

Alex put his mount into a fast walk over trails he remembered as a boy. The bright moonlight on fresh snow made it easy to read the way, while the four inches of powder muffled all sounds but his horse's breathing. With any luck, he would be at the Ural siding by early morning to turn the horses over to Lars. He planned on flagging down the morning train, paying for a ride to Eureka, and then hiking across the border into Canada. He would do this before the sun cast his shadow straight north.

He missed Morning Star and his young son. He planned to buy them each a winter coat, and would surprise Morning Star with a big ham, the white man's bear. She would laugh, and Alex could already feel her hands on him as she unbuttoned his clothes. It was good to return home with gifts, but he began thinking that Charlie was bad medicine, "Too much no good!" Alex winced as his horse jumped a log, sending a shot of pain through his body from his cracked ribs.

"Charlie drink too much, talk lie to Alex, make moose spook my horse. Maybe I still cut his throat. I will pray to the Great Spirit to have my black deer visit Charlie one night when moon is below the earth. I will look into my cooking fire in Canada, and I will have a vision. Alex Black Deer will know one night of no moon when Charlie visits his ancestors."

Walt was in good hands with Iver in camp. Richard and the two guides caught the evening train for Whitefish a couple days earlier to stock up on supplies and to let off some steam. The Dry Gulch Saloon was a lively place where a twenty dollar bill and a few beers would buy a man his bed with a shapely partner for the night. The steam disappeared rapidly in those rooms above the bar. It was enough to draw any hunter out of the mountains for a while.

Richard was in his glory at the moment. He created a certain curiosity in the Dry Gulch, and used his polished manner to persuade several ladies to keep him company. At the end of a day and a half, Richard came to the painful conclusion that he was no match for these two lovelies, when he staggered out of bed and creased his skull on the bathroom door. His bleary eyes watched the blondes take double their pay from his wallet, but his drained body could not respond. The blondes left the door open behind them, and wiggled their backsides in a parting gesture as they floated down the stairway. Richard gave out a low groan as he laid his aching body down and passed out on the floor.

Chapter 20

Chaps was expecting to get back in a couple days accompanied by J. T. Bidwell, the president of the Great Northern. Bidwell was a very powerful, very demanding man. He worked long hours himself, and expected total commitment from his staff. Chaps knew all about that, and he was blowing himself up while describing how he just raised the rates on grain being shipped from Montana. He forgot to mention just how much of the profit would find its way back under the table.

I could see that everything was under control so I left camp on my speeder the day before the big storm. I would return in a few days to take over operations again when Chaps and J. T. Bidwell showed up. I was secretly hoping that Teresa would arrive a day or two early. Maybe she awoke something in me that was too deep, too subdued for so long.

The memories of her were overwhelming sometimes. The faint perfume, her light touch, all seemed like yesterday, and I found it unnerving that my mind brought back every word, every sensation that I experienced that magical weekend. I had known fear, gut-wrenching fear on many a mission, but learned to fight it off until I got a handle on it. Was I again experiencing fear, or was it self-doubt, when conjuring up images of what life would be like with a warm, loving woman who seemed to want me.

I was somewhat of an explorer, even in boyhood, when my father had no qualms about sending me off by myself to fetch home a deer, or some other game. Often I would stay out for several days, and seldom returned empty-handed. I loved these trips with my old horse and my Labrador dog, and often made notes on what I saw, where I camped, and what I caught or shot. I knew then that I would write about all this in later years. It had never occurred to me to be lonesome, as I had a couple friends, but often we wouldn't see each other for days.

A hunter soon learns to respect life after he has taken a few animals, and shooting becomes a bittersweet experience. It is a necessity at times, and done properly is the same as harvesting a crop or thinning the cattle herd. I knew by then that the coming spring would replenish what was sparingly taken, but I never had any joy in killing. My satisfaction was in doing a better job than anyone else with my rifle, my knife, my horse and my pack mule. I was getting a lot of practice at that just before the Air Force recruited me to help fight the enemy in Europe and Asia.

My early experience with girls was limited at best, and in the military I was transferred every time it seemed like I was on the inside track with someone I could really like. Now that I was working for Walt, I purposely put in long, tiring hours in the woods. Some of my old nightmares from the war were returning, and I often woke up in a cold sweat, unable to get back to sleep unless I was physically exhausted from work. It seemed that I had my best luck when I rode my horse into the mountains and just camped out alone. Could I change my ways for a beautiful person like Teresa? Could she cope with me? I didn't know. My thoughts started drifting again back to the war when I was too young for it, but was there anyway.

Chapter 21

"Herb, a boat at two o'clock on the horizon." The captain was on the intercom.

"Roger, captain. I see it. Looks like a fishing boat of some sort," I answered from the nose turret.

"I'm going to buzz him, and see what he's doing here. Intelligence didn't mention anything about fishing boats in this quadrant."

We were flying a series of hunt-and-destroy missions, looking for German U-boats that were devastating our convoys of troops and supplies headed for England. Our bomb bays were half full of depth charges, and half full of fuel in special tanks that extended our range for hours. We had been successful in sinking two subs lately and disabling another, which one of our destroyers captured.

Some of the Allied convoys had been attacked far south of Europe, and it was obvious that those Axis subs were being resupplied somehow without having to return to base. The Germans developed a tanker submarine, but did not have enough of those to do the whole job. The war was starting to go against them, and they were taking desperate measures, sometimes gambling on refueling in South America and from there attacking the Panama Canal traffic.

"Dead ahead, captain," I spoke through the throat mike. "He's flying the Union Jack, and I can see nets and floats like he's catching salmon or something." We buzzed the ship at two hundred feet elevation and three hundred fifty miles per hour.

"He's fishing all right," was the reply, "but he doesn't belong here, and all the Brits know it. Let's take another look, and you be ready to strafe the bastards." I charged my twin fifties and fired a couple rounds at a whitecap to make sure everything was working.

The captain put our bomber into a long climbing turn, and came back around to the ship's stern. As we approached firing range, I could see a dozen men on deck pulling nets, but one man in the stern panicked and jerked the cover off a deck gun, swinging it in my direction. There was no way I was going to let him get away with that, and I fired a burst, allowing about thirty feet of reverse lead. A dozen rounds cut him down, and he went into the ocean for the sharks.

"Not bad shooting for the best in the Air Force," came through the earphones. "Let's see if you can get lucky one more time."

The captain circled around again and while we were about a mile off, I called, "Captain, radio in our position before we make another pass."

"Why for, country boy. We don't seem to need any help."

"Just do it for me, fly boy?" I said with disrespect. "I like to keep track of what I shoot and where."

"Roger, country boy, anything to keep you quiet, but we ain't rabbit hunting! Let's sink that tub and the Union Jack with it."

"You do the flying, captain, while I do the shooting. Make a pass about forty yards to the right of her, and see what happens."

"You got it, gunner, but I'm getting dizzy from circling around here. Let's get it done with, if you think you can hit that scow."

We made another pass, diving this time at four hundred mph and forty yards off the port beam while I fired a ten second burst into the water just off the ship's rail.

"What the hell you doin', gunner, sleepin'?" came an exasperated blast into my ears. "You missed the whole damn ship."

"I didn't miss, captain. Look at some of the crew going overboard. I need one more pass now, and then good-bye Krauts."

"You got one last chance, or your reputation is going down the tubes and I may just toss you overboard too. We're gettin' low on fuel."

Captain Gates brought us around one more time, and I fired a continuous burst from my twin .50 Cal. Brownings into the converted fishing boat, starting from five hundred yards out and finishing just as we reached the ship. I could see two lines of holes stitch the deck from stern to bow, right down the center.

"Pull up, captain, fast," I shouted into the mike above the roar of four engines. I noticed the deck of the ship start to rise, and I knew what was coming. My armor-piercing bullets and a few tracers made it into the hold, exploding a fuel tank, which set off a dozen torpedoes. The center of the fishing boat erupted like a volcano, the explosion tore the hull apart, and large pieces of burning wood and melted steel came rocketing up at our bomber like antiaircraft flak. Two dozen crew members never knew what happened, but I caught a fast look at a few of them, and that terrible scene burned itself indelibly into my mind. Black smoke filled my turret, and pieces of shrapnel hit our wings, punching holes here and there. Our aircraft shuddered, and rose about a hundred feet with the concussion of the exploding ship, but luckily we stayed aloft.

I hollered at Blake, our navigator, "Get out our life raft, and I'm coming to help you toss it out. Let's go around and drop it on the crew in the water while we get lined out for home."

The co-pilot lowered the bomb bay doors, and Blake and I shoved out a large yellow raft, which inflated when it hit the water. The captain put us directly over the swimmers at about a hundred feet, and as slow as he could safely fly. The life raft landed within a few yards of one of the crew, and we could see him climb aboard.

"That was a fine piece of work, mountain man," Captain Gates said into his mike, "but you nearly got us shot down. Lord, that was close. I guess you know that you are the first aircrew member who ever captured prisoners of war single-handed from a bomber."

Had I gone soft? I could have killed them all on the second pass, but I already had too close a look at death that day to ever forget, and I didn't need any more. We landed after the day-long mission with twenty minutes of fuel to spare.

A British destroyer picked up six survivors in a flat sea just before dark. They were a German crew who knew that the war was over for them, and they volunteered invaluable data on the workings of their submarine operations. They were expressing their gratitude to a Yankee bomber crew after thinking things over in a P.O.W. camp in Scotland. Hitler did not look so heroic to them anymore. The killing and destruction continued, unabated. My nightmares became a problem with no solution, although I knew I wasn't alone.

Chapter 22

When I hit town, I parked the speeder and checked in with Oscar to see if he had any messages for me. There was one from Chaps, from Chicago, who gave his arrival date with J. T. Bidwell. There was another from Teresa, who was arriving from Minneapolis a day earlier. She planned to debark at the camp site and stay in the private car. I was invited to a champagne and candlelight dinner in return for taking her hunting the next day. Lingering over dinner promised to be an exercise in restraint.

Oscar looked up with a knowing smile as he handed me the decoded message, written in his hand. On the back he scrawled, "Lucky." My face flushed a bit, and I felt my whole body warm up while considering that piece of good news. Never was there a greater incentive to go hunting, and I usually didn't need one at all. I started wondering just how a man could use up all his energy at night and still get up at dawn and put in a long hard day. I couldn't wait to find out. Charlie had not seen this telegraph message. He gave me no more than a scowl as I left the Great Northern Depot.

On the way home, I picked up a couple spicy German sausages and some dark bread for dinner. There wasn't a lot of time for cooking, paying a bunch of bills, and relaxing a bit with a good book before trying for a full night's sleep. Gerta beat me to my chores by cleaning up in her usual spic-and-span manner. When I opened the fridge, there sat a beautiful apful strudel with a note on top. "When you seeing that nice young lady again?"

Right now it was chilly in the house, so I headed for the woodshed to bring in a load of stovewood. When I built my woodshed, I made sure there was plenty of room for other things like a lawnmower, power tools, and my fishing boat. It was getting dark, but I could see an empty space where my boat normally sat on a pair of sawhorses. I thought that was odd, but sometimes Gerta's husband borrowed the boat for a bit of duck hunting, which was okay. He usually called me first, but I was gone a lot lately, and I dismissed it for the moment. My mind was busy enough with other thoughts.

Charlie was busy lately, too, planning his retirement. He gave Alex Black Deer fifty dollars and the promise of Johnny's horse, Blackie, to take the camp's stock up the Kootenai Valley about twenty miles to Ural siding.

Charlie told Alex, "Mr. Scharpe, a big chief on this railroad, wants to hunt up there for a few days, and he needs the horses and mules. He would be very grateful to Alex for this work, and wants to reward you with a new horse. The camp crew is gone for a few days, so they can't do it themselves. It must be done tomorrow night. My friend Lars will take the horses from you when you get there."

"Alex can do this thing, but he wants talk with Long Rifle. Find plenty elk. Need much bullets. Make jerky. Cold winter, plenty snow come now." Alex gestured with his arms spread out shoulder height.

"Herb is gone, seeing new woman, and we no can wait," Charlie lied.

Alex shook his head, "Herb Long Rifle plenty smart. Him kill elk first. Then lie on robes all winter. Plenty grub, plenty woman!"

The ground was bare, but there was a scattering of clouds blowing over the top of the Cabinet Range. It had been a very pleasant fall up to now, but Alex sensed a heavy storm brewing. Charlie wasn't even considering tracking snow in his plans. Everything was set for tomorrow night, so Charlie hit on the idea of offering Johnny's horse to get things rolling.

A gleaming eight-inch blade, razor sharp, appeared from nowhere, its stag handles grasped in Alex's weathered hand, and the point touching Charlie's chest just below his throat. Charlie was strangling on his own spit. His eyes crossed as he looked at that blade, and he could just feel his life's blood from a slit throat running down the front of his wool union suit.

"Charlie talk Long Rifle. Say, Alex Black Deer find two tens elk, need old pardner, good shot. No moose. Be back half moon, after deep snow!" When Alex turned, he and the knife disappeared in an instant, quiet as the shadow of a horned owl. Charlie was still choked up, hardly able to breathe, and weak in the knees. His eyes were the size of the bottom of a Great Falls Select, and just as glassy.

"Son of a bitch," he murmured, "That savage could've killed me without thinkin' about it. I wonder how he ever got friendly with, what did he call him, Long Rifle? He must have been huntin' with Herb and seen him shoot. What a combination them two makes." Charlie sat down and reached for a bottle that wasn't there. His heart was still up in his throat and he couldn't have slugged down a shot of Irish Mist, anyway. He barely made the John.

"Lars, you have to get up to Ural tomorrow night," Charlie said over a couple beers. They were at Charlie's place instead of the Mint Bar, where Ferd always poked his nose into everyone's business. Lars had been staying with Charlie, sleeping on an old quilt on the floor, and keeping out of sight. "A Kootenai Indian, who is a very good man with horses, is going to have some stock available for you the following morning. I already paid him, and he doesn't drink, so I know he's gonna show up. Take the rowboat I stashed in the brush below the county road and row across the river to the siding. Chaps' private car will be spotted there with nobody in it. I'll drive you close to the place and let you off."

"What the horses for?" Lars wanted to know.

"I'm explainin' that in a minute, if you just pay attention." Charlie was getting nervous now. "And for God's sake, don't cross that Indian, or he'll cut your throat before you take a breath." He shivered. "I never seen anybody so fast with a knife. Take the paintings I listed here, and remove the frames carefully. They are worth a whole lot of money, but if you damage them at all, nobody wants to buy 'em. Roll the canvases up and put them into these waterproof tubes here, and seal the ends. I checked with an expert and that's what he told me. You get a bonus for taking a custom-made rifle away with you. It's worth half a year's pay, or more."

"No, Charlie. I ain't stealin' a rifle from Mr. Scharpe. All I want is my money that I earned with my crops, so I can pay my bills. What are you doing with the paintings?"

"We are holding them until Chaps pays a bunch of people what he owes, including you, and then he gets them back." Charlie was thinking fast, now. He couldn't afford to alienate Lars at this point, after Alex was preparing his night raid on the camp's horses. That was a stroke of genius, he thought, creating a diversion in camp, splitting the crew, and getting a foolproof way for Lars to escape.

"You do what you want with the rifle," Charlie commented, wondering how a man could steal paintings, but not a personal item like a priceless rifle. He didn't understand how Lars could be honest enough to leave behind something like that, and he sure couldn't fathom a farmer's love of his land and devotion to his family. "The paintings are being picked up in three days by a man named Blaise. I have a map here, and this is where you have to meet him." Charlie traced the area on the map with a forefinger. "He talks with a foreign accent like he came from Europe, or someplace."

"I want my two thousand dollar, Charlie," Lars demanded.

"What makes you think I got money like that, Lars? You collect it from Blaise when you hand over the artwork."

"I don't like it, Charlie. Maybe he doesn't pay me, and I lose my farm."

"Don't worry none. Blaise is honest, just like you are. Now here is the deal. You take two horses that this Indian is bringin' up, and swim them across the river behind the rowboat. I got a couple saddles and some grub in a backpack and a sleeping bag hid there too. This map shows a trail that takes off right across the old road from where the boat is. It's about ten or eleven miles up Boulder Creek going west till you get to Lost Horse Mountain, where there's an old fire lookout tower with a cabin next to it. They always have a stove in them cabins, too. You won't find any hot women up there, so take your matches. There's enough grass on some of the open slopes for the horses." Charlie put away his third beer, and was starting to act like it.

"How am I supposed to get into the cabin," Lars wanted to know.

"I put in a hammer and a couple tools. You won't be havin' any problem with the door. On the third day, come down to the west, about fifteen more miles, to the end of the trail on Zulu Creek where it hits the Yaak River road. I got it all marked with pencil. Nobody will guess where you are, and Blaise will meet you there at dark."

"What I do about the horses?" Lars asked.

"Turn the horses loose after you hang up their saddles and halters on a good tree. Those ponies will remember the trail and make it home by themselves. Or maybe somebody will find 'em. Blaise will drop you off in Bonners Ferry, Idaho, and you can catch the train from there to anyplace you like."

Charlie did not mention that he was going to be at the end of the trail too, and collect from Blaise. Maybe he could get the two thousand back from Lars and just turn him loose in the woods, or worse. Charlie drained one more beer, and threw the bottle into a corner. The alcohol was quickly working now, and Charlie was thinking some dangerous thoughts. His face twisted into an evil grin. He could see Lars buried in a rockslide along with Blaise, then he would have all the money, fifty thousand dollars, and the paintings to sell once again, with no witnesses. It felt great to be so much smarter than those dumb foreigners. Nobody would ever miss a Swede, or a Hungarian, either.

Blaise was serving a customer in his Spokane art gallery when the phone rang. "This is Charlie, and I'm callin' from home."

"I told you not to call during business hours, and I have someone here now," Blaise replied in anger.

"I just called to tell you that the action is starting tomorrow night, and I want to be sure you will be doin' what we planned. It can't wait any longer. See you in a few days, and bring the package."

"You call again, and you will never see me. Now good-bye!"

Blaise had been busy ever since Charlie and Alice had dropped in on him the past summer. He had gone to extremes to find out if the paintings described by Charlie were authentic and actually registered to Ed Scharpe. Famous paintings and other artworks were nearly always kept track of by private firms like Sotheby's, and others, who auctioned off art and other assets of estates and wealthy collectors. It took a lot of money in the right places, plus trips to Vancouver and New York, to affirm that Ed Scharpe had indeed purchased a Picasso and a Russell in a New York auction. The other paintings that Charlie described may or may not be originals, but he could determine that after having them in his possession.

If Charlie didn't like the reduced financial arrangement, he could forget the whole business, or go elsewhere. Fifty thousand was a lot of money for Blaise to siphon off from his assets, but the payoff could be ten or twenty times that. He made some discreet inquiries around Montreal, Mexico City, and Miami, the places where he would have little trouble crossing the border or dealing with immigration officials. There were a few people who showed interest, but they wanted a hand to hand exchange for cash. It was wise to get as far from the scene of the theft as possible, but travel entailed its risks when one had a very valuable cargo with him.

Blaise thought back on his escape from communist-controlled Europe, and started making his plans accordingly. Past experience brought back bitter memories of friends who disappeared because of a single slip of the tongue. Others had simply been shot on suspicion of planning escape when the group became too large. Blaise got out alone, without consulting anyone. His plans were as complete as possible, including a way to finance himself for a while after escape, a physical fitness regimen, and absolute secrecy.

Charlie's plan was too complex. It had all the elements of disaster, with too many middlemen, too much elapsed time, and a less-than-brilliant mind behind it. Blaise planned on arriving at the scene himself, after considering the services of a runner. He started a physical fitness program at a tennis club, where he soon excelled at the sport. There was always the chance of an auto breakdown or other unknown circumstances. It was entirely possible that he would have to hike across the Canadian border and camp out for a week in the bush in winter weather. He bought a state-of-the art backpack, with sleeping bag, camp gear, dried food, maps, and a down parka. He also was going to carry a couple thousand dollars in Canadian money so he could get a train ticket to Montreal and stay for a time. A fine young lady was waiting for his return, after he charmed her on his summer trip. He could just as easily forget about Spokane and start up another gallery in Montreal.

A good place to pick up someone is at a bar, but a good place to make a friend is at an athletic club. Blaise was watching a comely lady on the tennis court, and managed to work his way into some mixed doubles. Yvonne DuMont proved to be friendly, bright, and alone. Her slender body with all the right accessories didn't hurt either, and before long, she was accepting help with her tennis during the day and listening to romantic guitar music after dinner. Yvonne's father had left her a fine apartment in an expensive development and a lifetime membership in several exclusive clubs, as well as providing an education at McGill University. She never thought much about marriage, and was sort of cruising, waiting for a perfect man, if such a thing existed.

Blaise obviously felt right at home in this situation, and moved in with Yvonne after a few days. She was amazed that he spoke French fluently, as well as several other languages, and kept plying him with questions about his past. He never told her much except that he had studied art. She knew from his trace accent that he came from central Europe, and this mystery excited her.

The first evening was going well. A nice meal and a glass of rare wine put Blaise into a talkative mood, but any questions about his past were expertly parried. Yvonne cleared the table and then disappeared without saying a word. Blaise, becoming curious, got up, and discovered a trail of discarded clothing leading into the back bedroom. He found a wide smile, a bared shoulder, and a thin blanket covering some inviting curves. After an exciting hour under the blanket, Yvonne found herself plotting just how to keep this man around for good. He was getting to her and she liked it.

"Want some dessert?" Yvonne whispered while looking down on him and marking circles on his chest with her fingers.

"I think we already had it," came a weary answer and a grin.

Breakfast with a man at the table was a very pleasant affair for a change. After a bowl of fruit, some toast and juice, the conversation turned back to ancient history. Blaise ended up with a whole lot more information than Yvonne did, and that helped her to form a new plan. She could not go on indefinitely this way, not knowing all she wanted about the diverse, exciting, and frustrating companion who was taking over her life. She would miss him more than she was willing to admit when he left on the business trip he kept mentioning.

The answer suddenly dawned on her. She needed help, and that meant but one person, Gregory Kromer. Gregory Kromer, barrister and longtime friend of the family, took it upon himself to be an advisor to Yvonne. When her father died, she went into seclusion for too long a time. Gregory was able to pull her out of her depression and get her back into the mainstream. He also did most of her investing, and was trying to teach her to take care of her own money. Gregory liked the good life, was very successful in his career, and had now branched out into collecting and selling antiques, artwork and restored automobiles. If anybody could get through to Blaise, it would be this man with his friendly disarming manner and sharp mind.

Gregory was a likable sort, with a blunt way of expressing himself. He grew up in London, then went to school at Cambridge, where he played rugby for three years. He earned his law degree and also had a minor in fine arts. Gregory specialized in insurance cases, sometimes defending International Guarantee Co. and other times bringing suit against companies who were trying to weasel out of a just settlement. He made a fortune, and was now pursuing the art business for the fun of it.

"Gregory and Blaise should meet each other." Yvonne was talking to herself. "A grand cocktail party would be just the thing, but I must talk to Gregory first and let him know my plans so he can be prepared. He will see that Blaise is no pushover. Maybe that is why he excites me so."

"Gregory, dear, meet Blaise Pulaski, my friend and tennis teacher. I've been telling you about Blaise, with his interest in music and art, and, oh yes, foreign languages. I swear he can speak Swahili if it interests him. I've got to leave you two alone now and see about all the rest of our guests." She gave Blaise a squeeze on the arm and Gregory got a peck on his cheek.

"Fine party, what?" Gregory said, looking Blaise over. "Wonderful girl, Yvonne. I knew her father as a close friend. Died early, poor chap, and left a very distraught young lady. I helped her some, best I could."

"It seems to me that you did a fine job, Mr. Kromer," Blaise replied earnestly, while watching a swirling gown disappear into the crowd.

"Just call me Gregory. No need to get formal among friends. Besides, Canada is a lot more casual than England or the Continent, thank God. Easier to talk to people too, without all that Royalty, don't you think?"

"I guess you're right, Gregory, but it is hard to discard old habits. Yvonne has told me about you, and she thinks of you as a second father. I am sure that we can find a lot of common ground."

"You do come from Europe, I surmise, with an accent that I can't place?"

"I'm Hungarian, actually, with a few problems in my past over there," Blaise replied. "I suppose I'm lucky to be here and alive, and even luckier to have met Yvonne."

"I cannot imagine how you ever got out of there, but my hat is off to you, old boy. I've read about the atrocities and such, and someday there will be an accounting with those people. Now, Yvonne tells me that you are an artist, and I just happen to have a lifetime collection of art that I am dying to bore you with."

"I don't know how much of an artist I am, but I do appreciate good work. I have studied many of the great masters and tried to learn from their paintings. Sometimes I feel like I'm making progress, and then I get discouraged and put it away for a while."

Gregory was really perking up now. "Let's get together tomorrow at my home, which is just down the street. You can give me your opinion on several of my latest purchases. I'm spending a lot more time on my collecting now that I'm semiretired from the law practice. Maybe we can do some exploring together, too. Who knows what may turn up."

Blaise was elated with this turn of events, but he let the conversation drift into sports, not wanting to press his luck. "We should get back to the party and find some of that great food, Gregory," Blaise said, as he started moving toward a huge table that was loaded to capacity.

"Tomorrow at ten?" Gregory asked.

"Wouldn't miss it for anything," Blaise smiled in return. "I wonder how Gregory would like a Charlie Russell and a Picasso?" he was thinking.

Chapter 23

Charlie had a lot of work to do, and the timing was important. The first thing was to get rid of Oscar for a day. He could never get away with firing him, so he had to come up with an excuse for giving Oscar an unheard-of day off. Oscar had never married, but the idea had never left him, either. His encounter with Teresa was still vivid in his mind, and he was ready to carry that a lot farther with someone else. He spent his week-ends off in Kalispell, socializing, and Charlie kept teasing him about that.

"Oscar, you been workin' too hard lately," Charlie was saying, as he stood looking over Oscar's shoulder at the account book for lumber shipments. "Things are slow right now, and I'm thinkin' about trying for a deer this weekend. Why don't you head for Kalispell this evening and stay a couple nights. You could make a connection this time with that lonely widow. She's bound to say yes sooner or later."

Oscar swiveled his chair and looked back at Charlie, hardly believing what he was hearing. "Okay, if that's what you want. I don't mind trading off a couple days." Oscar flushed a bit and could hardly conceal how eager he was. "I'll be back day after tomorrow. You may have to do the last couple pages on this ledger."

Johanson came into the depot later that evening during a break on his run west. Ever since his wreck and escape from death in the avalanche the previous winter, he had been working steady on the passenger runs. He usually let the fireman fill up the locomotive's water tank while he took a hike to the outhouse and then picked up a lunch supplied by Bill's cafe.

"When you comin' back through here again, Johanson?" Charlie wanted to know.

"I'm runnin' the evening train east, tomorrow, and den I get some time off," Johanson replied in his thick brogue. "I got to fix my roof before we get too much snow, or my wife's goin' to shoot me. We got dem paint buckets all over the floor already."

"Well, I got a special order for you for tomorrow," Charlie said, "and you better cut your break short here, so you won't be messin' up the time schedule. Ed Scharpe wants his private car moved up to the Ural siding where he is going to try a new hunting country. He's comin' back in a couple more days, and we want to have everything ready for him. Johnny is movin' some horses up there too. There ain't anybody around up there since the cook and that crew took off for Whitefish to do a little drinkin'." Be sure to put some blocks under the wheels, as we can't have that car movin' none."

"Ya, I do it, okay," Johanson replied. "It von't take me more dan a couple minutes to hook up and move him to Ural. I vunder yust how dey goin' find any deers in dem cliffs. Maybe goin' sheep hunting, ya?"

Teresa climbed off the westbound at the hunting siding and walked the short distance to Ed's car, full of anticipation. She turned and waved at the engineer as he cracked open the throttle and let the air off the brakes. A big plume of black smoke belched into the sky and whipped away in a rising wind. The weather was changing, and Teresa was glad to let herself in to the shelter of her luxurious quarters. She found the fire out in the heater, but there was plenty of coal handy, and she soon had the place warmed up and cozy. Teresa started humming a girlhood song that reminded her of the fall days in Vermont with her father. The contents of the big shopping basket that she filled in Whitefish, along with the champagne from Minneapolis, was put into the ice chest. Tomorrow night was going to be the start of a new life. She could just feel the vibrations.

Teresa knew what some of her assets were. After all, her modeling was successful because of a nearly perfect, sensuous body and a strikingly beautiful face. Much of her camera appeal came from within, as the plain-spoken country girl came through somehow in the filming. She was aware, also, that beauty fades rapidly. Many of her friends were out of the business at a still-young age, and were unhappy with their lives.

"What is it that I really want?" Teresa had been asking herself more and more. She looked down at her professionally groomed hands and wondered. "There has to be something besides money and fame. Maybe I can find it with this educated woodsman who completely disarms me. A small boy who looks just like his father, with an unruly shock of blonde hair and bright blue eyes might just do it. Montana would be a great place to raise a boy, an experience I will never have with Ed Scharpe."

A pattern was developing around an insignificant hunting trip in the wilds of Montana. Like ripples from a stone dropped into a pond, this hunt was touching everyone in its perimeter. Teresa wanted something of true value in her life, like making a home with a loving husband and bringing up a child. Modeling had its very good monetary rewards, and a certain pride at times in a job well done, but life with Ed Scharpe was becoming a charade. Maybe she had found a way to a new life in this isolated pocket of the Rockies.

Ed Scharpe had thought of himself as coming out of these mountains a changed person, a man's man, but his shortcomings were all too evident. He could never conduct himself alone in the wilds like Herb, nor would he ever get the respect that this quietly dominant enigma commanded. Perhaps his mission in the mountains was a failure. He knew he choked when the shooting of that oncoming bear might have saved his life. He even felt in his heart the possibility of losing a valuable possession, Teresa, to a man nobody had ever heard of. That was a blow he didn't wish to dwell on. Ed was a bad loser.

Johnny was looking for his perfect horse, and maybe he now had found it. Blackie was his alone, nobody else could ride him, but the two of them together could go just about anywhere, and quicker than most. Johanson, because of an avalanche, was now on a passenger run, and had become the pawn of a misguided agent who was setting him up to hijack a private car. Never would he consent to do something like that on purpose. All Johanson wanted was to work just long enough to be able to retire healthy, fix up his house for his "Missus," and go fishing.

Alex Black Deer needed meat for the winter, to take care of his wife and young son. He wanted Long Rifle to help him as in the past, which was really why he showed up in Libby. His needs were simple, and urgent, but now he was rustling horses and didn't even know it. What he did know was that he didn't trust Charlie, and would learn of Charlie's fate in another vision. Soon, his evening fire would burn fitfully in the tipi.

Blaise wanted security, after living under impossible conditions in a communist-ruled country, and risking his life in a gamble to reach freedom. He could see the clear trail through the Montana forests, north into Canada, ending in an eastern cosmopolitan area. Here awaited a beautiful woman who craved him, and a new life of country clubs, influential friends, and a first-rate art gallery, all paid for by one last major effort in a wilderness of mountains.

"I've been here before, but this is the last time," Blaise thought.

Charlie was looking for an easy street, full of money and women. His life had been filled with drinking, fighting, screwing, and bragging. Maybe he was finally going to get it all in a tropical climate, out of the accursed long winters on the Canadian border. Every one of his joints ached when the temperature dropped below zero, but he was about to end that condition.

Gregory wanted the respect that too often is withheld from a lawyer. He was honest in his dealings, but made enemies nonetheless. Too many barristers were labeled crooked by association. Now that he was getting more into the art business, maybe his image would change. All he needed was one or two old masters in his collection to gain recognition. He had no way of knowing that his big chance was awaiting him in a remote camp on the base of Hornet Peak in an unheard of area of the States.

Don always wanted to be a cowboy, and he actually lived the life for a year. The simple facts of financing a wife and kids drove him back into the family business. He always kept open the possibility of a short return to the mountains he loved; the horses, hunting, outdoor living, and comradeship that went with it. He took his opportunity, and in retrospect, it cost him part of his life. Don died happy though, finally a winner. His hunting companions on his big day would never forget the scene of a photograph with an obviously ailing Don and his elk. Johnny would never forget bringing him off the mountain, not knowing if it would be like the old posters, "Dead or Alive!" Don's last request to me had a good chance of turning his son around, making him a winner, too.

What were the waves in this pond washing up on my shores? Maybe the desires of my lovable neighbor Gerta to see me hitched to a nice young woman would come true. My own problems of sleepless nights could finally come to an end with a sensitive and understanding partner living my life with me. I was finding out that I really did not want to live alone. A classy hunting trip, as improbable as it seemed, was the catalyst for change in a lot of lives. I needed a bigger and better place for two of us.

Early day Chinese gold miners on Libby Creek were making it with extremes in hard work and deprivation, commonplace lifestyles in China. They were robbed of their gold, due to envy and greed, and then sent over the falls in the Kootenai River to their deaths. The first trappers here put up with falling demand for beaver. They starved, froze to death, were mauled by grizzlies and often disappeared unmissed somewhere in the Kootenai country. Homesteaders had a constant battle with early frost killing their crops, with isolation, deep snow, drought, and forest fires. The Kootenai Valley was overdue in changing its image.

Chapter 24

Walt and Iver decided to stay in camp for a day or two to bone out the three deer, and to take care of Buck and Sally until Johnny returned. The rest of the stock was gone upriver, chased there for some unknown reason, but Walt figured that Johnny would catch them in short order. Herb was due back anytime now, according to plans, and so was Chaps.

"I think I'll go up to the car and find us a small bottle of wine to go with dinner," Walt said. "We deserve it! Besides, Chaps has enough stored there for a year, easy. By the time you have the stove heated up I'll be back."

Walt walked across the small meadow and entered the strip of trees that hid Chaps' car from view. He stepped out onto the tracks and couldn't believe his eyes. "What in tarnation," he exclaimed as he looked both ways at the empty rails. The ground was mostly bare of snow where the car had been spotted, meaning that it had been moved just hours ago. Walt heard some noise on the main line, getting closer, which sounded like a speeder. Sure enough, it turned in at the switch. Walt finally recognized the operator when the speeder pulled up to him, out of the twilight.

"Howdy, Herb. I was sure hoping you'd show up. What happened to Ed's car?"

"Don't know, Walt," I replied, puzzled. "Nobody said anything to me about moving it, but maybe Chaps had it hauled to Whitefish for some sort of repairs."

"He wouldn't do that without letting us know, and besides, there isn't anything wrong with it, or Richard would be looking after the problem."

"I have the problem, Walt," I said, furrowing my brows, "and it may be worse than we think. Teresa sent me a telegraph through Oscar. She asked me for dinner tonight and an evening together in the private car." My face was turning a bit red when I added, "I guess you know how much I looked forward to that."

"No joking around?" Walt asked seriously.

"No joking. Teresa has a sense of humor, but she wouldn't do this. I know that she wanted to see me, and I sure as shootin' wanted to see *her*."

"Let's get down to camp and talk it over with Iver. He's about to cook dinner, and it's getting dark."

"Where's Johnny?" I asked, when we got to the cook tent. "And where did he take the rest of the horses?" Buck was nickering at me when he heard my voice.

"Did you find the wine?" Iver wanted to know.

"No, and I didn't find the car either. Somebody must have given Johanson the orders to move it," Walt answered. "It doesn't make any sense."

"Ya, and it don't make sense neither, that some rustler run off the horses," Iver exclaimed, raising his voice. "Johnny took out after 'em. Walt and I vas stayin' here to cut up the meat ve shot, and by golly you should see Walt's buck. Biggest horns I never seen. Good t'ing you put a tent up there, or ve vould have froze. It vas one hell of a storm!"

"There's too much going on to be an accident," I said, thinking things over. "Buck must have run away from whoever it is that tried to take him, and I see he brought Sally back, too." I was looking at the corral. "It's much too dark to go anyplace now, especially on the speeder, where a guy could get killed by a freight. I'm heading out at first light. I'm not sure what is going on, but I have an idea I won't be riding that speeder clear up to Whitefish. Iver, I think you had better stay at camp and look after things here. Walt, you could flag down a train and get your deer to town. That's the best head I've seen in years, and you should have it mounted. I guess you had better call Blue, the cop, but don't talk to Charlie. He wouldn't tell you anything, anyway. I'll get word to you if I need more help."

"Sounds like a good plan," Walt replied. "We may have a hijacking and a rustling going on all at once. I guess Blue should know about it. Maybe he can call the sheriff in Eureka to be on the lookout for our stock."

"Okay," I said, "but nobody is dumb enough to try running our horses and mules clear up to Eureka the way the country is now with the snow and all. They must be stopping off in between for some reason, and maybe Johnny has the answer by now. Why does somebody want that car? They can't drive it off anyplace."

"You said that Teresa was going to be here," Walt replied, looking me in the eyes. "Do you think somebody kidnaped her? Chaps would pay plenty to get her back. It's just a thought."

"I doubt if anybody but Oscar and I knew she was coming here, but it is a possibility I hate to think about. I would pay plenty to get her back, if I had it, but whoever is doing this will be paying more than he knows."

I looked down at my rifle, and set it carefully in a corner.

Dinner for me was a somber event, our conversation reverting to that of my military days when my crew members discussed the coming mission. We had a bit of grim humor in those times, knowing full well that we might be telling our last jokes, but not wanting to admit it. Now, another mission was in the planning stage, with my own personal interests at stake, and I didn't like it. Teresa had been on my mind lately, a lot more than I would have thought possible just a few weeks ago. It was quite some time now since we had spent our night together, and I supposed that the feelings generated during that episode would fade away, but it didn't happen. Now, it seemed that someone was directly threatening my future.

My planning for the following day included the possibility of an extended stay in the bush. "I may be catching up with Johnny and putting in some tough time getting our stock back." I was talking to myself, which sometimes helped in solving problems. "I may be tracking some kidnapper, or I may even be back home tomorrow to eat our planned champagne dinner. At any rate, don't take anything for granted."

I found one of our large backpacks and carefully stuffed it with all I would need for an extended trip in the snow. I even lashed on a pair of old bearpaw snowshoes that I had brought to camp in case we had heavy snow during the hunt. Now the high country was buried. I put out one whole tenderloin from Iver's freshly cut up deer, so it would freeze solid during the night. I could use this meat for a week if need be, and along with some dried food, I would do okay. A hand axe, hunting knife, down sleeping bag, waterproof small tarp, and extra ammunition for my .270 completed the list. I already had a topo map of the area, a compass, matches, and several candles. I could build a fire and a shelter anyplace I needed one, and could survive most of a week in the bush.

My sleep that night was anything but restful. I woke up with one of my recurring nightmares, which started years ago from wartime stress. By now, I knew why I was restless, but still I had trouble getting back to sleep. Well before daylight I had another dream. This time a buckskin-clad figure wrapped in a Hudson's Bay blanket emerged from a fire, asking for me. There was no food by the fire. The cooking pots were empty. It was Alex Black Deer whose face finally became clear to me, and I awoke calling out to him in greeting.

I lay in bed for a while with my hands locked together under my head, thinking about Alex. He had a way of seeing visions, which he claimed helped him find his way through life. Some of the things he had told me while we were hunting together seemed to come true. Who was I to question a practice that was centuries old? Was Alex trying to say something to me at this moment, or was it just this time of year when he always showed up to go hunting, and I would naturally be remembering that?

I met Alex on a mountainside one wintry day during the elk season not long after I took my discharge from the Air Force. I had spent an arduous day on a pair of bull tracks, and fortunately caught up with the two bulls before dark, and before the wind shifted and gave me away. The two old timers were traveling together as they sometimes do after the rut. They were smart, having survived many hunting seasons, bear attacks and tough winters.

On this day they kept moving, hardly stopping to feed. I picked up their trail where they crossed low down on the ridge I was climbing in predawn moonlight. After an hour of slow going, the moon set, and I waited a while for sunrise. From then until late afternoon I never took a break, and the bulls didn't either. Some days are worse than others, when a man will go fifteen miles on a track and get caught at dark without seeing a thing. I had about conceded, when I noticed the tracks start to wander quite a lot, indicating that the elk were about to bed down. All they needed now was good cover where they could see their back trail.

There was an opening ahead, but I was cautious enough not to walk into any clearing without looking things over very carefully first. After about a minute, a slight movement across a deep ravine caught my attention. It turned out to be one of my bulls, and then I spotted the other, the herd bull of this entire area. He carried an awesome six-point rack.

I rested my rifle across my left hand, which was holding a lodgepole pine, and tried to estimate the range. Counting by hundreds, I made it out to be close to four hundred yards, and slightly downhill. Then I went through the process another time. It took but a moment for my pulse rate to drop into my normal range, as I was in great shape. It was then that my sights were steady enough to come to rest directly behind a massive shoulder across the ravine. My bullet would drop two feet at that range, so I raised the sights slowly until the gold front bead lay on the hump of his spine. I would get no closer on this day. The six-point bull took a few steps after the shot, and collapsed in the snow. His companion disappeared in a flash into some heavy black timber. His would be the job of breeding the cows on this mountain for many years to come.

I was partway finished with my cleaning chores when I heard a faint crunch in the snow behind me. I whirled around, startled, and there stood Alex. His luck wasn't as good as mine that day, so he chose to come over to my shot and find out what was going on. He had never encountered another hunter this far in before, and wondered who it could be. Alex cut quite a figure standing straight and quiet there, his jet black eyes alert to what I might do next. He was tall and lean, obviously not tired from climbing into this high mountain pasture in deep snow. His clothes, mostly ragged denim, certainly weren't warm, but he showed no signs of discomfort. He wore a black hat with a bandanna covering his ears.

His battered lever-action .300 Savage rifle looked like it had been dragged clear across the county behind a horse. I guessed he'd have to be on top of an elk before making a killing shot with that relic, but in sizing him up, I had no doubt that he could do it. His feet were covered by knee-high elk-hide moccasins. From ankle down they were triple thick, adequate for the present conditions, and doubtless made by a master at working hides. He wore the historic winter moccasins of his tribe, leaving an apparent flat track in the snow, distinctive in form.

We stood without speaking for a seemingly long time, eyeing each other and learning as much as we would have with a long conversation. I knew from looking at his back trail that he had cut my tracks long before I reached the ravine, and would easily have figured out where I shot from. Alex now had a faint smile on his face. He looked at my bull, then touched his eyes with two fingers, while stretching his left arm straight out to its full length.

I watched this elk from a long ways off, across the canyon.

Alex touched his eyes again and looked at me while shaking his head.

I did not see you then. You were in the timber, on another mountain.

He put his hands over his ears, and looked up at the sky.

I heard your shot, but couldn't believe it. Too far.

Alex looked down at the bull, put his hands out, palms down, and dropped his hands forcefully along his sides. He looked back at the sky.

The elk dropped at your shot. How could this happen?

Alex reached for my hand, shook it vigorously three times, and gave me a new name. "Long Rifle," he said, and put his forefinger on my chest.

I put my forefinger on his chest and looked into his face. "Alex Black Deer," he said solemnly. I shared this bull with Alex in exchange for his help in packing it out the next day. He proved to be a natural with horses, as I would have expected. We became lifetime friends that day, and hunted often together after that.

Was Alex here now, or was he coming soon? Had one of his visions somehow reached me in this tent on this night? The sky was showing a false dawn over the black mass of Hornet Peak, and sleep was over with for me. I got dressed, started a fire in the cook stove, and headed for the corral to throw out a breakfast for Buck and Sally. It was just light enough to investigate the sign around the corral. I walked carefully, looking at the tracks, and suddenly stopped up short. There it was, a winter moccasin track, the kind I had seen a few times before. I knew Alex was here.

Why was this happening? I trusted Alex completely and I immediately decided that somebody had sold him a false bill of goods, and who else would do that besides Charlie? I knew then that Johnny, good as he was, would never catch Alex unless Alex willed it. I also knew that this string of horses would never show up in Eureka, at least not herded there by Alex, who knew better.

There was no reason for me to take off on the same trail. It was going to be the speeder for me, and probably the trail ended at the Ural siding. There was no other logical place, but logic seemed to be pretty scarce around these parts. There were no roads on this side of the river, either, and hardly any trails that an average horseman could follow. Something bigger was in the wind, but I wouldn't tumble to it quite yet.

When I put my nose back into the tent, Iver was cranking out the bacon and eggs alongside some hotcakes covered with huckleberry jam. His English was bad, but he sure cooked up a fine breakfast, which I proved by eating double what I should have. "I know how you feel about things," Iver said quietly, "and Walt and I want to do whatever we can to help."

"If I eat any more of this breakfast, I'm goin' to look more like Sally than anything else," I laughed. "One thing I discovered is that Alex Black Deer was here, and I can't figure it. He's my friend, and I trust him, but his tracks are all around the corral, and I couldn't be mistaken. I'm sure that when I catch up with him, there'll be some answers, and no trouble. Right now I'm ready to leave, and I don't know when I'll see you guys again. Take care of Buck for me, Iver, and give him some exercise."

Chapter 25

Johnny was feeling a lot of fatigue. The events of the past few days were catching up with him. His bout with hypothermia left him drained and the lack of sleep and all this hiking during the night took its toll also. He finally decided to tie Blackie up for a while, build a fire and cook a little meal. He slid off the horse onto a pair of numb legs, and groaned. This riding bareback with one thin blanket under his rear wasn't the greatest, either, even though it did beat walking in the powder snow. It was against Johnny's religion to walk if there was a horse within miles.

Johnny took off his backpack and found the hand axe. A short search turned up an old fir stump, which he kicked apart. The outer rotten wood fell away, leaving a center core of solid wood loaded with pitch. A few blows with the axe made enough chips for kindling, and soon a hot fire was going, with a tin pail hanging over it melting some snow. A packet of dried soup and a bit of coffee made him feel better as he sat on the horse blanket with his back up against a tree. In a few minutes, Johnny was sound asleep.

Alex wasn't allowing himself the same luxury. He was hungry, but did not carry any food with him other than a few strips of jerky, long since gone. He planned on eating something when he delivered the horses, and didn't want to miss the early morning train for Eureka. It would stop for a passenger if it was flagged down on a straightaway where the engineer could see far enough.

Alex was troubled a lot from his cracked ribs, but even more by the fact that these were Long Rifle's horses, and he began to wonder why anyone would want horses for hunting in the cliff country where he was going. He had been all night on the trail, and spent a lot of time thinking about this, and about his old friend with the sky-colored eyes. Alex needed help and would seek it in the best way he knew.

His horse lost the faint trail while Alex was dozing, and he stopped by an ancient ponderosa, waiting for guidance. Alex, alert now, noticed that the old tree had survived a lightning strike that made a twisting black scar for about sixty feet up the trunk. He reached over and broke off a piece of the charred bark. From a lot of practice, he painted an antler on each cheek, then threw the bark away and put his heels to the horse.

It was just before sunrise, with a faint light showing in the east, when Alex Black Deer had a vision of sorts. He saw himself by a cooking fire with nothing to eat. Maybe it was from pain in his cracked ribs, or from hunger and exhaustion, but his mind left his body and wandered to his friend. Was he angry at him for taking the horses without talking to him first? But then, hadn't Charlie told him that Long Rifle was seeing his woman and needed the horses moved? Who could understand a white man, anyway?

Alex Black Deer had never stolen anything in his life, and he wasn't going to start now with taking Long Rifle's horses. He decided that Charlie had tricked him, but he would get to Ural siding as soon as possible, talk about this with the man, Lars, who was to meet him there, and then head for Canada to sort matters out. He would tell Lars that he was coming back before elk season ended to talk with his friend about the horses, and hunt the elk once more. Morning Star would wish him to do this. As he thought about her, his groin took over the aching from his ribs. His empty buffalo robes were waiting.

Lars was as strong as a bull from a lifetime of physical labor on his farm. He thought nothing of working from daylight until after dark, doing everything possible to make a success of his life. He was faced now with a tough job, getting the rowboat into the water without dragging it across sharp river rocks, and then rowing across the wide Kootenai, which was suddenly carrying a heavy and very dangerous ice floe. If the weather got any colder, the river would freeze and the ice would be too risky to cross. He had to go now and do the job Charlie asked of him or he would never see any money. His farm was in jeopardy and his family depended on him to do something about it. He could never face Helga, his first and last love, if he came home empty-handed.

Lars managed to stand the boat on end and lower it onto his back while he stood inside. In that way, he carried the boat to the river's edge and let it drop into the water. He had the rope from the bow tied around his waist, as it wouldn't do to chase the boat downstream in this ice water. There was barely enough light to see when Lars started rowing, angling upstream so that he would come out on target on the opposite shore. A large ice cake hit the bow when he was in mid-stroke, nearly swamping the boat and wrenching the upstream oar from his grip. Lars cursed and made a fast grab at the oar, narrowly avoiding a disaster by reaching it just before the current took it away.

Capsizing in this water was signing your own death warrant, a fact that wasn't lost on Lars. He had seen boats ten times larger than the one he was in get into bad trouble on the Missouri during the ice runs there. One bad move, and it would be all over. Several times Lars took an oar out of its lock and used it to fend off an oncoming ice chunk, with the result that his boat was drifting too far downstream. There were dangerous rapids just below his take-out point, and he knew that he wasn't enough of a boatman to navigate them upright. Little did he know that the boat was designed for one man to be used during the summer for fly fishing.

Lars was soaking with sweat even though the temperature was below freezing and there was an icy mist rising from the river. A fleeting moment now and then was all he had, to see the opposite shore to get his bearings. He could tell that he was drifting too far downstream, so he put all his strength and stamina into fighting the current while moving toward the east shore. Finally he reached a small backwater behind the last boulder above where the white water began. Lars nosed the small craft up against the boulder, and sat there with his oars resting in the water and his head resting on his hands. He was exhausted, and he figured he was lucky to still be alive.

After climbing out, Lars dragged his craft upstream to where a path came down from the siding. He beached the rowboat on a patch of sand and headed for Ed Scharpe's private car. "By Gar," he muttered under his breath, "Old Charlie must think I'm Eric the Red, my Viking ancestor. No wonder he didn't want to do this himself. It's a miracle I made it, and now I got to do it again after I get the paintings. If I don't get paid, I'm going to choke that crook to death. You betcha." This conversation with himself made Lars feel better, and he continued it until he reached Ed's car. He had never seen a private railway car before, and he stood there gawking in amazement at the intricate paint job and the ornamental iron work around the rear deck before grabbing a handrail and climbing the steps to the doorway.

The heavy rear door swung on four perfectly set, massive brass hinges. It was made of laminated oak, two inches thick, with a mountain goat carved into the wood below the double glass windows. Even the glass was delicately etched with small scenes from Glacier National Park, a theme carried out in all the rest of the windows and the mirrors in the car. Lars pushed down on the swan-shaped brass handle and entered a living room the likes of which he had never imagined before. He gave the door a slight shove and it closed almost by itself, with hardly a sound.

There was artwork of great taste and beauty on nearly every available wall space. Lars was overwhelmed by this, as well as the antique

European furniture and the intricate handwoven oriental rugs his boots were sinking an inch into. His mind started to numb from what he saw, and he sat down to think this over. He finally remembered the list of paintings that Charlie had given him, and he pulled it out of his shirt-front to read the descriptions of the ones he was to take. He laid the two waterproof tubes on the table next to him and fished out his pocketknife, which held a small screwdriver and several other tools.

Lars eventually spotted what he thought was the Picasso, but he had to wander into the dining room before locating a Monet. He was quite undecided if that was on his list. Charlie was unable to describe all this in any sort of detail that Lars could understand, but he did insist that the Russell was the first one he wanted, if nothing else. The scene of Indians chasing buffalo over a jump to their bone-crushing deaths was one that he couldn't possibly miss, but it wasn't in sight yet.

The Russell painting was one that Chaps had coveted for years before he was finally able to make a successful bid on it. It was a powerful picture, depicting a savage scene of men's bravery and the highly developed skill of running buffalo on half-wild mustangs. There was danger, and man's disregard for it in this painting that plainly showed the emotions of the horsemen as well as the brutal end of the dying buffalo. Clouds of swirling dust and an evening tinted sky added almost a surrealistic effect to the painting by the West's greatest master.

Chaps never tired of looking at this scene, which always made him wish that he could be a man of this macho sort, unafraid of anything and tough enough to do whatever he wanted. He treated his employees this way, and tried to do the same with his women, but inside, he knew it was a sham. Maybe that was the reason he planned his elaborate hunt, to improve his image, and perhaps to actually learn something about making it in the wilds. Chaps hung his treasure in his bedroom, where it would be the first thing he looked at when he awoke in the morning.

Lars went through the dining room, where he noticed a fruit bowl on the table, next to an unopened champagne bottle in a sterling silver ice container. His stomach was telling him things, so he took a banana, which was rarely seen in this backwater, and ate it down before picking up an apple. He pushed open the door and entered a hallway that led past the kitchen to the back bedroom. The kitchen was sparkling clean, with an abundance of stainless steel, and cooking equipment that Lars had never seen before. It was obvious that the next door was where he had to go, and he turned the knob and stepped into the darkened room.

His eyes took a moment to adjust to the dim light filtering through the shades. When he looked at the huge bed, he noticed a figure under the covers at about the same time that the figure sat up and saw him standing there. Teresa was panic-stricken. All she could do for the moment was to stare at this large man, with his rough clothes and stocking cap that was pulled down across his ears.

"Who are you? What are you doing here?" she managed to shout in fear. "You get out of here right now, or I'll call Herb!" Teresa was now wide-eyed, and her hair was spilling across her face. She clutched her blanket to her chest, not wanting this stranger to get a better look at her. She was worried the previous night when the car was moved, and Herb hadn't showed. No one had spoken to her; they just moved the car and went on east in a hurry. Now with this man in her bedroom, she knew that everything was wrong. Her mind was racing; maybe Herb was dead. Maybe this man killed him! I know he would never just stand me up.

Lars was incredulous. Charlie told him that nobody would be around, and he never considered that someone was sleeping here, much less a screaming woman. "Shut up," he shouted back. "I got things to do." Teresa was getting her wits together now, and she grabbed an alarm clock off the side table and heaved it at Lars with all her strength while her blanket fell away. The clock was aimed perfectly at Lars' head, and he ducked sideways and forward at the last second to avoid being brained. His foot caught on one leg of the bed, and spilled him across the bed on top of Teresa. Lars was still more or less in a state of shock himself, and not being of a violent nature, wasn't prepared for what happened next.

Teresa dug her left hand into Lars' hair and with the right, raked him with her nails across the face, inflicting four painful wounds that started flowing blood. She then drew back a fist and plunged it into his nose. Lars suddenly had enough. He caught her hand, and pulled back, lifting Teresa bodily from the bed. She tried to kick Lars, but he caught her by the sheer nightie she had on and stripped it from her body. One backhanded slap to the side of her face from that work-hardened hand knocked her onto her back, stunned. Lars gasped at what he saw. Teresa's sculptured breasts, heaving from exertion and glistening with perspiration, were the first thing he noticed. After that, was her strikingly beautiful face, her eyes glaring with anger from behind a screen of shining chestnut-colored hair. Lars looked down at her belly and then her legs, and then he felt an overpowering desire for this woman, the beauty of which he had never dreamed.

Teresa was not going down easy. She sat up and took another swing at Lars' face, but he blocked it, and held her in a bear hug, pinning her arms to her sides. All he had to do, now, was to take her. Lars could feel that struggling, sensuous body beneath him, and it was driving him crazy. He had seen Helga a thousand times, but she was not built anywhere near like this woman, who was just the second female he had ever seen undressed.

"No, no, don't do this to me. You'll be sorry, forever," Teresa was crying, while continuing her struggle against this pile of muscle. Her anguished voice penetrated somewhere, and Lars started regaining his senses. Helga, who had worked beside him in the fields, Helga who had nursed him through pneumonia, Helga who had given him two kids, would one day find out, and his life would never be the same. He couldn't trade ten minutes of passion for a lifetime with his family.

"You quiet down, now, and I ain't goin' to hurt you," Lars said, while still holding Teresa helpless. "I got a wife and I don't want any more women. I'm sorry, but nobody was supposed to be here, and I got a job to do. Old Scharpe ain't goin' to get my farm, and that's all there is to it. I'm goin' to tie you up for a while so I can get done and get out of here."

"What have you done with Herb?" Teresa was still sobbing.

"I don't know nobody by that name, and I don't see nobody since two days ago," Lars replied.

"Then he is going to come after you, and he will probably kill you. I know he is looking for me right now."

"I don't come here looking for trouble. I just come to save my farm."

Lars ripped a sheet into strips, and tied Teresa's hands to the headboard, then fastened her ankles to the foot of the bed. He took one more look at what might have been, shook his head, and tossed the blanket back over her now quiet body. With that done, he took the Russell off the wall, removed it carefully from the frame, and moved back into the dining room. He located what he guessed were the paintings Charlie wanted, put the rolled-up canvases carefully into their tubes, and left the car. Teresa lay still now except for a few sobs, and she started thinking how lucky she was not to be violated. The remark that big Swede made about Scharpe taking his farm was a puzzle that she would work on.

Lars was just stepping on the ground again when he heard the noise of horses, and looked into the woods where it was coming from. Sure enough, here came an Indian with a string of horses and mules, right on time and according to plan. Lars raised his right hand, palm forward, and held it in greeting like he had learned from the Blackfoot in Eastern Montana. He then moved his hand to his chest and back forward.

I am happy to see you.

Alex raised his hand, and immediately reached down to hold his sore ribs. His face was peaked, and he looked very tired, which Lars could well understand. Charlie had told him where these horses were coming from. Alex reined in next to Lars and slid off his horse, handing Lars the reins. This was never done unless the rider wished to give or lend his horse to someone. There was a moment of complete silence before Alex put his finger on his chest and said, "Black Deer."

Lars looked curiously at the antlers painted on Alex's face with charcoal, wondering what the meaning of that was. He then responded by pointing to himself, and said, "Lars. I need two horses."

Alex waved his hand in the direction of the now-tired band, which was pawing away the snow to find a little graze. "Plenty horses. Plenty mules. Belong my friend, Long Rifle. You hurt, Alex kill you." A knife with a gleaming eight-inch blade appeared like lightning in Alex's hand, and waved dangerously close to Lars' midriff. Alex's face had no expression, except that his obsidian eyes were boring a hole into Lars' face where four ugly wounds were caked with blood. He recognized what they were.

Lars gulped, and knew that he could be gutted in a flicker if he made a wrong move. "Who is Long Rifle?" he asked, while standing motionless.

"Herb Long Rifle. Hunt elk with Alex Black Deer. Best shot. Plenty fast. Him friend." With that, he stalked off toward the car. The last words Lars heard before the Indian opened the door were something like, "Find grub now."

A sickening thought just occurred to Lars. The woman in the bedroom had mentioned the name Herb, and so had this man. There had to be a connection here that Charlie hadn't told him about. If this damn Injun finds that lady tied up, and naked, before I get out of here, he'll figure I raped her, and then he sure as hell will kill me as he says. I don't believe how good he is with that knife. Helga, Lars thought, you saved me. If I had spent a few more minutes in there and screwed that lady, this wild Injun would've caught me and I'd be stone dead now, sliced up like watermelon! He wiped his sweating face with a sleeve. That was far too close, but it taught him a lesson. No one needed to tell him now to move his rear end.

Lars took the halter ropes of two horses and raced to the river. He tied the ropes to a cleat on the back of the boat, pushed the boat into the river and jumped aboard. He had to row like his Viking ancestors to put enough pressure on the lead ropes to get the horses to plunge into the icy Kootenai behind him. Lars spent far too long getting away from the current that washed this shore, and dragging two reluctant horses with him made things a lot worse.

A heavy ice cake bounced against the side of his boat and slid up onto the gunnel. That formed an incline for the current to run up on and pour water over the side, soaking Lars and threatening to sink the boat. Lars leaned away from the current and with all his strength managed to push the ice away and balance the small fishing boat once more. Cold fear of drowning made him see what had to be done. He reached back and unhitched the two halter ropes, turning the horses loose. The horses reversed direction and headed for the shore they had just come from. Upon reaching dry land, they shook themselves, then rolled in the snow and shook again, throwing spray and ice crystals into the morning sunlight. They were safe now, but it was a wonder they were alive. They could never have crossed successfully to the other side in this weather.

Lars could feel cramps coming into his back and arms. He never remembered working so hard for so long, and this was to save his life. He was more and more regretting his involvement with Charlie. There had to be a better way of dealing with a greedy railroad man, like paying someone of Alex's character to make him see the errors of his ways. He managed a smile, just thinking of the look on Chaps' face when Black Deer was carving the form of an antler onto his bare chest with that wicked-looking knife.

These and similar thoughts kept Lars' mind off his cramped-up body for the rest of his long ordeal. The boat was heavy with water that he had no way of bailing. It was difficult to keep heading into the current while maintaining the proper angle. Lars was getting close enough to see the shoreline through the perpetual mist that would never leave unless the river froze over solid sometime in the next day or two. He was going to make it, just barely, with a little more luck coming his way. There was one thing about Charlie, though; he chose the right man for this part of his plan.

Alex Black Deer entered Chaps' private car, and just like Lars, he looked things over in amazement. He had no appreciation of fine art, but he did like the paintings of mountain flowers that he recognized, and the scenes of elk, and beavers and other Montana game animals. One particular picture caught his attention, and he studied it for quite some time. It was done in the prairie badlands of central Montana along the Missouri River breaks. It showed the vast country, broken by canyons, crowned by square-topped buttes and endless sky. There was a herd of antelope feeding on bunch grass in the foreground next to a whitened buffalo skull. A group of mule deer was moving out of some juniper in a sheltered gully. There were no trees in this prairie, but small islands of brush amidst an ocean of tall grass waving in the never-ending wind.

Alex's tribesmen had gone to such a country for centuries on trading expeditions with the feared Blackfeet, and sometimes even skirmished with them. It took his people about a year to make the trip to the upper reaches of the Kootenai, east over the Crowsnest Pass, and out into the treeless country that reached to the end of the earth where the sunrise lived. They traded for buffalo robes, mostly, but they also found pottery from the tribes in the Southwest, and even ocean shells sometimes from the Gulf of Mexico. His family's many horses dragged laboriously peeled tipi poles behind them for exchange. The nomadic tribes of the Northern plains would go to almost any lengths to secure their supply of poles. Without them, they could not erect their lodges, and they would perish.

Alex had never been out of his mountains, or very far from timber, but he remembered stories told in the tipis about this country, and now for the first time he could see what it was like. Alex wondered if antelope tasted like white-tailed deer. He questioned the wisdom of living where there was no water or firewood or tipi poles. Where did the tribes find these things?

The bowl of fruit on the dining table received Alex's attention, and he quickly finished an apple, then took out his knife and cut an orange into quarters. He loved oranges, but seldom had one unless he was in camp with Long Rifle, who ate many, and always seemed to have more. He wandered down the hallway past the kitchen, when a curious smell came to him. It was like summer flowers, but it was no longer summer. Alex had to find out what this new wonder was in this house on wheels. He carried a quarter of orange in his left hand and pushed the bedroom door open with his knife in the other.

Alex possessed a very sharp mind, and he was quick to see and understand an entire scenario. A smell of distant honeysuckle came from the bed, where tied up was a fine-looking girl. The bed was a mess, a chair was overturned, and a white man's sun clock was broken, lying on the floor. He picked up the clock, and set it on a dresser. There had been a real battle here between two people.

Teresa had been struggling to untie herself, but it was futile. The thrashing around had uncovered most of her body. She was breathing hard and covered with sweat from her efforts when she looked up and saw what was undoubtedly an Indian, tall, lean, and topped with a black hat. Her eyes riveted on the dangerous-looking knife in the hand of this stern-faced, war-painted man who didn't make a sound. She screamed, "No, not twice in one morning." She thought she was in more danger of being killed at any moment than being assaulted.

Alex knew already that this was the woman of his hunting friend. He could plainly see that Lars had tied her up so he could have his way with her, and he instantly regretted not carving up Lars' privates when he had a chance. His instincts told him to do it, but for some reason he had not. He advanced on Teresa with his knife ready and she fainted. Alex looked into her face and approved of the perfect teeth and long hair. He removed the blanket and studied the rest of her with an impassioned stare. Not bad breasts, but body too skinny. Not like Morning Star.

Maybe Long Rifle had bad luck hunting, maybe no money. He starving his squaw. Needs plenty meat for winter, rice, too.

Alex gently inserted his knife under the ties that held Teresa helpless, and with a slight lift, severed the cloth holding her wrists and her ankles. He picked up the blanket by the end corners, and giving it an easy flip, settled it down on Teresa, full length. It was then that he noticed the sheer nightie that Teresa had purchased in an exclusive store. She was planning to do a little tormenting of her own after the champagne dinner.

The garment was badly torn, but Alex thought that Morning Star could sew it together somehow. Right now he needed it to bind his ribs, that were again hurting like wasp stings. He folded the cloth into a long bandage and wrapped it tightly around his chest. His coat just made it over the wrap without buttoning. Already he was feeling better. Teresa woke up about then and noticed that she was free, and covered. She was still afraid and whimpered a bit.

Alex looked down on her and asked, "You Long Rifle's woman?"

"I don't know Long Rifle."

"Everybody know Herb Long Rifle. Alex Black Deer friend. Send you plenty grub. Too skinny." Alex turned to leave. "Going Eureka now. Walk to Canada, see Morning Star."

"Yes. I am Long Rifle's woman," Teresa said in a low voice after a moment of thought. She tilted her head up, giving the Indian a curious look.

Alex nodded his head, raised his hand in salute, and moved through the door. He took a couple more oranges with him and walked into the middle of the tracks. He sensed the vibrations of a train approaching, and now he could see it rounding the curve from downstream. He took off his wide-brimmed black hat and waved it back and forth until the engineer acknowledged with two blasts of the whistle. After several huge puffs of black smoke and a loud hiss of vapor coming off the air brakes, Alex was on his way to Eureka and Canada. The conductor took a couple bucks, and Alex found an empty seat.

There had been about fifty dollars on the dresser where Alex set the clock. This must be money for him because he was not going to have a new horse. And hadn't he carried out his end of the bargain? Nobody would set money out when they knew he was coming unless it was for him. He could make it all winter on his hundred dollars and some fresh meat. He felt good about himself, but as he laid back into the seat, his ribs gave him another shot of pain that left him breathless. The trip hadn't been easy.

It didn't take long before the monotonous clicking of the train's wheels put Alex to sleep. He needed rest badly, and didn't wake up until the train came to a jerky stop at the Eureka station. Alex climbed off, dodged a couple hand-pushed baggage carts, and headed up a rut-filled street toward the Mission Mercantile. Here one could find all he needed in the endless supplies of the pioneering establishment. First on the list was a good backpack, and then a pair of winter coats for his family. Next was a huge ham, which he bargained over until the price suited him. Nobody else had shown an interest in this monster, so the clerk made him a bargain. Last was a ten-pound sack of rice and a fifty-pound bag of potatoes. These were for the skinny woman who belonged to his hunting partner, and who would likely starve before springtime when the fishing was good again.

Alex carried the potatoes and rice with great difficulty, due to the pain in his side. He eventually made it down to the depot and gave them to the agent. As an afterthought he threw in a big handful of licorice sticks. He had no problem telling the agent that the big house on wheels with the white goat painted on its side needed these supplies. They arrived at their destination the same night. Alex crossed the Canadian border and walked out of harm's way about an hour after dark.

Johnny heard the train whistle when he was still a half mile away from Ural siding. By the time he arrived on his tired and hungry black gelding, the eastbound had left with Alex aboard. He was gratified to see Chaps' car parked on the sidetrack, but all the horse and man tracks that led to the river commanded his attention. Johnny ground-hitched the black, slid off onto a pair of stiff legs, and hobbled toward the beach. The swirling mist coming off the ice-choked river gave him glimpses of the opposite shore, where he could see Herb's boat and an unfamiliar figure kneeling beside it. It was Lars, who was resting from his exhausting and lucky trip across the Kootenai. He decided to wash the blood off his face before preparing to leave the area when Johnny spotted him.

"Here's a good chance to get that crook," Johnny thought. "It looks like he stole Herb's boat, and who knows what else." Johnny pulled out Iver's .357 Magnum, sat down and rested the pistol on his knees, gripping it with both hands. The mist was opening and closing like a curtain, giving tantalizing glimpses of his target, but before Johnny could fire, Lars would disappear again. Johnny was tired and hungry. His all-night trip didn't improve his disposition any, either, and he was determined to get something back in return for all the trouble he'd gone to.

Lars finished washing his face and moved up the riverbank to where Charlie had stashed the supplies for his escape. He picked up the backpack and was about to put his arm through the strap when a bullet hit a boulder two feet to his right and splattered him with rock chips. Lars jumped back in surprise, but his recent experience with Alex had him conditioned to danger.

He had everything he needed here, and within three or four long strides he was running all out for cover. In an instant, Lars made the trees. He dodged behind a large old cottonwood and heard a bullet strike the trunk where he had been a moment before. Once again he was safe, but probably not for long. It was time to find the trail up Boulder Creek to Lost Horse Mountain. He needed the horses, but he would make it on foot somehow. The big Swede farmer would soon need all the endurance he had built up in his entire lifetime.

Johnny knew he had missed, and cursed his bad luck. He figured that the Indian he had been following had vanished somewhere, and he knew he would never find him. That Indian was just too good, and during the long night he had gained Johnny's respect. That man across the river, though, was another matter. What was his part in all this, and why did he steal Herb's boat? That boat was one of a kind, and known by everybody along the river. He couldn't get away with it for long.

It was a long way back to town and up the other side of the river, but there was no other way to pick up the crook's trail. Then, there was the matter of all those horses and mules. It was very possible that they could wander onto the tracks and cause a major accident, or get themselves killed. Johnny wanted no part of that, and he would have to keep an eye on the herd until help showed up. He wasn't inclined to trail that bunch all the way downriver to the hunting camp without some help, or at least without a saddle. He would get something to eat in Chaps' car and maybe take a nap in there. He didn't doubt that Herb would be along soon, after he figured out what was going on around here.

Johnny climbed the steps to the car's rear platform, and pushed on the heavy door. His eyes opened wide in disbelief at what he saw, and his jaw dropped open. "What in blazes?"

Teresa was standing there, dressed in a plaid shirt and jeans, with sheepskin moccasins on her feet. She didn't look so good, with eyes puffy from tears, and an angry bruise across the side of her face. "Oh, Johnny, I'm so glad to see you," Teresa said in a halting voice. "It's been just awful."

"It's okay now," Johnny said as he stepped forward and put his arms around her. "All them bums is gone. You're gonna be all right." Teresa finally relaxed and sat down.

"You look hungry, Johnny."

"You guessed it," came the reply. "Tell me all about it over breakfast. I figure you'll be gettin' another visitor before long, too."

"I hope so," Teresa perked up a little. "I miss him so much." She was starting to feel better now that she was safe again. Her sense of humor returned, too. "I'm giving you rice and potatoes for starters, with a licorice stick for dessert. I received a year's supply last night from an unknown admirer."

Chapter 26

A hundred-car freight train came rumbling by, headed upstream. It was being pulled to the continental divide by two steam behemoths that were soon to be the last of their kind. Everything in Chaps' car vibrated and rattled while heavily loaded cars of lumber, ore, and scrap steel and Washington apples rolled past. Johnny's coffee was making waves like someone was dropping marbles into it. The ground finally quit shaking after the freight went out of sight and the commotion subsided. The sound of a small motor could be heard coming up the tracks, but this time there were no vibrations, and suddenly the noise stopped, with a speeder parked on the siding. The driver had to follow close behind a freight so he wouldn't meet a train coming downriver and be forced to derail the speeder, or worse. A few moments later, Teresa was in the arms of the man she wanted, the man that she wanted a new life with.

"Hi, sweetheart," I greeted her in-between kisses. "I was really worried about you after I saw that this car was moved. I couldn't figure out why it happened. Hello, Johnny," I greeted him next with a big grin. I was looking over Teresa's shoulder, still holding her melting body. "It's good that you made it okay. I saw Blackie outside, too. I'm glad that Alex didn't take him, but I never thought he would, either." I finally let Teresa go and she headed for the stove again, to heat up some more rice and potatoes, she said.

"How did you know it was Alex?" Johnny asked.

"I saw his tracks in the snow around the corral, and knew them right off. He wore the same style moccasins while we hunted together at different times. Nobody else in this territory uses that pattern. I believe that Morning Star, his wife, makes them from our elk hides. She's really good at it, and I've been thinking about paying her to make me a pair."

"You mean that Indian is really your friend?" Teresa asked from behind the stove.

"Sure is," I replied. "We've spent a lot of time in the bush together, and I trust him completely. It's important, though, for you to know the differences in thinking with a man like that to keep from having a problem."

"When I first saw him standing in the doorway, he had a big knife in his hand, like he was going to kill me. He looked quite severe, and he didn't talk. There was war paint on his face, too. Like a design."

"I can believe you were scared, but Alex makes very few rash moves. He knows what he is doing, and can figure out most situations without talking about it. What you saw on his face was antlers, his totem. It helps him to have visions, somehow, and I feel like he reached me in one this morning. In fact, I know he did, now that I think about it."

"I just fainted because he was the second one in here this morning, and I knew I was done for. Besides, that first gorilla tied me up and I couldn't even move." Teresa recounted everything the way she remembered it, including her fight with Lars. "The last thing he did was to take some of Ed's paintings because he thought Ed was trying to steal his farm from him. I really don't understand that."

"What did Alex do?" I asked, believing that the Indian would never have hurt her.

"I can't really remember, except when I came to, his knife was gone and I was cut free. He mentioned something about my being skinny, and said something about Morning Star, which I didn't understand, either. He must have had a good look at me without my blanket on." Teresa blushed.

"Now I know where all that rice and spuds came from," I laughed. "He took one look at you and decided that you were starving. See what I mean about Alex Black Deer? I suppose I'll have to fatten you up now."

"He took fifty dollars from the dresser, too." Teresa was smiling again.

"There was a reason, I am sure. First, he went to the trouble of sending all this rice and potatoes, and he must believe he was being paid for delivering the horses up here. Notice he didn't take Johnny's black."

"There was a different guy across the river when I got here," Johnny recalled, "and when I saw he had your boat, I took a couple shots at him with Iver's .357, but I missed. He took off a runnin' into the woods, and with all that fog around, I never got another chance at him. He likely hitched a ride to Eureka or someplace else by now, on the old county road. "Funny thing, though," he continued after some thought, "when I went to move the horses away from the tracks, I noticed that two of them was soakin' wet. I just remembered that."

"You know, Johnny, that could mean that this thief was taking two horses across the river to help him escape. Either they got loose from him, or he may have untied 'em to keep himself from drowning. I doubt if any horse could swim across the Kootenai now with all that ice floating down. It's hard enough in summer. It's a wonder he didn't capsize my boat."

"Nobody is goin' to use horses on the county road, neither, if they want to disappear," Johnny remarked.

"You're right about that." I was becoming thoughtful now. "We should look on the Forest Service trail map for a place he may be planning to go."

"Since we're talking about thieves," Teresa said as she dished up my breakfast, "that ruffian took the Russell painting and a couple others. He seemed like he was after a few particular ones, and didn't bother with anything else. Ed's rifle is right here in the corner, and he didn't even touch it. The paintings are priceless, but the rifle is one of a kind, too."

"Try to remember what all he said, and maybe we can make some sense out of this. How long was he gone before Alex got here?"

"It was just a few minutes. I thought he was going to force me." Teresa folded her arms around her sides and closed her eyes while the memories of that awful moment flooded back. "I really scratched him good, and then something changed his mind at the last moment. He mentioned a wife, and a job he had to do here. He had quite an accent, and didn't really say much more than that. He took the paintings out of their frames after he tied me up, and then left in a hurry. I'm sore all over from wrestling with that brute. He was very strong." Teresa was on the verge of tears.

"It seems like his lucky day," I said in anger. "I know if Alex had caught him with you, there would be a corpse lying right here. Johnny must have just missed him with the pistol, too. I wonder where he's headed with those paintings, and how he knew they were in this car? Who wrote out the orders to move the car up here to Ural, anyway? Not that guy, for sure. It all comes back to one place."

I just remembered that my boat was gone from the woodshed when I went there to bring in a load for my heater. No stranger in the community would know of my boat or where I kept it. For sure it wasn't Gerta's husband who did this, but somebody else, who knew I was away. It was somebody who knew where to find a portable boat for this purpose, and who could coordinate the delivery of our horses at the proper moment.

"There's another thing I'm wondering about." I was looking at Teresa now as she cleared off the breakfast dishes and refilled my orange juice glass. "If this guy is as rough and uneducated as you indicate, he won't have any idea what the paintings are worth or where to sell them. That means he has to meet someone else fairly soon who does. He will be paid, or maybe killed, and the paintings will leave the country. It's too dangerous for anybody to sell them near here, and there isn't enough money in this area either."

"I better check the horses," Johnny said as he stood up from the table. "They could be feedin' too close to the tracks."

"Tell you what, Johnny," I replied, "It's time we move out and do something about this robbery. I think I'll take Teresa to town with me on the speeder, and she can stay at my house if she wants. I'll send Iver up here with Buck and Sally, and he can help you herd this bunch back to our camp. He can pack your saddle and some more clothes on the mule. It's important we get this car moved right back to our spur, too, since Chaps and Bidwell will be arriving shortly for another hunt."

"Ed is going to be surprised, and very angry," Teresa said.

"Surprised about more than one thing," I replied, seriously. "You'll be better off at my place 'till all this blows over. Oh, and thanks for the great rice and spuds," I winked at her, "but the bacon and eggs were a whole lot better. Did I hear Johnny say something about licorice?"

A bright morning sun was dissipating the mist rising off the river. The mist had frozen instantly to anything it touched, including the millions of fine needles on the surrounding firs and pines. The effect was like an endless supply of tiny Christmas tree lights, decorating the river's edge in a dazzling display of natural beauty. The river was running a wide carpet of ice, reminding me of a glacier, but broken in places with emerald green water. The natural beauty was a deception, a cover concealing the danger just beneath its surface. Four or five minutes in there was all that a man could survive.

Teresa and I bundled up for the windy speeder ride to town. We waited for a passing train, and moved right in behind it, knowing that the engineer had the schedule of all the oncoming traffic. By the time we reached the hunting spur, we were shivering with the cold, but enjoying each other's company and the picturesque scenes that changed with each curve in the tracks. I turned the switch and backed into our spur.

Iver was happy to see us and wanted all the news. We told him all that we knew, or suspected. I helped him saddle up Buck, who took his usual apple out of my pocket and chomped on it noisily. Sally seemed eager to go, too, and soon we had her loaded with Johnny's saddle and necessities.

I told Iver that I was heading up the other side of the river as soon as I could to retrieve my boat and do some scouting around. If I could find the tracks of the man with Chaps' paintings, I would take my pack and run him down. That may take some time, but it wasn't a whole lot different than chasing bull elk all over the mountains. The more we discussed it, the more unlikely it seemed that he would head for Eureka, where the law would be waiting. There was some special place he was headed for, with or without the horses, and I aimed to find it.

It was late when we turned into the sidetrack at Libby, and we were about half frozen. The sun was going down over the Cabinet Range, creating shafts of golden light between the shadows of the high peaks. I never tired of looking at those mountains, in any of the four seasons, when they always gave a new view to be enjoyed, or better yet, painted.

The day was too far gone to think about going back for my boat. There was always tomorrow, and more important things were on the schedule for this evening. We cooked our special dinner together, and savored the vintage champagne. We actually managed to linger a bit around the low light of an antique lantern on the table. Teresa mentioned the fine nightdress she had purchased to impress me with, but it turned out that she didn't need it for any reason after all. We did a good job of staying warm without it. Maybe Morning Star was getting some mileage out of that sheer piece of cloth by now.

The following morning dawned clear and cold. A high-pressure area settled into the valley, guaranteeing a few more days of the same zero temperatures and cloudless skies. It was good weather for tracking, if that is what I had to do. I described in detail to Teresa what I had in mind, and marked on the map several options for searching out a tall man on foot in the vast roadless area to the West of Ural siding. We discussed his height and weight so that I could get an idea of his stride, and how deeply he would sink into loose snow. Any bit of information about one's quarry is useful in tracking it, as I learned early in life when studying the fine points of following deer, cougars, and elk.

Gerta was delighted, when she answered my call, to hear that I had finally come to my senses and brought back that lovely girl. She was happy to visit several times a day while I was gone to make sure Teresa was okay. After what had happened to her, I was concerned for her well-being, and Gerta would make great company.

Chapter 27

My first move was obviously to retrieve my fishing boat before it washed away or was crushed by an ice floe. I managed to drag it across the snow to my old pickup, and loaded it in upside down. When looking across the river, it seemed to be a miracle that anyone had made it across both ways in my fragile plywood craft. One oar was cracked where Lars had used it as a pry to remove an ice cake from his path, but otherwise the boat was okay.

I was already learning something about my man. He was not just an everyday thief. He was desperate, to do what he had, under very dangerous conditions. A casual burglar would never risk his life like that. I remembered what Teresa repeated about her attacker's remark, that Scharpe was trying to get his farm away from him. If there was some truth to this, it would explain why he was angry, but it did not explain a lot of other things. It was obvious that Charlie had a hand in the hijacked car and the removal of the paintings, but why would he risk his own neck to help some unknown farmer? There had to be a lot in it for Charlie, too, no doubt about that. I finally concluded that somewhere on the other end of a trail through the snowy peaks, I would run into Charlie once more.

There were a lot of man tracks in the loose snow where my boat had been abandoned, and I memorized their shape, size and tread marks. The thief was wearing a pair of L.L. Bean shoe pacs, with a chain link tread. There were a lot of loggers and hunters in our valley who wore the same thing, but not many wore an obvious size twelve, or so. The tread looked brand new. Johnny said he had shot at this man a couple times, so I looked for running tracks and found them where they went through the woods and onto the county road. Unfortunately, the county chose to plow the roads that day, so all the footprints were obliterated.

Lars considered hitchhiking to Eureka, where he could hop a train for eastern Montana and then call Charlie for instructions. Without horses, he wasn't sure he could ever make it up to the old lookout, but the police might have been alerted and waiting for him in Eureka, and Libby, too. Then there was the problem of meeting Blaise for the transfer of the paintings and money; if he didn't show, he was broke and in worse trouble. He didn't have much time to waste, so he located the Boulder Creek trail on the map and headed up the road a couple miles to the trailhead, thinking it over while he walked.

Even if he had horses, their trail would be a snap to follow, and when he got up into higher country, the deep snow would have all the feed covered. His mounts would never last in the cold and the belly-deep snow, with all the work required of them. Without plenty of grass and a sheltered resting area they would give up and die, or maybe turn back. It was probably better that he turned them loose when he did instead of risking drowning himself and the horses, too. Charlie's scheme was made for bare ground and difficult tracking conditions, but the early storm changed all that. His lack of an alternate plan proved to be a costly omission.

Lars reached the sign marker for the Boulder Creek trail and stepped out of sight just in time to see the snowplow come barreling up the road. The driver had a lot of miles to cover that day, and he wasn't letting anything slow him down. The snow was arching twenty feet into the air alongside the truck, carrying thirty feet or more into the timber. By the time the noise ended and the powder snow rainbows settled out of the morning sun, no sign of Lars' passing was visible.

"Ya, I got this far and nobody seen me yet." Lars was talking to himself. "Maybe I just head up the creek as far as I can go and see what happens."

My best chance to pick up a man's trail, if there was one, would be at the trailhead nearest where my boat was beached. That trail would be going southwest up Parsnip Creek, running a mile south of where I was standing. My old pickup truck groaned to a reluctant start after sitting in the cold. One of these days it would give out on me altogether, probably at the end of some remote logging road, twenty miles from help. The snowplow had opened up a turnout at Parsnip Creek, in an otherwise single track road. If a driver met another car, he was sometimes obliged to back up a half mile to the nearest place where there was room to pass.

I parked in the rare wide place in this primitive road and got out to investigate the possibilities. Heavy snow thrown out by the plow made it tough going for a ways, but when I bulled my way through that, I found a set of tracks heading up, and none returning. Maybe I was getting lucky. Stepping in my own footprints, I returned to the truck and put on my pack, checking to make sure that I didn't forget anything important. The first mile was relatively easy going, the trail following the creek along a mild grade. Too much powder snow was in the tracks to accurately identify them, but two things were certain. They were made by a very large boot, and the maker was still in front of me.

The sun was shining on a clean white landscape, spotted green by firs and blue green by spruces in the creek bottom. Tracks of snowshoe rabbits were numerous, indicating a successful winter season ahead for bobcats, coyotes, and other predators. At this point, the hike was an enjoyable change from the pressures of the past weeks, with all the hunters, guides, cooks, and horse rustlers getting my attention. It wouldn't be long, though, on this trail before things could get sticky. I was running numerous scenarios through my mind. It wouldn't do to stumble right into someone who was desperate enough to have risked his life already. If he caught sight of me first, who could tell if he would shoot at me, just run me a race, or try some other way to escape.

Two hours and three miles up the trail, I stopped for a break. It was time to load my rifle, and that I did with six rounds. I slid the safety on, hung the rifle over my right shoulder again by its military sling, and bent to the task of finding a certain wilderness traveler. This man had not stopped once for a break, and he was definitely getting my respect. My own pack was over fifty pounds, which had me wondering how much the farmer was carrying. Something about this man's performance bothered me, though. How many farmers from the prairie were this good in the mountains? Ten minutes later, my question was answered. A bobcat track crossed the trail where there were was an unusual amount of rabbit sign. The man tracks veered off to the right for twenty yards, leading to a newly built cubby, a small narrow shelter fashioned from short saplings. Inside was a freshly killed rabbit, partially frozen, hanging over a concealed steel trap. Soon there would be a bobcat caught there, and a couple days from now, the trapper would retrace his steps, pick up his take and haul it to town for skinning and fleshing out. The trapping season had begun, and I was likely following the first man out. Why didn't I tumble to it earlier? I knew why there wasn't any vehicle parked at Parsnip Creek, either. The man's wife would no doubt be waiting there for him just at dusk, in three or four days' time.

I wanted to meet this guy, share a night in camp with him, just to talk trapping and hunting, and have a simple meal. What I did do was turn around and head back to the road. Sooner or later I would find out who the trapper was, and have a good visit. Right now, there was time to look at the Boulder Creek trail before dark, but I had to hurry. Sunset was at four thirty, and dark by five. The days were very short this time of year, with morning light coming sometime after eight. My outer coat was too warm, now, and I didn't want to fall into the trap of getting my clothes wet with sweat. I took the coat off, tied it to my pack, unbuttoned my wool shirt, and hurried downhill on a well-broken trail.

One push on the starter button was all it took this time to fire up the truck, which was waiting for its own time to sabotage my plans. A bit of slipping and sliding around on a road that was rapidly icing up kept my attention. The more traffic there was on snow, the sooner it turned to ice. The roads would get worse until the next snowstorm, when for a time, the ice would be covered, but there would be plenty of wrecks until spring thaw came. Some people never learned the art of driving safely on sheer ice.

It took longer than I figured for me to shovel out a parking space for my pickup, but I finally managed to dig up a place wide enough. It was foolhardy to travel the roads in that country without a shovel, axe and crosscut saw handy. It didn't bother me much that my boat was resting loose in the back. Hardly anyone would steal from his neighbors around here, and it seemed that I was the single boatman on the whole river anyway. Since there was some daylight left, I was going to make use of it. The berm thrown up by the plow was quickly freezing into a solid pack, which made it a lot easier to cross. At least I wasn't sinking in to my waist on every step. It took a few minutes before I discovered the tracks that I was sure belonged to my quarry. It was doubtful that two trappers were operating in the same general area. The prints were big, and the stride was long, indicating that a tall man was making them. Once, he stepped under a spreading fir tree where he left a sharp track in an inch of snow. The readable tread marks he left were Bean's chain link!

It had been some time since I last fired my Winchester, so I decided to test it out before leaving the truck. There would be no time, or opportunity either, to fix any problems with ice or dirt in the action when I was on the trail. Before leaving home, I took the precaution of removing all the oil from the action and wiping the moving parts dry. Too many times I had witnessed a misfire when the firing pin spring of a companion's rifle was clogged with frozen oil. I slipped a round into the chamber and rested the rifle on my backpack, which lay on the hood of the truck. The scene looking across the river was right out of Currier and Ives, and I could almost see fancy horse-drawn sleighs with laughing children climbing aboard. I wondered why some famous painter hadn't done work in the Kootenai country. Nothing I had seen in Europe was any better.

After a short wait, a large ice floe came down the current and moved into an eddy about two hundred yards out. On one edge of the floe rested a piece of older, blue-colored ice, about the diameter of a base-ball. A wave from an upstream rapid must have tossed it up there where it made a perfect target, sparkling in the afternoon sun. One shot disintegrated the blue ice, throwing a powdered spray across the entire flow. Two distinct echoes reverberated back and forth across the valley, audible for miles. There was no need to shoot again. I hoped that the farmer was far enough away by now that he couldn't hear the shot.

About a mile up the trail, I found out another interesting fact about the maker of these tracks. He was undecided about what to do, as he would stop and turn around, retrace his steps a ways, then turn and head uphill once more. The trapper I followed earlier that day had no hesitation at all, and stuck right to the trail. The man I was now after evidently could not read the old trail blazes, some being made forty years earlier and quite grown over. A few side trails blazed with one axe mark took off for some old hunting camp, or an elk kill that a packer wanted to find again. This seemed to confuse him. The government trails were always marked head high, with a small six-inch blaze on top and one twice the size directly beneath it. A flatland farmer would not know this.

The more wandering around that Lars did, the sooner he would tire, and the sooner I would catch up with him. Several plans of action were forming in my mind, none of which involved killing him, but then he did terrify Teresa, give her a big black eye, and tie her up with no clothes on. I would teach him a lesson for that, even if he hadn't stolen some very valuable art works. It would be interesting to find out, too, what the problem was between him and Chaps. I was going to have plenty of time to ponder this, but I also needed to stay alert. I wondered again, was the man armed and desperate enough to shoot me on sight? Maybe he was counting on having enough head start to finish his business and leave the territory before anybody found him. Surely he knew that the woman he tied up would get help before very long. Someone would sooner or later be on his trail.

The lower the sun dropped in the west, the colder it became. My coat was still tied to my pack, but I buttoned the wool shirt I was wearing. A lot of layers made it possible to adjust the clothing to the amount of heat put out by my body. There was a lot of hard work ahead, and it would be impossible to stay warm in a sleeping bag with damp or wet clothes on. The backpack I was using had an inner frame that contoured itself to my back, preventing sore spots from rigid pressure points. A newly designed padded waistband put much of the pack's weight on my hips, thus relieving my shoulders. It also gave my arms greater freedom of movement. Several deer had fallen to my rifle because of this, where before, it was next to impossible to handle a rifle properly while wearing a conventional pack frame.

Sunset created a different splash of color, the snow turning luminous where it angled toward the west, and charcoal where it sloped east. A few cirrus clouds at high altitude moved along in giant fleecy white fingers, pushed by a jet stream bending down from the Arctic. There would be no snow tonight, but a deep cold was sure to settle down when the stars came out. I planned on finding a sheltered bench above the streambed for my camp, where it would be at least ten degrees warmer. I could find dry firewood in such a place. It would give off little smoke, and more heat than anything that lay along the stream, where the sun and wind never seasoned it properly.

A series of small waterfalls created a pleasant noise in the otherwise muffled quiet of a forest covered by loose powder snow. Waterfalls meant a canyon, which trail engineers avoided because of the rocky cliffs. It was at this point that the trail made a series of switchbacks out of the canyon to a more open ridge. My bench was on the third switchback, where I made a comfortable camp on a small level area surrounded by young firs. Green fir boughs made a good cover on the snow, and an insulated pad under my sleeping bag kept the cold from invading from underneath. A light tarp stretched into the shape of a lean-to over my bed caught the heat of a small fire while I cooked my meal in comfort. It took a lot of melted snow water to quench the inevitable thirst in this cold dry air. Hot lemonade made from powder was more welcome than Chaps' wine.

Nothing disturbed my sleep after a horned owl signed off for the night. For once in a long time, I was free of nightmares. I thought about Alex Black Deer, and decided that he was home safe and having a good day also. At least he wasn't trying in his strange way to communicate with me. He could be of great help to me on this trip and maybe he would be, yet.

Lars was having a difficult time of it, losing the trail numerous times before finally discovering it again in an obvious lane cut through a heavy stand of trees. He had two days start on me, but at the rate he was going, I would be up with him before he left the mountains. By now, it seemed obvious that he was headed for Lost Horse Mountain and the lookout cabin there. If he was planning to camp out a short distance from the road for a few days, he would have done so before now. The question that came to me was, did he plan on returning this way, or was he going over the pass to come out on the Yaak road? Whatever the plan, he had a nearly impossible trip ahead of him. No wonder he was first going to use horses.

By midmorning, I came onto Lars' tracks again. He had left the trail at the canyon, choosing to follow the stream up through the rocks and over the cliffs in a vertical assault on the headwall where two branches of Boulder Creek joined together. From what I had already seen, it figured that Lars missed the switchbacks where they turned abruptly out of the stream bottom. He would never get lost, he thought, by staying with the stream, whereas if he bypassed the tough going, he might never find the trail again.

It must have taken all of his strength to come the way he did, I knew, especially with a pack on. It wouldn't surprise me if I found a camp very soon. Within a half mile, I smelled wood smoke, and immediately left the trail on the south side. Fifteen minutes of hard walking through the brush took me in a semicircle back to the trail, where I cut his tracks again. I was above his camp, but he was gone. It was a natural decision to go back and see how he had spent the night.

Lars had rolled a large log, half rotted and punky, into the fire, where it would smolder for days. The prevailing downstream breeze carried that smell to me. Not too smart for a man trying his escape from the law. There were no boughs under his bed spot, and I wondered how much he slept that night. Cold from beneath can be more uncomfortable than cold from above. It takes a lot of good rest at night to keep going for several days under the winter conditions we were traveling in. I doubted that his fire ever got hot enough to boil water for coffee or chocolate, either. Early in life, I discovered the misconception that a person must be miserable any time he is living in the bush someplace. I had to admit, though, to learning a lot of lessons the hard way.

The government trail stayed on the ridge for a long ways at this point, to keep out of the canyon with its constant windfalls and snowslides that create too many maintenance problems. Lars was making pretty good progress now, but we were gaining elevation rapidly on the ridge, and the snow was suddenly getting deeper. Lars had to break trail, making it tough on him, but easier on me. I finally reached the decision that knee-deep snow was bogging me down too, so I stopped long enough to put on my bearpaw snowshoes. The walking became somewhat slower, but a whole lot easier with the snowshoes on. I was breathing easier and quit sweating.

We were emerging from a dense forest into much more open terrain, good summer range for elk, above the heat and the insects that plague them. There was evidence of a lot more wind in the higher country than we had along the Kootenai. All the larger trees had snow plastered to their western sides where the wind had driven the heavy clouds out of the Pacific. There was drifting in places, also, where the snow was piled up three feet deep. Lars was able to skirt some of the drifts, but in other areas, the deep snow covered the entire ridge. I could see the struggle taking place where a heavy body forced its way through the worst places, and rested in between. If conditions kept getting worse, he would never make it to the mountaintop.

My eyes started watering as the brilliant sunshine reflected off the snow, forcing me to squint in order to see. Now was the time for dark glasses, which I found after emptying most of my pack on a rectangle of snow compacted with my bearpaws. Snow blindness was rare in the deep timber, but up here, above the haze, and in endless snowfields, it was a real danger. I felt better right away, and knew that I had avoided a major problem.

Lars was feeling great fatigue. He wanted to lie down in a snowbank and sleep, but he knew he would probably freeze to death if he tried it. The previous night had been bad enough, with his underwear clammy with sweat, eating a half-cooked meal, and shivering all night. This deep snow on the flanks of Lost Horse Mountain was defeating him, but he would keep going as long as he could, as long as he was alive. Lars had overcome a lot of problems in life, but this time he was alone with the elements. Helga was four hundred miles away, and might as well be four thousand. He could hardly see anymore, and finally avoided complete blindness by pulling his stocking cap over his eyes and tearing a couple small holes in it to look through. Lars knew that he had to have food in order to keep going, so he ate everything in his pack that didn't absolutely require cooking. By this time, he developed a raging thirst that was impossible to quench with snow.

Twice he caught sight of the lookout tower, perched on a high point an interminable distance above him and to the north. It was these tantalizing glimpses that kept him going, like someone following a mirage in the desert. Sundown came unnoticed to the high country, with the temperature immediately dropping to zero, carrying a promise of minus ten, or colder, by morning. There was a twilight on the mountaintop, above the timber, which lasted just long enough for Lars to stumble the remaining few yards to the door of the cabin. He nearly fell out of the chest-deep powder onto the bare ground under a roof overhang. With the few minutes of daylight left, Lars took the hammer from his pack, pounded the lock and hasp from the door and collapsed when he finally staggered inside.

He lay there for five minutes before gaining the strength it took to move toward the stove and get a hot fire going. Lars pushed the door shut, then turned the wooden stopper into its slot. He had done it, he had survived the toughest experiences in his life, but with every breath he was cursing Charlie and Ed Scharpe. "Twice in the past couple days,

I've cheated death," Lars started thinking. "I could easily have drowned when crossing the river two times, and now I almost didn't make it to this cabin. There's no doubt that I would have died outside tonight. Maybe I should take these paintings somewhere else and sell them myself. That crook Charlie owes me a lot more than he wants to pay me."

The table and two chairs in the cabin were placed around the stove in a half circle. After about ten minutes, the stove was kicking out a lot of heat, and Lars began hanging his soaked clothes on the chairs and the hewn plank table. Steam started curling around the room, fogging up the windows as the moisture evaporated. One pot on the stove was melting snow for drinking water, and the other one was cooking a can full of Dinty Moore's beef stew. Lars needed all the food and water he could hold, as he was exhausted and dehydrated, and was too sleepy to stay up for long. He first had to dry his sweat-filled long johns, though, and bring in some more wood before he went to bed. It was a lucky thing that the last man at the cabin during summer had laid in a good supply of dry larch stovewood. He was thoughtful enough to stack it under the eaves.

Lars woke up once during the night when he had to empty his bladder from all the water he drank at supper. He pulled on his partially dried boots and stepped outside into a night faintly lighted by the myriad stars that seemed to reach right down to the mountaintop. The Milky Way, the galaxy that contains our solar system, stretched in a lighted band across the entire spectacular night sky. It required about a minute or two for the subzero temperature to force Lars back inside, where he added some more wood to the stove. He turned down the damper and went back to sleep. Tomorrow would be a day of rest and a time to plan the next move. Lars dreamed of finding another way out of these infernal mountains.

My own camp that night was in a grove of stunted firs that gave some shelter and provided enough firewood to get by with. If I climbed any higher, I would be in the open, on a mountainside that had burned hot and clean in the great conflagration of 1910, and once more in 1936. Maybe a century would pass before a wet, cool summer allowed seedlings to prosper and start a forest on the exposed slopes of this mountain again. In the meanwhile, the open grassland provided endless forage for mule deer and elk. There were dozens of game trails leading to the area, out of the brush below, and I put that information into my memory bank.

With one snowshoe in hand, I piled up a three-walled snow shelter over which I stretched my tarp, a quick way to build an igloo. At least I would spend the night out of the wind, and keep the frost off my down sleeping bag. Snow stacked on the tarp's edges would keep it stretched tight, giving me some room to move around inside. For dinner, I ate boiled sausage and carrots and drank the soup that formed in the pot. A large portion of banana bread made a tasty addition to the simple meal, but for sure, it wasn't Thanksgiving. I slept warm on top of another bed of green boughs and my insulated pad. My contoured down sleeping bag was good for about minus 20 degrees, if I kept the hood over my head and let the warm air from my breathing stay inside. Tomorrow would bring me to the cabin, where I might have a confrontation, or maybe a short break followed by another chase. I had to stay alert. It would never do to get careless at this point.

Once before, I had been on this mountain, and that was as a boy, accompanied by my father. We were looking for mule deer and blue grouse, both of which were numerous and virtually unhunted in this entire range. A man could ride the crest trails between the peaks for forty miles north and south from the east fork of Pipe Creek all the way to the main Yaak River. The numerous peaks lay pretty much in a line, paralleling the Kootenai River from Libby to the Canadian border. There are hundreds of long finger ridges leading from both sides of the main backbone to the drainages thousands of feet below. One could easily spend an entire summer exploring the whole area, which contains vast canyons, high peaks above timberline, old burns, new lodgepole jungles and impenetrable brush-choked north slopes. If someone wanted to disappear, this was as good a place as any. All he had to do was to leave one of the main trails on some navigable ridge, and in minutes he would be gone into the center of eight hundred square miles of grizzly country.

It was obvious that my quarry had no intention of taking off along some ridge where there was no trail to follow. He was having enough difficulty sticking with the main route to Lost Horse Mountain, and I knew that he would soon head down the obvious Zulu Creek trail to the west. I remembered the long glacier-carved cirque that lay just below the lookout tower. The trail led south along the rim of the cirque, which plunged a thousand feet straight down to a wet, boulder-studded valley, a perfect hideaway for a herd of moose. From there it curved down for a ways and led through a saddle beyond the south end of the cliffs.

Pink Mountain formed the west side of the saddle. A narrow, timbered ridge was the logical route to the top of it and into the headwaters of Zulu Creek. Zulu Creek, with its several forks, was a long, steep drainage that eventually crossed the road on the south fork of the Yaak, far out of view of Pink Mountain or the lookout tower beyond.

Altogether, it was a formidable trip, going east to west through these peaks in the deep snow. But the worst was over for Lars, except for the one steep climb to the top of Pink Mountain, a somewhat lower elevation than the lookout cabin. He would be confronted by less and less snow as he eventually worked his way west. I knew that I had to catch him before he met Charlie or somebody else on that road, otherwise he and the paintings with him were likely gone for good.

No one in the police department would think of making this trip even had they been able. Crime was never much of a factor in Libby, which led to a complacent attitude among the cops. There were no murders, and anyway, who would worry about some old paintings that were missing from a greedy millionaire's fancy car. The man didn't even live around here, he didn't pay any local taxes or vote here, and besides, he must have his own railroad detectives. Right? The guy who stole the paintings, if he actually did, could hide them anyplace in the mountains, and come back to pick them up a year or two later, and never get caught with the goods in his possession. The value of the art is grossly overstated. Who ever heard of paying half a million for anything, especially a picture of a buffalo with some redskins chasin' after it? My Uncle Jude's kid, who never even went to high school, painted a danged good picture of a buffalo down at the Bison Range, and he sold it for twenty bucks. Hell, I could buy a cattle ranch for half a million with a lot left over for booze and loose livin'.

As for an attempted rape, and beatin' up a female, there was no proved rape, and most women need a good whack across the chops at times to let 'em know who's runnin' things. I could never hang around with a bossy woman, and this here one is pretty high and mighty by the looks of her.

Thoughts along this line by our local law is what had me up in the hills on snowshoes, sleeping out in the bitter cold. I didn't like it any more than anybody else, but if something were to be done about the manhandling of Teresa and the theft of Chaps' artworks, it had to be done now. I had a very personal reason to try, and what's more, I was still on Chaps' payroll at double my normal pay. He gave me discretion to do what I thought necessary, at the time I was hired, and I convinced myself of the urgency of this matter. Ed's hunt, at the moment, would be handled nicely by Johnny and Iver, along with the rest of the crew when they came back from Whitefish.

Lars woke up in the pre-dawn when the fire burned out in the stove. Sharp cold penetrated his inadequate sleeping bag, forcing him to get off the bed and start the heater going again. It was just as cold inside as it was out in the snow, except there was no wind in there, and he was dry once more. A painful leg cramp attacked Lars, forcing him to sit on a chair while he massaged the lumps out of his afflicted muscles. There was too much unaccustomed climbing yesterday, as well as dehydration, and that did the damage. His whole body could easily have cramped up, making him helpless, and dead. It took him a long time, but he eventually worked the knots out with a grateful sigh of relief. Lars knew that he was lucky it hadn't happened the day before, or he would be a frozen addition to the landscape.

It was getting along toward morning, and breakfast time, which Lars met with a frying pan and a coffee pot. He decided to spend the day eating and resting, and then leave the cabin a day ahead of his planned schedule. Charlie told him that the cabin was at the halfway point on the route to meet Blaise. That meant that he had more deep snow to plough through, which would take a lot of time and energy, but it must be mostly downhill from here on out. Reaching the top of Lost Horse Mountain was a five-thousand-foot lift from the river bottom, a hike that would tax 'most anyone in dry weather, but in the deep snow it was sheer agony. Why didn't he have a pair of trail snowshoes along with the junk Charlie had given him? The food he found in the backpack wasn't much to brag about either. Lars wanted nothing more than to be safely home with his family, and with his bills paid. How could one greedy tycoon, whom he had never met, be causing him so much trouble?

He had time after breakfast to finish drying out his clothes around the cherry-red stove. He was going to pay a lot more attention to staying dry from here on out to the end of the trail, a very dear lesson learned, which would not be wise to repeat. Sunrise brought with it a pink glow, setting the unbroken snow on fire with its filtered light. From the windows of the cabin facing north, Lars could see a dozen Canadian peaks jutting into the cobalt blue sky. To the west, the high country near Priest Lake in Idaho appeared to be within reach, as it emerged from the night shadows to become backlit by the rising sun.

Lars was impressed with the new sights from his hideaway, but soon his thoughts returned to the lady in that luxury railroad car. How had she gotten there, and why did Charlie tell him that the car was deserted? His first reaction was a bit of shock at seeing someone, but when he had a long look at that rare beauty, all undressed, he lost his senses and almost did a terrible thing to her. Lars thought about his own wife and daughter, and wondered what he would do to someone who treated them in a similar manner. He was becoming sorry for the lady, and felt bad about what had happened. Maybe there was something he could do to make up for it. Who was this man, Herb Long Rifle, that the lady and Alex Black Deer both mentioned? He remembered the young lady saying he would likely kill me if he ever caught up to me. That wild Indian also said something about Long Rifle being the "best shot, and plenty fast."

It didn't sound good. Probably, a guy described like Long Rifle is a mountain man, capable of finding me up here, and doing what comes next.

"I'd leave right now if I thought I could make it," Lars said out loud, surprising himself with his own sound in the complete silence of the snowcapped mountain. "I'm feeling better already, and by daylight tomorrow morning my strength will be back, and I have to get out of here. It won't take that guy Herb too long to figure out where I am after he sees the boat and gets going on my tracks. I'm lucky enough to get a head start on him, but I sure can't sit around waiting for a bullet, or maybe get carved up like Black Deer would do." Lars felt his skin tingle, just remembering that wicked-looking Bowie knife pointed at his stomach. He knew the Indian had seen the bloody scratches on his face and had an idea how they got there. His scarred face broke into a sweat while an involuntary move put his hands down onto his crotch. Maybe Providence was all that stayed a vengeful blade. Lars had his own blade, but he wasn't very good with it.

"I wouldn't be surprised if that man Blaise was early, too, since it is hard to know just how quick I could make it over these mountains. He could be camped out there for a week, just like any deer hunter, waiting for me to show up." Lars ate a cold breakfast the following morning. When daylight arrived, it brought with it a cloud cover, and the smell of another storm. It was leave now or be hopelessly trapped when it snowed again. He shuddered as he remembered the woman's promise. The hunter would kill him, no doubt, and toss him over the cliff where nothing but the ravens would ever know. Lars looked at his two water-proof tubes full of paintings and just shook his head. The prospects looked grim, but he was out of options.

The backpack was lighter now without the tools, and much of the food was gone also. Even with that, the going was very slow, with the deep snow hanging up his legs at every step. It was destined to be a long day before he reached some lower country, with half the snow cover that lay on the alpine maze of ridges and peaks. It took about two hours for Lars to reach the saddle before he started up the back of Pink Mountain. He was already tired, but the map clearly showed it was just a mile to the top and then downhill all the way out. He could make it if he beat the oncoming storm. Two days, and his ordeal would be over, a thought that kept the rugged Swede going.

I arrived at the top of Lost Horse Mountain in mid-afternoon, the same day that Lars left the cabin and headed southwest. Before I came into clear sight of the cabin, which sat on a round knob on the summit, I made a circle completely around the area. It wouldn't exactly be prudent to walk right up to the door and take the consequences. There was no sign of smoke coming out of the stovepipe, which was both good and bad news. I hoped to surprise the man while he was still in the cabin, but he may already be gone, and my search would continue. My circle was nearly completed when I found his southbound trail close above the cliffs. His boots made prints more than waist deep in the powder, and sometimes deeper than that. Damn! I must have just missed him.

Ever since daylight on this morning, it was becoming apparent that Lars was in trouble. His trail through the ever deepening snow showed a man in stress. His rest stops were more frequent, and he was unable to keep a straight line. Too often there was an imprint of his whole body where he had lain, or fallen, before taking up the struggle once more. It seemed to me that I would be finding an incoherent stranger, or maybe a frozen one before I reached the lookout, but his obvious determination got my respect. A lot of different thoughts kept entering my mind as I listened to the soft rhythmical swishing of powder snow as it sifted through the rawhide webbing of my bearpaws. Every tired step lifted six inches of the endless stuff, a burden that often caused disabling cramps, with dire results to those unfortunates who were out of shape.

Teresa had mentioned that her attacker was very strong, and the proof of that was right here. My own emotions ranged between feeling sorry for him, and anger for what he had done. Walking a distance through snow like we had, here, is a slow and silent killer. It beats you to death with hundreds of light blows. You have delusions that you will soon be on dry ground, or that the snow will disappear, and all the while it keeps sapping your strength, like drowning you without water. Exhaustion and hypothermia catch you in their net without your knowing it, and become your master, your enemy, your executioner. I once threw out a life raft over the middle of the Atlantic Ocean, for an enemy that soon became a friend of my country. That memory never left me, and I wondered now if perhaps the same type of scene would repeat itself.

I couldn't let a man drown in an ocean of saltwater, and I couldn't let one drown in an ocean of snow, either.

With the need for caution gone, I hurried up to the cabin. Maybe I could get a clue in there of what was going to happen next. It seemed obvious, though, that a pickup man had to be waiting on the other end of the trail. The lock and hasp were still on the ground next to the door where Lars had pounded on them. The screws finally pulled through the wood, thanks to the hammering, which scattered splinters of fir all around the doorway.

There was nothing much inside the cabin except the few essential pieces of furniture, a stove, and a couple pots and pans. I did find the hammer and screwdriver and pliers that Lars left on an apple box shelf.

"Charlie must have given these tools to the art thief, or else how would he know that there was a cabin with a locked door on a very remote mountaintop." I was asking my own questions out loud, and wishing that a special, good looking woman was here to voice the answers. My many lone expeditions into untracked country used to be a tonic for me, but more and more I was feeling a long-suppressed need for companionship on a permanent basis. Who could tell if Chaps, as unpredictable as the weather, would appreciate this unscheduled and difficult job that I was doing for him? What was going to set him off, the loss of the fine artwork, or the money it represented? How about the loss of a woman?

The sky darkened with the rapid approach of a bank of storm clouds. In a matter of minutes, snow was pelting down, then blowing across the open slopes before a rising wind. Visibility dropped to near nothing. There was one course of action for me, and that was to bring in a load of firewood and wait out the blow. Lars had reached lower ground by this time, where travel was somewhat easier, but he was completely done in. He made a sheltered camp in some dense timber where it was possible to survive another bitter night. He would get but little rest, and nothing much to eat. A few scraps of food was all that remained. Time was running out for Lars, and he knew it.

The storm ended about midnight, after dropping another foot of snow in the high country. The stars came out, but the moon was just a sliver now, and would not show itself until morning. I had a night's sleep done by four a.m., when one of my nightmares woke me up with a shout.

The aircraft I was flying in ran into some violent turbulence that disabled the controls and forced a crash landing. I shook my companion, but he was dead. Gasoline started dripping into the cabin and I had to get out of the wreckage or risk an explosion and a deadly fire. I managed to unhook my safety belt and slide out of the seat into some tall grass before the aircraft disappeared in the roar of a white-hot inferno. For some lucky reason, we crashed into a tiny meadow instead of shredding ourselves into fragments in the heavy timber. We were on the side of a large mountain, away from any settlement.

There was nobody around for miles, but a movement caught my attention. It was a cow moose looking at me from the edge of the clearing. By her side was a newborn calf, trying to stand on wobbly knees, but too early in life to travel. I called a friendly greeting to the new mother, and woke myself from a vivid dream. Before my eyes, a life was started. Another was taken.

Why was I having a dream like this? If I could not stop these all too real nighttime dramas, at least I wanted to understand them. Alex was able to integrate his visions into his life quite naturally. He never questioned their meaning, but interpreted them for his own benefit, often to my amazement. Maybe some of his ability would rub off on me, and that got me to thinking about Alex some more. The least I could do was to thank him for the rice and potatoes, and help him get his elk put down for the winter. I knew that he would never shoot a moose, and he held the bulls in a special kind of reverence. Maybe Alex was communicating with me again, as a blood brother. I didn't attach much credence to the mystic, but then there were times . . . .

We had mixed a few drops of blood from our thumbs, once, in a solemn ceremony. It came after a particularly trying and ultimately successful day when I downed an elk with the last rays of light. We spent the night with the elk, and ate fresh meat together, along with a couple of oranges left over from lunch. We were to share this young bull, a fact that meant more to Alex than I could imagine until that time.

Alex put the edge of his knife to the flames of our cooking fire, and then cut a thin line across his thumb, and across mine. We pressed our thumbs together, and became blood brothers, a lifetime bond of friendship and help, more binding to an Indian like Alex than an oath in court. Alex would never have touched my woman, stolen my money, or my horses. He would die before dishonoring himself in that manner. I had to admit to similar feelings.

Sleep was out of the question. There was a bit of wood next to the stove, so I started a fire and cooked breakfast, and drank a lot of melted snow water. Starlight on the new snow created a pale luminescence that I felt I could navigate under, and I wanted to get on with it. I took up Lars' trail, which was very faint, with the drifted snow filling most of the tracks. The temperature was so cold that the snow squeaked every time I put my weight on a snowshoe. It must have been minus twenty, or maybe more. The continuous effort of breaking trail kept me plenty warm, though, and I unbuttoned my outer jacket in order to stay dry. There was little margin for mistakes on top of Lost Horse Mountain during a deep freeze.

It was hardly getting daylight when I topped out on Pink Mountain. Lars' struggle was plainly written in the drifts. Had he spent one more night in the cabin, he would be dead by now, and could never have reached this point. Luck, if that is what one could call it, was still holding for the rawboned Swede, but I knew now that I would see him before this day ended. His was a trip of attrition. Lack of sleep, a poor diet, and days of extreme physical effort would drain anybody. The tracks leading up to the last high promontory told the true story, like reading it from the Bible.

Alex Black Deer sat by his evening fire, which was a habit he acquired as a boy while listening to his father relate tales of their family and tribal history. This evening, the fire was not burning cleanly. It spit and sputtered, while throwing off more than the usual amount of smoke. Alex spent much time gazing into the fire, trying to poke it into a clean burn. He was concentrating on his efforts and was vaguely aware of Morning Star, as she sat down next to him. Alex watched intently as a figure gradually revealed itself in the center of the flames, a dark form growing into a moose. The apparition finally walked out of the forest and stood by a road. The tall, well-fed moose had a sleek, nearly black hide, but no antlers, since it was an old cow. A large bull was tracking the ancient cow as he had been since leaving the heavy snows in the valley below Lost Horse Mountain.

Winter was always severe in that valley, which forced the herd down to their winter range along the lower ridges bordering the Yaak River. The cow was done running away, as it was her time, and she stood passively for the bull as he helped create a new life. The strong, now mating with the best, obeyed the timeless laws of survival. A strange man appeared on the scene. The bull, still excited and possessive, lowered his head in preparation for running his long brow-tines through the intruder.

The vision faded, and Morning Star laid her hand in Alex's lap. She had on a much mended sheer nightdress, the firelight revealing her body through the fabric in a way Alex had never noticed before. The moon would not rise tonight, but the dancing flames added to the passions of the moment.

His hands started a gentle caressing of his loved one. Morning Star responded to Alex's attentions, and soon they were consumed with each other in the creation of a new life. They finally lay cradled together, on a softly tanned buffalo robe, which Alex had obtained that fall. He always took part in the annual buffalo roundup near Moiese, on the national bison range. It was an ancient custom with the Kootenai tribe that a new life be brought into being where an old one had been taken.

In the short time before sleep overtook him, Alex started thinking about his blood brother, and wondered if he also had a vision tonight. He wondered if Long Rifle's woman had recovered from her obvious attack, and was it this enemy that the bull had targeted for death? Was it that tall man called Lars, or maybe it was Charlie, who was full of lies. Charlie, who had cost him much pain, and a couple broken ribs.

Noontime arrived with a bright sun shining on the south slopes of upper Zulu Creek. I was making good progress since the trail was all downhill. The radiant heat of sunlight reflecting off the perfectly white background soon had me tying my heavy mackinaw to my backpack, even though it was still below zero in the shade. Lars' trail from the previous evening was one of a desperate man trying to stay alive. The human body needs good fuel to keep warm, as well as the proper clothing. Lars, having neither, was hungry, cold and exhausted. He managed a prayer.

I followed his tracks when they left the trail and went into some timber. A crude camp made it obvious that Lars waited out the storm under the spruces in a small gully. Sometime during the late morning, he had gained enough strength to head for the meeting place with Blaise, and the end of his mission. He was so close, and yet so far. I was rapidly closing the distance, and after a couple hours the trail was fresh. No frost from the morning fall lay in the tracks, and bits of snow were still dropping into the depressions made by his boots. He would be in sight at any time, and I would have no difficulty in taking him my prisoner. The bottom of the canyon where Zulu Creek emptied into the Yaak River was already in plain view.

Around the next corner lay a body, covered with snow. I almost stepped on him, but stopped in time and removed my snowshoes. I rolled him over, and saw that he was alive, but I couldn't revive him. Spots of blood lay scattered in the snow where his head had been, indicating some foul play. There were tracks coming up the trail, a lot of scuffling around where the two men met, and fast-moving tracks heading downhill. I must have been in view of whoever had done this. I shook off my pack, took my rifle and ran down the trail as fast as I could manage with sinking knee deep at every step. I cleared the last of the timber and almost fell on the icy ruts of the South Fork Road.

One glance downhill showed a car with Washington plates parked in a turnout. Uphill was nothing, until a record-class bull moose and a heavy, slick-looking cow stepped off the hillside into the narrow, steep roadway. I couldn't help notice their hoofs slipping a bit on the ice as they walked. A car started up about then, and I heard the driver shift gears, as he accelerated down the hill and into view. It was Charlie's old Chevy. I could recognize it anywhere, and it looked like Charlie was driving, or flying. He was leaving the country, and fast. The bull and his cow were in the middle of the road, where Charlie had no choice but to knock one of them down, and dead, to get past. Charlie's moment of truth was arriving.

With hardly a second to waste, I sat down on the bank of the road, rested my elbows across my knees, and shot out Charlie's right front tire. When the tire exploded, the Chevy made an abrupt skid toward the right. With a smooth, often-practiced motion, I reloaded in an instant, swung with the left tire until I saw a couple inches of lead, and shot it out also.

The battered Chevy skidded on the icy road, picking up speed. The car did a complete turn, just missing the unperturbed bull, and went into space, over a bank above the river. Twenty-five yards into flight, Charlie came to a literal dead end, crashing into a monarch of a larch tree that had started life in that spot before the days of Columbus. The shifting lever, which extended from the floor of the car to waist height, had long been without its decorative knob. The steel rod impaled Charlie through the heart, just like a sword, or like a herd bull's long, ivory-tipped brow tine.

I walked up to where the car went over the side, and didn't need more than one look to know that the big dreams of a small crook were over. I wanted to hurry back to where Lars was lying in the snow, and see what I could do for him. There wasn't any activity by the other car, so I left it for the moment. The man was coming around when I got back to him, but he was in bad shape. His two weeks of beard was frosted, and he looked gaunt. His mittens were wet, and it was likely that his fingers had frostbite. Maybe his toes did, too.

"What is your name, farmer?" I asked him after getting him into a sitting position. "I know quite a bit about you after following you all this time."

"Name is Lars," he replied thickly, barely able to speak. "How you know of me?"

"You tried to rape my woman, and then you stole some paintings. I swore I would track you down, and it looks like I damn near got you killed doing it. I've been thinking all along about shooting you on sight, but maybe I'll knock you out again and let you freeze to death instead. Nobody could ever put the blame on me."

Lars was thinking this over as carefully as his cold-numbed mind allowed. "Your name is Long Rifle? You friendly with that Injun? I thought he was going to knife me to death when he looked at my face."

"Yeah, that's what he calls me. I can still see where Teresa worked you over, and I'm sure that's what Alex saw, too. He must have figured that you got it from some woman, but if he had known that she was mine, you would be dead and buried under the ice in the river."

"Charlie warned me about Alex and you. Said you were a bad combination. I figured one of you would be on my trail, and that's about all that kept me goin' the last two days. I thought I just heard some shots, and maybe you was shootin' at me."

"If I were shooting at you, you would never hear it. I don't miss. It was Charlie trying to get away, and I shot out his tires. His car went over the bank and he's dead. Speared to death. Now tell me what you are doing stealing these paintings. I'm going to help you down to the road where there's another car, and see if I can save your ornery hide."

"I'm real sorry about your beautiful woman. I never saw anything like her before. Charlie said that nobody would be there, and it surprised me. She was in bed, and I just lost my mind, but I stopped before I hurt her bad. I never done anything like that before, and never will again."

Some things started making sense after Lars told me how Chaps was manipulating the freight rates, which threatened his farm and his life.

Charlie had arrived at the trailhead before Blaise showed up, and decided to hide his car around a corner, uphill. He started up the trail with a hardwood walking staff, which he used to help keep his balance. When he saw Lars staggering up to him, he asked for the paintings. Lars refused, saying that he wouldn't give them over until Blaise got there with the money. Charlie saw right off that Lars was so used up he could hardly stay on the trail. Lars came through a lot more than most men could endure, but Charlie wasn't thinking about that. He was thinking about putting the screws to Lars, who normally could take him apart, joint by joint.

Without warning, Charlie raised the tip of his staff and jammed it into Lars' stomach. Lars doubled over in excruciating pain, and nearly blacked out. Charlie saw his chance. He raised the staff straight up and brought it down on Lars' head with all the force he could muster. There was a sickening crunch, as the hardwood broke over Lars' skull, dropping him like a stone into the snow. Charlie opened the backpack he had supplied for Lars, and quickly removed the two waterproof tubes containing the priceless paintings. He had all he wanted from this half-dead Swede without paying him a dime. Lars would soon freeze to death and the winter's snow would keep him hidden until April. Charlie had no way of knowing that retribution was just a few minutes up the trail.

Blaise Pulaski made sure that he was on time, or a little early. He rented a car in Spokane, paying for a week in advance to make certain that nobody would come looking for him too soon. It was easy to find the trailhead leading up Zulu Creek, as the Forest Service had one of their rare trail signs bolted to a post next to the road. He was surprised, though, to find a set of fresh man tracks leading into the forest, with none returning. He looked around for Charlie's car, but he just missed seeing it by minutes.

"Something is wrong here," Blaise was thinking, "and I don't like the idea of walking into some kind of a trap." Blaise was unusually cautious, having dealt with people a lot more devious and vicious than Charlie, and he had learned much from those masters of deception and torture. Blaise stopped for a moment to remove a .38 Colt revolver from his shoulder holster. He checked the loads, and pushed the gun into the wide slash pocket in the right side of his heavy wool coat. He took a handmade fanny pack loaded with fifty thousand dollars in hundreds, strapped it around his waist, and made sure it was concealed.

There were two large old ponderosas by the trail, growing nearly together as they often do. Their great size formed a convenient place for Blaise to wait in concealment for a time, while he thought about his next move. It didn't take long for the sound of crunching snow to tell him that someone was coming out of the timber in a big hurry. Charlie passed the two big trees without noticing the tracks leading behind them.

"Hold it, Charlie," Blaise commanded as he stepped onto the trail behind his partner in crime. Charlie stopped like he had hit a stone wall. When he turned around, his eyes bugged open at the sight of a .38 Colt pointed at his chest. Its hammer was thumbed back, giving Charlie the same kind of stomach cramps that he had just dealt out to Lars. "Open those tubes, Charlie, and be careful about it, or I'll shoot you now and do it myself."

"What is this, Blaise, don't you trust me?" Charlie whined. He felt a sudden, painful urge to urinate, and had to fight to hold it back.

"Oh, sure, I trust you, all right, as long as I have this loaded gun stuck into your guts. Did you ever see a gut-shot man, Charlie? They die very slowly, and usually beg to be shot again. Where is the guy who brought these paintings all across the mountains? What did you do to him, you snake?"

"He's coming along shortly, soon as he gets his camp picked up," Charlie lied.

"I want to see you pay him off, Charlie. I don't like unhappy people looking for me. It could be bad for my health." Blaise backed away from Charlie and unrolled the masterworks, studying them with an expert's knowledge. Blaise replaced the canvases, still holding Charlie at gunpoint. He took off his fanny pack with the money in it and tossed it to Charlie, who could hardly believe this turn of events.

"I'm not like you, you two-bit cheat. I keep my word, and you are going to keep yours. Go get that man and pay him what you owe, or you won't be leaving here alive."

Charlie turned and started back toward Lars, when they both heard me come up to the unconscious Swede and exclaim, "What the hell happened here?" I had been talking to myself so much lately that I was hardly aware of my own voice.

Neither Blaise nor Charlie wanted any confrontation with me, and they both bolted for the road. Blaise made it over the bank into cover behind his rental car, and knew enough to remain motionless. Charlie ran out of sight just as I came out to the end of the trail. I spent a precious moment looking for danger before stepping into the open. After a minute or two, I heard a car start, a couple gears ground like they would break, and here came the old Chevy on its final trip.

Blaise stayed hunkered down in the brush behind his car, watching the next scene unfold. He was fascinated with the display of shooting, and horrified at the results. He didn't know anything much about me, or where I had arrived from, but he wasn't going to hang around long enough to find out. Nobody with a .38 Colt was going to intimidate this rifleman.

Blaise saw me look at the wreck, and then turn back up the trail. He knew that I was going after Charlie's runner, which might take a few short minutes. Lives are made and lives are often ended in just a few moments, and those who are ready and willing to take a calculated risk can sometimes win a game or two. Blaise took his backpack out of the car, but left the keys in the door. He didn't want to be seen in the car, which the woodsman would describe to the police. He knew that it would find its way back to the proper agency before his week's rental expired.

It was a risky job, getting into the front of Charlie's wrecked car, but Blaise managed to find his fanny pack with the money still intact. He shuddered at the sight of Charlie, dead as a mackerel, just like he himself could be at any second. Blaise knew he would never hear death coming on this mountainside. He had to get his tail out of here, and fast, but there was one remaining item.

"I have to pay off the runner, one way or another. I don't know what the rifleman will do when he obviously comes back for another look, but I can't take the man's money after all he went through to earn it." It took a couple precious seconds to count out twenty-five of the century notes, and lay them on Charlie's shoulder. Blaise slid down the embankment to the mouth of Zulu Creek, crossed the South Fork of the Yaak, and disappeared into the wilderness. He headed north, having a low-elevation route already planned. Two days later, Blaise crossed the open timber strip marking the Canadian border. A small rocky outcropping formed a series of dry, waterproof holes, frequented by pack rats and squirrels. Blaise chose the best one, and deposited the Colt revolver and the ammunition in there, away from rain and the elements. He had no more need for the gun, but maybe some lucky hunter would have use for it in the future.

The camping and cold-weather gear that he so carefully assembled was working just fine. Another day in the bush brought him to the Canadian National Railway. A few miles east, he walked into a small village with a depot and a family restaurant. He made sure to pay for everything with Canadian money. By evening, Blaise was on his way to Moosejaw, Saskatchewan, and from there to Montreal. The money he retrieved from Charlie went to pay off his debts in Spokane, and to close down his business. One gamble, one win. Yvonne was still waiting, and Gregory would be exceptionally happy to hear what he had to tell him.

I was able to get Lars to his feet long enough to help him to the rental car. With the heater turned on, his mittens and boots off, and his coat unbuttoned, the danger of hypothermia was over. Lars started feeling a lot of pain as his frosted fingers and toes began thawing out. The pain was hardly exceeded by the hurt in his head where Charlie had tried to brain him. It would be months before all the feeling came back in his fingers, but at least he would save all those extremities.

There were some raisins left in my pack, and an orange and a candy bar. I gave these to Lars, who gobbled them up before the heat and comfort of the car seat put him out. He told me how Charlie had knocked him cold, and was never intending to pay him.

My emotions had to be choked back when I went down to look at Charlie once more. Neatly stacked up, lying on his jacket, was a pile of hundred dollar bills. Below the wreck was a new trail, sliding down to the creek, and crossing into the forest. I wouldn't follow it. That man could run forever as far as I was concerned, since I had better things to tend to.

It hit me that Blaise must have known that Charlie was robbing Lars, and wanted to clear his conscience of this fact. Exactly what kind of a man was I dealing with now? Did he really trust me to do the right thing with the cash? Just what was the right thing, anyway? Did the money belong to Lars, or to Chaps? When that thought entered my mind, I knew what I had to do. Ed would never miss it, and nobody would ever tell him what happened here. He probably was incapable of understanding what I was going to do next, and it was better if he never heard of it.

The trip to Troy was mostly a silent one, giving me plenty of time to ponder the events of the past week. Before I put Lars on the evening train going east toward his farm, I discussed his future. I had a lot of respect for this farmer, and decided that one mistake wasn't enough to destroy his life for him in jail. I ended up giving him twenty-two of the bills, which brought tears to his eyes, and lifetime gratitude. He never failed to send me a Christmas greeting from the farm, which one day he would leave to his kids. The other three bills I kept for expenses, combat duty, and a way to pay one of the guides to deliver the rental car back to Spokane. He could catch the Great Northern train back to the hunting spur.

Driving on solid ice on an old forest road kept my attention, but certain things kept puzzling me. My dream of a plane crash was virtually what took place on this icy road. The wobbly calf was a newcomer to this world on the same day that Charlie left it. The massive old bull on the road, along with his cow, was in a way responsible for Charlie's wreck, which actually took place a short time after the two animals made an heir of their kind.

Was my dream a message of sorts from Alex? Maybe he had another vision that reached me in part, several days travel away. Life as a hunter had already taught me more than relentlessly following a fresh trail. I learned that out of death comes life. Many times I had come across the carcass of a deer pulled down by a cougar. The big cats ate meat, and fed their young on it. The deer ate browse and grasses, which would spring up again after each rain, and during the long growing days of spring. Snowshoe rabbits bred early in life, ate a lot of brush, and produced a lot of young. Rabbits were the food of bobcats, coyotes, owls and hawks.

Deep snow in the winter buried the grizzlies and black bears, keeping them out of danger during their cold-weather sleep. The snow turned into life-giving water when the sun changed its angle after a long winter. High water in the Kootenai River scoured the gravel bottom, cleaning it so that insects had a proper place to spawn and create food for the cutthroat trout. Alex was fully attuned to this rhythm, but I was still learning. Don was happy, even though he had nearly died on our hunt. Don would be with his ancestors soon. Lars was headed back home to pay off his farm, Charlie was gone for good and Alex had disappeared into Canada. Was it my turn to start my own continuation of life? It looked like the planets were now lined up in my favor. My plan for Ed Scharpe came into focus.

Chapter 28

Ed Scharpe was livid. His private car was moved up and down the tracks without his permission. Richard, the cook, was gone, the paintings that were his pride were scattered around, and three of his best artworks were missing. To make matters worse, Teresa had disappeared, and nobody had heard from Herb for days. Oscar was filling in for Charlie, who arranged this exchange long in advance because he wanted to go deer hunting all weekend. Rumor had it that some big uneducated Swede wanted to talk to him, but even that person was nowhere around. Blue, the cop, knew nothing. Iver and Johnny were off someplace with the horses. Walt claimed no knowledge of anything, but he was obviously being evasive.

For once in his life, Big Ed was totally frustrated. His rapid rise in the railway company hadn't given him much time to learn about taking orders, but he practiced giving them. There wasn't a humble bone in his body, either, a characteristic that made him a lot of enemies, but Ed was smart enough to keep those people at a distance. His biggest critics seemed, for some obscure reason, to always be working in another department, where they had little chance to do more to him than complain. When Ed barked out an order, he wanted action at that moment, or else. Now, he had no one to shout at but the local cop, who apparently was waiting for Herb to come up with some answers. Either that, or he didn't care about any old paintings, which "most likely were used to hide knotholes in the paneling."

Why did everyone keep depending on Herb to do things, Ed asked himself. Who actually was this man that stuck his nose into everything, from guiding, to police work, to ordering around my own railroad crews. The minute I give an order, somebody says, "We can't, right now, because Herb told us to do this first," and, by God, they run off and do it. Now he and Teresa are both gone someplace, and it could be that he spirited her away to a cabin somewhere for a little fun. She sure has been acting strange lately, come to think about it.

On the other hand, Teresa isn't tough enough to enjoy camping out in this bloody cold weather, and I'm not either. I guess he couldn't have talked her into it. I wonder, though, if Herb was trying to get me killed by the bear that ran me down. He could have shot it, but he just let it keep coming right over the top of me, and then laughed about it. I'd fire that barbarian if he were working for me! Damn it, he is working for me.

Ed was on the phone to Blue. "I want you to put out an arrest warrant for Teresa Parker. She is missing, along with a million dollars worth of my paintings. It looks like she waited until I was gone for a few days, and then set up this fake robbery. Nobody else knew anything about the value of this art, and none of the rest of you around here are smart enough to pull this off. She is probably in Portland with her sister, getting rid of the loot right now. Make out a warrant for Herb, too. Nobody has seen him lately, which means that he is running my paintings to California someplace, or Mexico."

"Now, Mr. Chaps," Blue responded, cool as a cucumber, "We can't just start issuing arrest warrants to our best citizens. Why, Herb has helped half the people in this valley at some time or other. He has a good military record, too."

"The name is Scharpe, not Chaps," Ed shouted back. "Don't you have brains enough to see how he and my, ahh, secretary set this up. They could take off together and live a hundred years on the money from those masterpieces. Nobody else but my cook could have been responsible, and he just returned from Whitefish with the rest of the guides."

"Now, Mr. Chaps," Blue repeated, "We have to start an investigation about all this, and that may take three or four weeks. We got a heavy case load here, what with a lot of kids playin' hooky, and such. We even caught a couple of 'em smokin' yesterday, and had to call their folks down to the station. There was a lot of fightin' over at the Mint, too, when Ferd had to toss out a few gold miners what got out of hand. Seems like he knocked two of them tough buzzards out cold. They took the door and the hinges off before they landed on the sidewalk. Disgraceful for this quiet town! Things sure ain't like they once was. Why, I remember when there was at least three or four days between fights around here."

"When are you getting off the pot and doing something useful," Ed broke in, screaming into the speaker.

Blue continued talking as if he didn't hear Scharpe's outburst. "We had to lock 'em up for a while to let 'em sober up and pay some damages. Ferd's hardwood bar top got all split where one of them old miners sunk a pickaxe into it. My back is still sore from tryin' to pull it out so's it could be used for evidence. I'm tellin' you, Mr. Chaps, we ain't got any room in the jailhouse for Herb and that young woman at the moment. Wouldn't look good, nohow, to lock 'em up together. The Ladies' Circle at the church won't stand for that sort of carryin' on."

Blue winked at his deputy as the air around the receiver turned purple with Scharpe's response to that speech.

"Find those two, you idiot."

"Well, I was up at Herb's place this morning, wantin' to pick up a piece of meat he promised me, but his truck was gone, and his boat too. I think he went duck huntin', or fishin'. He generally stays out a week or so, where nobody can locate him. He is sure some loner, that mountain man is." Blue artfully dropped the receiver back on its hook as he looked at his deputy. A thin smile crossed Blue's face.

"That old Chaps is a real hard case, ain't he? We'd best get over to Judge Hegler's office and work out something with him. I ain't about to arrest Herb. Couldn't do it unless he wanted me to, anyway. Wheeoo! Ever see that man shoot? I seen him pick a raven right out of the air with his .270, one time, when that old thief was stealin' some of his venison. All I recall lookin' at was a big red spray in the sky, and a bunch of black feathers floatin' down. I ain't goin' near him with any crazy warrant, particularly when he didn't do nothin' ag'in the law to my way of thinkin'."

J. T. Bidwell was having the time of his life. The one guide that was available had shown him a dozen shootable deer, none of which he bagged, but J. T. did manage to take a nice bobcat, fully furred in its winter prime. The bobcat would look great in his office, a real conversation piece next to the whitetail trophy he hoped to bring home. The food was edible, but the day that Richard returned, chastened from his experiences with a pair of Whitefish's best consorts, the cuisine began to rival that of New York City.

Never mind that Ed Scharpe was completely out of sorts these days. The missing art did not belong to the Great Northern Railway, so wasn't really any of his concern other than the insurance. He was here for a holiday, and was making the best of it. Herb and the rest of his crew would be back at any time, and J. T. was sure that his trophy buck would be forthcoming. After all, the reputation of this hunter had found its way into their corporate offices clear back to Chicago and New York.

Iver and Johnny finally rode into the hunting camp with all the horses and mules strung out between them. It made the place look like a thriving establishment again. Johnny took J. T. Bidwell for a long ride on Buck one morning, starting before daylight. J. T. knew 'most all there was about railroading, and loved it, but he had never been around horses much. He was converted after that ride.

Several hours of slow climbing brought them into a game-feeding area about the same time as the sun brought them good shooting light. Buck suddenly stopped before entering an open ponderosa park, turned his head sharply to the left and swiveled his ears forward. He was motionless, concentrating on something unseen. Johnny slipped off of his black gelding without saying a word, and motioned for J. T. to take out his rifle and do likewise. Johnny dropped Buck's reins to the ground and motioned J. T. up the trail eight or ten steps where they knelt behind a windfall. A moment later, right on cue, a group of mule deer wandered into sight, nipping at the tender tops of huckleberry bushes poking out of the snow.

A heavy-beamed buck trailed the herd, and Johnny didn't need more than one look to know that J. T. had better try for this one. He tapped his hunter on the arm and nodded toward the big old four-pointer. One shot across the steady rest of the windfall, and the president of the Great Northern had his first wall hanger, a bragging mule deer.

The brilliant blue sky sparkled with small flakes of frost lazily drifting down. High peaks to the south poked up through the valley fog like islands in a vast ocean. Temperatures had moderated after the blizzard, making travel in the mountains brisk, but pleasant. It was a time to savor, a time to reflect on the reasons for being out in God's country hunting game in the snowy peaks near the Canadian border. Buck created a slight diversion for the moment, rattling the roller on the bit in his mouth.

Johnny started a small fire with a few pitch-filled branches off the windfall. They really didn't need it, but something about a fire makes a person own that little piece of ground for a short time. It becomes a personal place, a place to rest and talk some. J. T. wanted to talk, and Johnny listened as he prepared the deer for Sally to pack off the mountain.

"How do you men get along with Ed Scharpe?" J. T. asked.

"He gets a trifle demanding, but he ain't much good in the hills. He knows that, so he listens to what Herb tells him, even if he don't like it. How come you asked that?" Johnny wanted to know.

"Ed is more than angry about losing his paintings, and he is looking for someone to blame. He called the police and demanded that Herb and Teresa be arrested. He says that nobody else was in the position to do this, and they both have disappeared. He's really frustrated about that."

Johnny stopped working on the deer and looked up in surprise. "I tell you what, Mr. Bidwell, I've known Herb most of my life. Been huntin' and fishin' with him, and runnin' horses in these mountains since we was kids. I never knowed him to take somethin' what he didn't own, but I sure don't want to be the guy who stole anything off him, neither. One way or another, he will get it back, if you see my meanin'."

"Do you know where Herb is right now?" J. T. was leading up to this question.

"Yeah, I know, but I shouldn't be talking about it," Johnny mumbled.

"Why is that?" Bidwell raised his eyebrows.

Johnny debated with himself before answering. "Herb had quite a war record, and it's been takin' him a long time to wind down from that. He puts in a lot of time alone, just him and Buck campin' out in the hills." Johnny broke off a couple branches and fed them to the fire. Sparks and smoke curled lazily into the calm air, and drifted off to the east. "He and Teresa kind of hit it off, and I think she's good for him. Somebody rustled our horses a few days ago, and when we found 'em up at the Ural siding, Teresa was there, all beat up and cryin'. I got into Chaps' car first, and sort of quieted her down till Herb showed on his speeder. He didn't say a hell of a lot, but I knew right off that he was goin' after the guy what did it. He'll surely track him down and take care of the problem. I doubt if Herb will ever tell us what happened, but Alex and I will both know. There ain't a man alive that's a goin' to outrun him up here."

"What about the missing paintings? They're worth a fortune."

"To my way of thinkin', Herb don't give a damn about any paintings," Johnny said quietly. His accent was a long stream of sizzling brown juice directed into the center of the flames.

J. T. Bidwell sat for a long time, contemplating what he had just heard. He intently studied the burning fir branches as bubbles of melted pitch boiled out of the bark, spitting and crackling when the flames caught them.

"It looks as if Ed is going to lose his lady friend that he brags about so much. Quite likely it's that which is getting to him. She is a real stunner, and Herb will be a lucky man if he catches her for good. I'm beginning to think that the paintings are a matter for our insurance company, though. Your local police won't have a chance as I feel that those stolen paintings are thousands of miles from here by now. I plan on having a long talk with Ed over a glass of French wine and one of Richard's dinners tonight."

J. T. thought for a bit, and then asked Johnny, " How did you know that these deer were up there, anyway?"

"I was watchin' Buck, and he just pointed them like a bird dog. That horse has a real nose for game, and he's seldom mistaken."

"It would really be nice to have a small place around here with horses like that for my grandchildren. I'm not long until retirement, myself." J. T. was smiling as he removed a pastrami on rye from his saddlebag.

I pulled into town late in the evening and parked on the ice-coated street in front of the police station. Blue looked up, not all that surprised as I walked in. "Howdy, Herb. Where you been lately? Old Chaps is sure lookin' for you. Says he wants me to arrest you for stealing' his artwork and kidnapin' his lady friend."

"What about you, Blue? Want to lock me up?"

Blue swallowed kind of hard. "No way, Herb, but tell me a few facts."

"I came in here to report a death. Charlie died up in the Yaak."

"No fooling? Did you shoot him, or something? How did you know he was up there, anyway?" Blue was suddenly wide awake, and all ears.

"Never mind how I knew. I didn't shoot him, either. A bull moose got to him, got him speared to death. I saw it coming a day ahead of time. You better get a crew up there at Zulu Creek." With that said, I turned and walked toward the door.

"Hey, what about old Chaps? He says you stole his paintings," Blue called after me. He was totally baffled by all this.

"Tell him to come over tomorrow and arrest me himself if he is man enough. I have a full schedule tonight, and I'm heading for the hunting camp tomorrow morning. I don't have any idea where his paintings are by now." I was badly in need of a shower, a good dinner, and several other things that I felt a warm glow thinking about.

Blaise stepped off the train in Montreal and headed for a phone booth. An eager voice answered his call, and soon Yvonne had her arms around him, asking him a hundred questions. It was a warm reunion, for which Blaise was duly grateful. He knew that it could have been a fatal experience at Zulu Creek. Timing was everything, and he was lucky, but his thorough planning made the difference.

By the next morning, Blaise couldn't wait to examine the paintings. Yvonne went out to do some shopping, which gave him plenty of time to relax and start a detailed examination. The first thing he checked for was damage, but by some stroke of fortune, there was not a blemish on any of the three canvases. The Russell was magnificent, and much different from any works Blaise had ever studied in Europe. The wild interaction of Indians, horses, buffalo, and life and death gave him much reason for thought. His own life had been a series of escapes and survival. He wondered what sort of a life Russell had lived, and he planned to study about the cowboy artist.

The early Picasso was like an old friend. Blaise looked at it, spread out on a coffee table, remembering every brushstroke. The painting was the missing Picasso that Blaise had researched for so long before he painted one of his own. How did it ever make it to the U.S.A., after being lost for all those many years? Strange things happened during and right after the war, and here was a mystery from that period, sitting right in front of him. The picture was small and detailed, unlike some of Picasso's later work that was too impressionistic, and very bold. It seemed remarkable that a Picasso that was missing in the old country had been stolen from a railway car in the wilds of the Rocky Mountains in the United States. It was already a continent away from there, resting on his table in Montreal.

The longer Blaise studied the canvas, the more intrigued he became with it, and finally he turned it over to look at the fabric and whatever gallery markings there were on the back. The fabric was old, no doubt about that, and in one corner was a minute gallery marking that he recognized from his days in Paris. It was a tiny circle with an S hardly visible in its center, done with an oil paint. Curiosity finally got the best of him. He just had to see what was under that circle. Blaise took a thin pen knife blade and removed the hardened paint.

He could hardly believe his eyes. There was no doubt about it, his own mark was right there, quite dim, but visible. It was a near microscopic star with a P overlaid. An average gallery would not question the mark, if they ever noticed it, believing that Picasso was eccentric enough to put his own mark on a few early works of his. Some dealer subsequently applied his own seal directly over it, for reasons of his own.

Blaise began getting flashbacks to the time he was planning his escape from the Nazis, and then the communists. All the killings, the forced labor, starvation, the whole scene nearly made him sick. He had deceived people in order to survive, but he wanted no more of that, especially with Gregory, who had befriended him. Blaise planned to tell Gregory that a man brought the paintings to him and wouldn't say where they came from. The problem at that moment was to decide what to do about it. Maybe Gregory would like to buy them, he thought, or maybe make it known to the International Insurance Company that there was a deal to be made for a reward.

The forged Picasso was another matter entirely. It obviously passed through several hands before Scharpe bought it, and evidently nobody questioned its authenticity. That made Blaise feel good about his abilities, but to pass this off on Kromer was out. To fool a panel of insurance experts may be nearly impossible. Those people were quite reluctant to part with their money, and they would do major research on these stolen paintings before making an offer. Blaise had no wish to take a risk on losing everything he had going in Montreal. If he were found out, he could be tossed into jail on a fraud charge. It seemed that his gamble had suffered one loss, but he could still end up way ahead. He decided to pass up a chance for a hundred thousand dollars and keep his own work out of sight. He didn't have the heart to destroy it. Maybe some day it would occupy a place of honor in his own living room as a reminder of what once was.

Dealing with the other two paintings was a delicate situation, best handled by Gregory Kromer. He was quite familiar with the ways of insurance buybacks, which saved everybody a lot of time and problems, as well as substantial money. A person who found some stolen art and turned it in for a reward was usually happy to settle for much less than the insured value, and still come out far ahead. There would be no difficult questions asked.

Gregory lifted the phone on the third ring. "Hello, Gregory, Blaise, here. I just got back yesterday, with some interesting news to talk about."

"Glad to hear from you, old boy," was the reply. "Come on right over, and have a spot of tea while I find out what you've been up to. I have a couple new items that need your evaluation. It seems like I'll never stop looking for a good addition to my collection."

Blaise put the two remaining paintings back into their tubes, and walked the half mile to Gregory's place. The cold air and exercise felt good after his long, confining train ride across Canada. His welcome last night more than convinced Blaise that he was making the right decisions in his life. That lady was getting to him, and he wasn't trying to figure a way out of it, as so often happened in the past. Blaise was feeling upbeat, but still somewhat apprehensive about Gregory's reaction when he got a look at the two masterpieces. Gregory couldn't easily be fooled, but he didn't have to be told everything, either.

A jangling doorbell was answered immediately. Gregory grabbed Blaise's hand and shook it in welcome. "Come right in. Nice to have you back. I was starting to wonder if we'd be seeing you again," he said with feeling.

"Yvonne said something along those lines, too," Blaise replied. "I like it here a lot. I think my traveling days are probably over. Maybe a business deal will help my plans for the future, and I'd like to talk that over with you."

"Sit down at the table, here, and I'll get us some refreshments. You have me all curious now." Gregory pulled out a chair and motioned Blaise into it.

Blaise took the two paintings out of their protective covers and laid them out on the table while Gregory was in the kitchen. The beauty of the small Monet contrasted with the stark reality and the violent action of the Russell. Both were worth a fortune in themselves at any auction house. He had been reluctant to study these works while on the train, as any slip could have ruined the entire enterprise. Blaise knew a master's touch when he saw it, and now he couldn't take his eyes away.

"What have you got there?" Gregory wanted to know as he set the tea service on a side table. He came rapidly around the table and stood next to Blaise with a startled expression on his face. "Good Lord," he exclaimed, "Are those real? I'm no great expert, but that sure looks like a Monet, and I think the other is a Russell. I have to sit down before I fall down!" Gregory pulled up another chair. "These paintings are priceless, and here they are in my own house. Some people would do anything to own one of these." Gregory looked questioningly at Blaise.

"They're real, all right, and no, I didn't shoot anybody or rob a gallery to get them."

"I didn't believe you could do something like that. I have news for you, though. A report on three missing paintings from a private residence came through to the insurance company that I do some work for. The description fits these two. Whenever there is a theft of this nature, all the insurance people in the U.S. and Canada are notified immediately. It's surprising how often the stolen goods are recovered without any fanfare, and returned to the owners. Most of the time, they go through three or four parties before someone makes a phone call and does the proper thing. We almost never catch the original thief." Gregory was staring at the two paintings with a longing aroused in his heart. "Tell me about it."

"I had a visitor come to my store in Spokane last summer. He asked a bunch of strange questions about the value of different works of art, including a particular Russell that he was going to buy. I didn't think he was for real until I got another call to meet with him at a certain place, so I went, and he had these paintings with him. I don't know who it was that stole them, but I know it was not this man who called himself Charlie.

He wanted a lot of money, but we were interrupted by a third party with a rifle. Charlie ran up the road, jumped into his car and came too fast down the icy hill. A big bull moose and his cow stepped right into the road just then, and he would have run into them and wrecked the car, but the rifleman shot out both his front tires. I've never seen anything like that. There was hardly a split second between shots. Charlie's car skidded, and went over the bank, and he was killed. The woodsman took a quick look and then headed back into the timber. I sure didn't want him shooting at me, so I just headed north through the forest as fast as I could go. I suppose that man could have easily run me down, but for some reason, I don't think he cared about me or what I was doing. It was Charlie that he was after, and also there was someone else back up the trail where they came from."

"Did that woodsman with the rifle get a good look at you, Blaise?" The lawyer in Gregory was coming to the front now.

"No. In fact, he never saw me at all because I was in the brush behind my car. There's little doubt, though, that a man like him would read my tracks in the snow, and quickly know just what I was planning to do. Lucky for me, he just decided to leave me go."

"I guess there's no way to connect you with this affair unless you talked to somebody about it."

"I stayed alive in Europe by keeping my mouth shut, and I haven't changed my habits any," Blaise replied. I haven't told Yvonne anything much about my past, either. You can't imagine what those work camps are like. A lot of people don't survive the first two months."

"I don't want any part of that lifestyle," Gregory opined. "Now to get right at our problem. We have to sit on these pieces for a few months at least, so nobody will suspect us of being in on the original theft. These paintings have to appear like they filtered down to us over a period of time, and by coincidence, came to my attention. Insurance people know that I have handled similar matters in the past, so nobody will question my involvement. A few officials may wonder just how or why I was contacted instead of someone else. I'll just say that my reputation for dealing with these matters discreetly is well known."

"What do you have to do next, Gregory? I want to stay as far away from the negotiations as possible," Blaise said, thoughtfully.

"I will start by calling for a copy of the insurance policy, which will tell us the insured value and probably the approximate market value of the goods. It is doubtful that the owner would insure them for less than they cost him, and the value has assuredly gone up a lot since then. I would guess, one million, with a reward value of one third, or three hundred thirty three thousand U.S. dollars. A tidy sum, at that."

"What happens when you announce that you have found these paintings, and someone wants a reward?"

"We have to keep the police out of it, and deal directly with the officers of International Insurance Co. I will tell them that if there is an official investigation, the paintings will disappear in Argentina where they are now, and where we have no extradition treaty. I will let the company have an expert of their own choosing evaluate the paintings to make sure they are authentic, but it will be at an undisclosed location. I usually do this offshore, out of the hundred-mile limit, but on a Canadian fishing vessel where the customs people don't bother it. The expert will charter his own craft, and meet us offshore. He will then accompany us back so we can keep him from calling the police or the Coast Guard until you have the paintings hidden in a bank vault safety deposit box."

"How does the owner get them back after all this," Blaise wanted to know.

"I will have myself bonded for the appraised value, and then deliver them myself. By the way, what do you suppose happened to the third painting they mentioned?" Gregory looked hard at Blaise.

"That's a good question," Blaise replied a bit cryptically, "but, sooner or later, I'm sure we'll find out."

"In the meanwhile, I'm going to frame these two pictures, and hang them out of sight in my basement gallery. At least I can say that I've had a couple of world-class artworks in my collection. It'll be difficult to part with these beauties, but the penalties for knowingly keeping stolen goods aren't exactly to my liking, either."

Chapter 28

The trip across Canada was a learning experience, but there were a few logical conclusions to be made first. A major insurance company, International Insurance, was the underwriter for the company that dealt with the Great Northern. I found out that their main office was in Montreal, and I followed the tracks from their source right to their end. I did take a two-hour hike along the trail leading from Charlie's wrecked car. It led me straight north, and I concluded that the man tracks terminated on the Canadian National Railway, Columbine station.

I drove across the border at Creston, and caught the train to Columbine. Hardly anyone gets aboard there, and the agent remembered the description of the man who could be the one I was looking for. I already had his name and a lot of other information from Lars, who talked a lot while he was half-conscious during our ride out of the Yaak. From Columbine to Moosejaw, to Montreal, the natural end of the trip, was an interesting but long ride across a winter wonderland.

One visit to the International Insurance office brought out the name of their chief legal counsel.

The doorbell jangled, and I said hello to Gregory Kromer. He wasn't exactly overjoyed to see me, but my introductory papers, which the New York insurance agency had sent to Montreal, were enough to get me inside. It took a lot of persuasion, but he seemed to trust me, and finally introduced me to Blaise at a private dinner the following evening in his basement gallery.

I was fascinated by the life story that Blaise told me, and agreed to forget the forged Picasso that meant so much to him. I would have to tell Chaps that the third painting was missing forever. He would be out a lot of money, anyway, if I came clean and disclosed the forgery.

There was no reward for Blaise and Gregory to collect, but Gregory did have a sizeable legal bill that he submitted to International Insurance. He was going to set up Blaise with a new gallery, at Christmastime. Life never changes. You gamble to win, but you can't count on it

Teresa had her own way. I wanted a small affair, but she wanted to invite friends from all over the country to our wedding. We worked like slaves in getting the new house ready for an early summer ceremony. All Teresa's guests from her modeling business loved the idea of coming to Montana, where none of them had ever been before. My old hunting partners came through with some unusual gifts, including a new buffalo robe from Alex and Morning Star. The thought behind this was obvious, and we all heard some interesting theories on how to use it.

Blue sent me a framed arrest warrant for myself, and one for Teresa, all legally signed by the judge. Ferd brought over a case of champagne, and Gerta made enough food to feed an army. Ingvar spent many hours hand-carving a beautiful speeder out of nicely grained hard maple. I guess we both had a tear in our eyes when he handed it to me. Oscar showed up with his new wife, and gave Teresa an antique telegraph key, all polished up and in working order. That sat on our mantle for years.

The buffalo robe must have had some of Alex's magic left in it. We gave it a good trial, and about a year later, along came a blue-eyed boy. For some reason, it seemed to me that Lars should be here, but for other obvious reasons, he wasn't. Time went on, and we settled down to a routine of working, hunting, raising a boy, and harvesting a garden.

The mailbox was down the lane from our new house, just far enough so that I could read most of the mail before I took it inside. I recognized the rough handwriting of Lars on the envelope, and sat down on the lawn to read what he had to say.

"Dear Herb and Teresa,
I know of your marriage some years ago, but I was never brave enough before this to write to you. Hardly a day goes by that I don't think about what happened in those mountains, and I am sorry for what I did.

I have two ranches now, and my boy runs one where he raises horses down in the breaks. It is grazing land and good hunting, but too steep for farming. I have not shot a big buck or an antelope there for many years, and I am inviting you and Teresa and Black Deer to hunt. You will see many bucks that will sooner or later die of old age.

I want to do this for you and I have to talk to you before I get too old and something happens to me. I never told Helga anything about what went on over there, or how I got the money to pay off our debts. I did tell my boy that it was you who saved my life.

Lars

A long family discussion took place before we finally decided to go. Alex was excited to see the country where his ancestors made their long treks, trading with the plains tribes, and hunting buffalo. Teresa was willing to forget past problems and wipe the slate clean. She even practiced with her rifle, hoping to get an antelope to mount in her study. Our son could stick to a horse like a saddle blanket, and he wanted the chance to do his cowboying on a real prairie ranch.

Lars picked us up at the Great Northern depot in Malta, and drove us south to his first spread, which now sported a beautiful house on a bluff overlooking a thousand square miles of Missouri River breaks. It was down there that his son, Leif, would guide us through the endless canyon country.

Helga took to Teresa right off, and hated to see her leave for a few days of hunting. We all had good luck, seeing deer and antelope in great numbers, and shooting some real old-time trophies. Teresa got her antelope with sixteen-inch horns, which was better than mine, and I never heard the end of it. Alex shot a few deer, and decided to take off on his horse to see the country. He returned about four days later, with his own stories to tell.

It was time to leave, but Lars had a dinner and some sort of celebration planned for us. We ate the finest Swedish dishes I had ever tasted. When it was time to say goodbye, Leif headed for the barn, and then rode back on a classy, well-conditioned young mare. Leif dismounted and handed Teresa the reins. I understand good horses, but this one had them all beat. I had never seen a mare to match that one in my life. Teresa climbed aboard, and proceeded to put that horse through its paces, which were flawless. When she was finished, she dismounted, and gave the reins to Lars.

"Lars, I want to thank you for a wonderful time. You couldn't have been any nicer to us." She gave Lars a smile that tugged at his heart. "I don't even remember seeing you before. It must have been someone else. And thanks for the ride. That's by far the best mare I have ever been on."

"Missy," Lars said to Teresa as he gave her a hug, "I have been hurting inside for too long, now. I want you to have this horse. It is yours. Leif has been training her for four years, and he always knew that it was for the man that saved my life, and my family. We have been waiting for her to be ready, and we can't do any more." He turned away, wiping his eyes.

"What is her name, Lars?" Teresa asked, her voice deep with emotion.

"Cleo," was all he answered.

"Cleo?"

"Ya. I didn't go to school much, but my teacher told us once about the most beautiful oriental woman called Cleopatra."

"She was Egyptian," Teresa said softly.

"Ya, you are right. I named her for you. I don't know any other beautiful women." Lars handed her a bill of sale, completely made out.

"Thank you, Lars. God bless you," Teresa whispered, all choked up. "Come visit us, Helga."

Chaps heard of a request from his agent in Malta for a specially equipped stock car to ship a single valuable mare to Libby. He took it upon himself to handle the details. Everything was done to insure the comfort of the horse, and there would be no charge. Ed was in the bedroom-office of his private car, looking at the Russell painting, with the Blackfeet on their horses, chasing buffalo over a cliff. He had been doing a lot of thinking for a long time, now, about the one man who had the nerve to stand up to him, steal his woman, and then go and retrieve his painting against considerable odds. Ed finally had to admit to himself that the hunt with this man was the high point in his life. His memory of the bear running over him was still clear as a crystal. He reached his hand up and thoughtfully touched the scars on his neck.

The train pulled in to Libby after a long two day run from Malta. The car with Teresa's mare was spotted in the siding behind the depot. Oscar was there with a box for me, and a small package for Teresa.

Johanson climbed down from the locomotive. "By golly, Mr. Herb, I been glad to see you." We shook hands and I smiled at my old friend. "I heard somebody vas shipping you a horse, and Aye signed up for the last part of the run. I yust retired, but dey let me do it. I don't vant nothing to happen to your fine horse, by golly. I never forget how you come to the hospital to see me."

"Thanks a lot, Johanson. I really appreciate it. By the way, did you ever get rid of the buckets in your living room?" We had a good laugh over that.

Oscar stood by while I signed the slip for our two parcels. I pried mine open, and there lay a beautiful Winchester custom rifle. It was built to fit me, a bit shorter than the one I had made for Chaps. The stock was carved from beautifully grained Circassian walnut. On the floorplate, which covers the magazine, was an angry bear, inlaid in gold, standing over a deer he had obviously killed. On the trigger guard were my initials, set in Old English script lettering. There was a note attached to it from the same gunsmith that had worked on Chaps' rifle, years before.

"I have heard about you from Mr. Scharpe, who ordered this weapon. This rifle shoots as good as it looks. I would like to watch you use it some day. Good hunting. L. Mews, Gunsmith."

I was at a loss for words. Now my son would shoot my old .270 when we hunted together. Teresa opened her package, and there, glistening in the afternoon sun, was an intricately worked private railroad car, of the finest craftsmanship imaginable, done in pure gold. It had a perfect, sterling silver mountain goat inlaid along the side. The piece was made like a pendant, to be placed around her neck on a heavy gold chain.

Teresa looked at Oscar, and then Johanson, who were speechless at what they had seen. She put her arm around me, and said, "Lets get the mare home. I guess our hunt for the Great Northern is finally over."

Buck was glad to see me, and nosed at the apple I had in my pocket. We put the mare into the pasture, and he took off with her for the far end of the field. It was obvious that he wasn't coming back.

"Well," I said to Teresa with a laugh, while I pulled her enticing curves up against me, "It looks like we've been deserted."

After a few preliminaries, I slept the best I had in years.

The autumn sun reflecting off the Kootenai lightened up our front deck where I was eating my breakfast orange.

"Come on, Walt," I called to an eager, tow-headed boy, "I can see a cutthroat rising out there. You need some practice with your fly rod."

Maybe, life along the river would get into his blood like it did mine.

The phone wouldn't stop bothering us, and I grabbed it on the fifth ring. It was tough trying to talk with a mouthful of Teresa's light pancakes, but I did manage to mumble a little.

"Hello, Herb, this is Oscar." He was talking loudly enough for everyone to hear. "We have us a bad derailment in the canyon down by Kootenai Falls. There won't be any traffic goin' through there for days unless we get some help. Mr. Scharpe told me to call you."

"That figures, Oscar," I replied while using my sleeve to wipe some syrup off my face. I smiled knowingly at Teresa. "Tell old Chaps that I'll get on it in about fifteen minutes."

"There's more," Oscar said in an agitated voice. "Ed Scharpe is in the Lutheran hospital in Minneapolis, where I understand he isn't doing well at all. Some guy tried to rob his house and Ed got hisself stabbed in the process. He called the cops before he fainted, and they found the crook sprawled out in the front yard with a .30-06 hole through his chest. A detective answered my phone call and gave Ed the message when he came to again. This just came off the line. Ed says that if he makes it he is retiring to New Orleans."

"Thanks to you, Herb, I didn't miss this time. I won't be needing my rifle again, and I want young Walt, who is the fine grandson I never could have, to use it and remember his railroading 'Grandpa,' for better or for worse. Take care of that boy for me."

After winter comes spring. One well-worn life that would not be duplicated was ending, but now a young one was getting a good start. Teresa pulled me up close and blotted her tears on my soft flannel shirt.

"There'll never be another one like him, thank God," she whispered, "Or you either."